MISUNDERSTOOD

BRIDGET E. BAKER

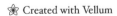

For my mother
I have known during every moment of my life that she loves me.
There has never been any doubt in my mind. If every child on earth
was this lucky, the world would be a much more beautiful place.

FOREWORD

I am a Christian. Many of my readers are also Christian. I believe that God loves all people.

I know a story about a gay character might be difficult for some people to read. I hope you will give Melina a chance to tell her story.

And I hope that you'll listen to the stories of the Melinas who may be hurting in your life. The suicide rate in gay teens without a supportive parent is unbelievably high.

We must do better for our children. They deserve our support.

THE PRESENT

D earest Chancery:

You surely know by now that I abducted and nearly killed Judica. I still worry that she needs to die to keep you safe. But I also trust your judgment and hope that I haven't epically failed you by allowing her to live.

You probably also know that I tried to kill you when you were a newborn. I don't deny either of these things. I hope that my attempt to eliminate Judica was as misguided as my attempt to eliminate you. In both circumstances, I can honestly say that I saw no other path at the time.

Those two confessions alone may be enough for you to throw this missive into the trash bin without reading any more. That would be a mistake, but I would understand your reaction. Sadly, these aren't even the only major miscalculations I've made in the forty years that I've been alive.

But my mistakes have also made me an expert at finding the right path.

You never met your father, Eamon ne'Godeena

ex'Alamecha, and you may already know that Mother didn't think highly of him. In fact, they pretty much fought non-stop. Notwithstanding that truth, he was a great man. You could even call him a visionary. He taught me many things, from facts to feelings and everything in between. Unfortunately, his life was cut short, and he wasn't able to teach you himself. He was also unable to finish his life work, but you are carrying on his legacy without even knowing you're doing it. Father dedicated his life to making the world a better place for all people, human and evian alike.

Almost everything I hear about you convinces me that he is beaming down at you from heaven right now. He loved those that others considered flawed. He cared about the genetic anomalies among us. And he didn't worry about whether someone was pure in his determination of their worth. He loved all God's children, and he believed we should love them, too. He believed the evian birthright wasn't to rule. According to Dad, our task from God has always been to protect, to shepherd, and to teach.

Eve set us on that path, but even Eve didn't understand quite how our lives would play out. As her children became more and more fragile with each generation, we sought to learn more and more about *why*. Why were we weakening? Why were we dying more easily? Why did life grow harder, scarier, and shorter? These questions led to the dawn of the scientific age. Instead of turning to our creator for the answers, evians ceased praying. Our pride turned us inward in our pursuit, toward our own understanding.

We forgot these questions had already been asked and answered by someone much smarter than us.

Eve and Adam had been given a set of keys to a place they did not understand or need at that time. Just as an eagle would believe a car to be useless, our parents did not understand the purpose of the Garden of Eden. Sure, it was perfect, but it was so small, it was so limited. What could a place that predominantly featured two large trees—one that provided knowledge, and one that provided immortality—do for the perfection of evians? We already had intelligence and quite a bit of knowledge. Their long lives felt almost the same as immortality. So our great great great great great grandmother left that little garden for the wide, wide world, seeking who knows what. Perhaps something new and exciting. Perhaps she had tasks to perform. But the knowledge that humanity needed remained behind her, untended.

She was wise enough to leave us with her prophecy, and in addition to that, she left messages inscribed on the gates into the Garden. She tasked her second oldest daughter, Shenoah, to watch over the garden, but Shenoah failed to see the importance in the gate inscriptions. In fact, she felt that her mother had quite overlooked her when she assigned her that task. Millennia later, our dad dedicated his life to following the breadcrumbs left behind. He methodically pursued the path of knowledge back to the warnings Eve left.

You've already seen Eve's main message. You're the Eldest—I really believe that. I don't know how I didn't see it before. Wishful thinking, perhaps? But the staridium's reaction to you clinches it beyond doubt. You are the one, the empress who will reunite the fractured evian descendants and right the rudder on this ship.

Before he died, Dad did a lot of work and made a lot of progress, even without Mother's help. I might have disappointed him with some of my decisions, but I have dedicated all my resources and effort to pursuing his leads now that he's gone. From his research and mine, it appears there were three additional messages left by Eve, one on each gate.

The first, carved into a gate that opened to the east, predicted and taught us to prevent a flood that would decimate the world as we knew it. Sadly, we ignored that one.

Whoops.

The second, the gate that opens northward, allegedly provides the timeframe for the final danger.

And the third gate, the one that opens to the west, tells us precisely what we're endeavoring to prevent.

Dad spent his entire life seeking the answers to the location of the Garden, which Mother was also desperate to find. He pursued the text of the prophecy of Eve, which Mother had in her possession all along and refused to share. He also doggedly sought for replicas of the gates and their inscriptions—which most believe are merely legend.

I always believed in their existence. After all, as long as people have been alive, they've made duplicates of anything they thought was valuable. It stands to reason someone would have copied these as well, even if they abandoned the real ones. Dad says they were supposed to be inlaid with precious gems—and I think that would only increase the likelihood of copies.

He found what he believed was a faithful replica of the Eastern Gate. I've attached images and information on it for your review. I've spent the past twenty years tracking down possible locations for the other two gates and the Garden itself. Most of them came to nothing, of course.

I have one final lead to pursue on the Northern Gate, one I haven't followed due to its location—within the geographical boundaries of Alamecha holdings. Many years ago, Mother forbade me to leave Austin, Texas. As a result, my wife Aline has tracked down lead after lead for me, but I haven't let her pursue those located in Mother's territory. Usually Angel would pursue them for me instead, but this is allegedly heavily guarded. I humbly ask your permission to follow that final lead. I promise that, if successful, I'll bring the information I recover directly to you. I'd include more details, but I don't know who might see this letter. It's the third I've sent, and I'm increasingly concerned that they're being intercepted.

I don't know who to blame, but I'm guessing it's Judica. If I'm right, then this is for you, sister. If you don't convey this information to Chancery so that she can fulfill her destiny, I'll take more drastic steps to ensure she hears from me. Chancery may not want you dead, but if you're working to prevent her fulfilling her destiny, I will go against her wishes and kill you anyway. It's better for one person to perish than an entire world to endure 'utter destruction.' Consider this your final warning.

Yours through whatever may come,
Melina Alamecha

✵ 2 ✵

THE PAST: 1990

For the last eight years, two months, and six days, I have played a game of chess against my mother every single morning. That's two-thousand, nine-hundred, and sixteen games, all concluded before breakfast. Just once, I'd love to eat a roll or an apple or something before I'm expected to focus on a game of strategy.

But in all that time, I've never won. Not once.

Thirty-two pieces move in various directions across a board composed of alternating wooden squares. Humans believe that chess originated fifteen hundred years ago, but evians have used it for millennia to train their children. Every single possible combination of moves has been played over and over and over.

In my three thousand games, I've tried every opening gambit listed in the books in the Alamecha library: the Latvian, the Elephant, the Albin, the Budapest, the Danish. Loss, loss, loss. I spent more than a month starting every match with a Center game, another two months on the popular Sokolsky, and a full three months on the Sicilian Defense. For a while, I alternated my openings, hoping to throw Mother off, hoping to surprise her. Then I wondered if maybe I just wasn't trying for long enough. So for the last year, I've used Ruy Lopez for every single game.

"You know, Inara beat me when she was only six." Mother sets up the board.

Like I could ever forget.

"You turned ten two months ago, Melina."

Two months and six days. Today must be *state the obvious* day.

"And you still haven't won."

Or maybe the theme is *twisting the dagger*. My heartbeat doesn't accelerate, no matter how much my stomach roils. My hands do not clench in my lap, in spite of the heat of my blood. My breathing remains steady, even though I'm fuming inside.

Because this is all part of my training.

She's goading me so I'll do something stupid, like open with Budapest again. That was one of my most epic losses, and Mother still jokes about it with Inara.

Mother's best friend Lyssa bursts through the door with a manila envelope clutched in her hand and a snap in her step. Mother's head whips to the right. "What's wrong?"

"The first images are in from the Hubble." Lyssa beams and extends the envelope to Mother. "I thought you'd like to be the first to see them."

Mother holds out her hand, her heart rate slightly elevated.

I should be giddily impatient to catch a glimpse myself of our first photographs of far-away stars, taken from outer space. If we're lucky, they'll show us things from a thousand light years away. Maybe more. The hairs on my arms stand up, and a shot of adrenaline punches through my heart.

But it's not because of the telescope or the blurry images of stars Mother's examining.

No, it's because I'm about to defeat my mother for the first time—and she has no idea. To defeat an opponent who's stronger than you, you need skill, knowledge. . . and good timing. Surprising someone like my mother is hard, but I've had a strategy up my sleeve for a while, waiting for the perfect moment. In the past eight years, there's one well known opening gambit I've never used, mostly because chess analysts widely consider it to be terrible. For just that reason, Mom won't expect me to open with the Grob, the extremely unpopular opposite of the Sokolsky.

I finish setting up the board and then slide my white pawn forward to C4. "Your move."

Mother barely glances my way. She slides her pawn to D5, a half smile on her face at my bumbling open.

I shift my bishop to G2, and I can barely believe it when she takes my pawn with her bishop absently, leaving me to move my pawn to C4.

I'm clearing a path.

And she takes the bait, eliminating my C4 pawn with hers, and leaving me a clean shot at her rook on A8.

After I take it, Mother sits up in her chair, the photos wobbling in her hand as she shifts her attention to the board. A smile steals across her face. "The Grob? Really?"

I shrug.

She moves her knight to D7, but I'm still ahead. This time, she's the one scrambling.

Lyssa clears her throat. "How do you want to disseminate the photos?"

Mother turns her attention back to the photos.

Lyssa winks at me—she's helping. I should feel guilty, or pathetic, or something else, but I don't. There's no room in my heart for anything other than hope. And possibly a pinch of elation.

Mother rattles off the tiering of the release of the

images, starting with US news outlets, since the United States was the one she used to launch the Hubble, and flowing down to international ones. I don't care about any of that, but I do appreciate the ongoing distraction.

Mother fumbles another move. She arches one eyebrow at Lyssa. "Out."

Mother's bestie ducks out so quickly she forgets the photos, but it's too late for Mother to redeem this game. I already have her. When the path for the final foray opens, I can't quite suppress my smile. Soon enough, my thirtieth move is a checkmate. I want to leap up and scream at the top of my lungs. Or maybe wave my arms in the air and hoot. I long to dance around and around and jump into the air repeatedly.

Of course, I don't do any of those things. That would as good as negate any positive impression I made on Mother with my win.

"I began to worry you'd never beat me." But Mother's sparkling eyes belie the sting in her words.

Even with the distraction and the innovative opening, it's still possible Mother let me win. Either way, it's done. I may have taken four years longer to pass this test than Inara, but we can't all be flawless replicas of Mother. Certainly I'm not, no matter how hard I try.

"Your father will be pleased," Mother says.

I shift on the hard wooden chair. "He will?" Dad doesn't seem to care about my chess games. I've asked him for help, and he simply laughs and tells me to be patient.

"I made your father a promise long ago."

"About what?"

Mother quirks one eyebrow. "He hasn't told you?"

"Something about chess?" I shake my head. "No."

"Once you've beaten me, you're finally eligible to train with him at Sovereignty."

Because he's a master of strategy and regularly wins at Sovereignty tournaments. "I thought you hated those."

Mother sighs. "It's one of the things that first drew me to him, his skill at politics, his burning passion for government and domination. But the things we love the very most are often the things that circle back around to annoy us later in life. You're too young to fully comprehend that, I imagine."

Why wouldn't she like his skill at *the* only truly evian game? Chess actually came from Sovereignty—its designer was asked to create a watered down version for beginners. But now I've graduated from the baby game to the real thing. Instead of two players, Sovereignty has up to six players—representative of the six evian families. I can't suppress the tremble in my hands, but I'm not sure whether I'm nervous or excited. "When do I start?"

"Today, I suppose. After we've eaten breakfast and run through your melodics forms, and after you have completed several matches, you may meet your father in his office."

Mother threw me a tremendously large birthday party when I turned ten, but this graduation to the next level of my training feels more significant somehow. Maybe it's the time with Dad, which is a rare treat, or maybe it's that I'm finally making progress toward becoming a capable heir.

I struggle to concentrate during my forms while Mother plays the same songs I've heard a million times. "Keep your eyes straight ahead," she says.

I focus.

"Bring your hands through the entire arc."

I lengthen my movements.

"Those strikes should be sharper," she says.

I redouble my efforts.

Even so, it's one of my worst melodics practices ever. And then I lose three sparring matches in a row against

Mother. But finally, she folds her arms. "You'd better not be this distracted tomorrow."

I can't help bouncing a little on my toes. "I won't be, I swear." My mouth doesn't curl up into a smile, but my eyes are far too eager.

Mother sighs. "Fine. Get out of here."

I bow and scramble out of the courtyard, beelining for Dad's suite of rooms. As I approach the solid mahogany doors and wave at Holden and Rupert, Dad's guards, the tension slips from my shoulders. The nervous energy evaporates, and I realize I wasn't worried about learning something new. I was fretting because I thought Mother might change her mind.

I'm excited to spend time with my dad. I know Mother loves me. She pushes hard *because* she loves me, and she wants me to be the very best I can.

But Dad's different.

Even if I took three decades to defeat Mother in chess, his eyes would crinkle up in the same way when he saw me. He's never disappointed, or critical, or judgmental. Dad loves me, no matter what. I'm excited to move to the next level, but I'm euphoric to have a dedicated chunk of time every single day with him. A break from disguising my emotions. An hour where I don't need to guess what will please Mother or tremble under the weight of the consequences if I pick wrong.

"Can I go in?" I ask.

In his always-gravelly voice, Rupert says, "He's expecting you."

I've never met anyone who reads as much as Dad does, so of course he's reading. But when I walk in, he leaps to his feet. "Darling! Congratulations!"

Dad stinks at hiding his emotions. Maybe that's why I struggle so badly. "Thanks, but I couldn't have done it

without the Hubble telescope photos distracting Mother."
I shrug. "Use what you can, right?"

"Always. In fact, that's the first rule of Sovereignty.
You're already learning that understanding people's motivations is the most important weapon in your melodics arse-
nal." Dad crosses the room until he's standing right next to
me. "Those lessons will form the foundation of your ability
to evaluate the people around you, and I think that's the
most important ability of any monarch."

"You sound like Mother."

"Your mother is a very wise woman."

"Then why are you always—" I gulp. I shouldn't have
even begun that thought, but now I can't think of any way
to fix it.

"Why are we always fighting?" Dad's eyes widen. "Is
that what you were going to ask?"

I look at the top of his head, a trick Inara showed me
once when you don't want to meet someone's eyes, but
you're worried they'll notice.

Dad slings an arm around my shoulders and drags me
across the room to the corner where a Sovereignty board is
already prepared. "Listen kiddo, I shouldn't fight with your
mother. I'm sorry you've seen that."

"Pretty sure everyone on the island has heard it," I
grumble.

Dad pins me with a look.

"It's nothing. I'm sorry I mentioned it."

"Being married is complicated," Dad says. "And your
mother and I don't always agree. In fact, we disagree on a
lot of things."

"I know."

Dad grins, his eyes lightening. "You're ten. You may
know, but you won't understand until you're—"

I groan. "Don't say until I'm older."

He snorts. "I was going to say more experienced, which isn't always the same thing. Love is complicated, and life makes it even more so."

I bob my head, even though I have no idea why it's so complicated.

"One of the reasons I wanted the opportunity to train you, nugget, is that there are some things we should discuss."

Something about the word *discuss* vibrates with an odd kind of weight. This isn't a normal conversation Dad wants to have.

"Okay."

"I suppose it's good that you've noticed your mother and I don't always get along, because this is probably the core of our. . . discord."

Acid churns in my belly, but I can't explain why, even to myself, so I repeat myself instead. "Okay."

Dad stands and pulls a slim book from the top shelf and places it on the highest level of the Sovereignty board. "At the completion of this lesson, I'm going to give you something. I'm not asking you to hide it, but if your mother didn't notice it the next time she walked into your room, or ever, it might spare us some trouble."

The idea of hiding anything from Mother terrifies me.

Dad proceeds to summarize the basics of Sovereignty, as though the book I need to hide isn't hovering a foot above my head on the fourth and highest tier of the game board. "The full game begins with six players, and they never start any game with even footing."

I know that already. "Because no one in life is born in the same circumstance as anyone else."

Dad smiles. "Even so. And as the daughter of Enora of Alamecha, you essentially begin at the top of the highest board. But in life, things won't always be easy, even with your huge advantages. So when we learn the basics of this game, you'll always start—"

"At the bottom." It's my turn to smile. "I figured."

"Your mother has trained you well, and we've already established that you *listen*." Dad's little jab at me for listening in on their disagreements is well aimed.

I glance at my feet.

"Each player begins with one main opponent." Dad points at the pieces and tells me what they do, one by one. "As in life, the queen is the strongest piece on the board, and she's stuck protecting her people, but in this case, her people are represented by her king, much as in chess." Dad's wry smile tells me he knows he's not as important to Mother as her people. I wish it didn't hurt his feelings.

"I've read books on this, you know," I say.

"But if I miss anything that matters in these lessons, your mother will eviscerate me." Dad points at the second board, positioned six inches higher and a few inches to the right of the bottom board. "This is the Second Level. Two more players would begin here. You can ascend to the second board before you've eliminated your opponent, but it's risky."

Dad walks me through the rest of the rules and refuses to be rushed. I worry he'll never reach the final rule set that governs the throne—the topmost level. No one can ascend to it until they've completely destroyed at least one other opponent. And once you've ascended the Throne, you can't descend, even to defend. Which means in rising, you lose your greatest defense against any opponents below you.

When he finally reaches that last stage, almost an hour has passed. "Our time is nearly up," I whine. "How am I supposed to earn that?" I toss my head at the book I still haven't been able to see clearly.

Dad shifts backward in his chair and stretches his legs out in front of him.

"I'm not getting it today, am I?"

"What do you think your mother and I disagree about, fundamentally?"

Everything. Not that I can say that. I try to think of particular conversations and can't think of a common theme. Dad's always arguing that the evian way is wrong, but the issues about which he complains vary widely. "Progress?" I finally ask.

"You're more astute than your mother realizes." Dad leans toward me and rests his elbows on his knees. "We're evian. The name signifies that we are the literal descendants of Eve and Adam, right?"

I nod my head.

"Where do humans come from?"

My eyes widen. "I mean, well, they come from us."

Dad's eyebrows shoot straight up. "Do they?"

"No?" I don't know what he wants to hear. "Or, well, I guess they come from Eve too."

I'm rewarded with a smile. "Correct. They do. So why aren't they 'evian' like us?"

I open my mouth to tell him that it's because their DNA is corrupt. They have less value, because they aren't nearly as good as we are. But what he asked was why they aren't evian, or 'of eve.' And they are. I close my mouth with a click.

"They are as evian as we are," Dad says. "And that's the heart of every disagreement between your mother and me. That simple fact, that no one could really contest, not if they examine the truth of the world, causes us fight after fight after fight."

I don't understand.

"Your mother doesn't believe humans are evian."

I swallow. "But they aren't the same as us. If you really look at it, they're totally different. Their DNA is degraded. They can't heal, they're slow, and they aren't nearly as smart as we are. They're not pure, so they aren't really Eve's children, not anymore."

Dad's eyes swim with sorrow. "Only perfection has value?"

"Evians are perfect."

"Your mother actually believes that, I think. But how arbitrary is that line?" Dad stands up and begins pacing. "If you were one hundred generations removed from Adam and Eve, do you know what you'd be?"

"Uh."

"You'd be evian. But if you had a child, a child who was one hundred *and one* generations removed from Eve, then what?"

I shake my head.

"Your child would be human."

"Why?" I ask.

Dad scowls. "Your mother and the other empresses had to choose a bright line. They insisted at the time that it was based on research. They explained that by the hundredth generation, the deletions to the DNA resulted in conclusive flaws. The child of an evian who falls below that threshold is suddenly worth. . . nothing. But mark my words. That line was drawn nearly two thousand years ago. Soon, they'll be forced to move it, and this time, they'll cite new evidence that has justified drawing the old line into question."

"Science."

"Sure," Dad says. "They'll use 'science' to justify their position, even though you and I both know it's nonsense. Their position is based on keeping the 'haves' big enough to operate, and the 'have nots' in line. It has to do with how far removed we have become from Eve and Adam—and nothing to do with the actual 'value' of any of the individuals affected."

That feels wrong.

"And the fact that they need to draw a bright line where none exists tells me this entire business is misguided at best, and evil at worst."

"But if we're all the same. . ."

Dad stops pacing abruptly and drops into the seat in front of me. His eyes are practically burning, they're so bright. "Say it."

"Then we don't really have a right to be in charge, do we?"

Dad beams. "Precisely. Which means the only reason we should be in the position we are in at all is. . . if we are earning the right. We are supposed to be here to do a job— to protect all of God's people."

"How do we know what God wants us to do?" I ask.

Dad picks up the book and holds it against his chest. "You begin by asking what He wants. Then you actively seek for that answer." Dad holds out his hand.

I take the plain, brown leather book from him. I flip it open, desperate for the answers to all the questions Dad has spawned.

It's empty. Nothing but blank pages.

"I don't understand," I say again. It feels like the only thing I've said today.

Dad places a hand on my shoulder. "You have the Bible. You have the Koran. You've got the Vedas, the Talmud. You have all the religious texts of humans of the past seven millennia. You also have our religious texts, including the written prophecies of Adam and Eve. They're all part of your basic course of study."

I shake my head. "But Larena and Inara say that the human belief sets aren't right."

"We haven't had total control over them, in any case. But what if they're wrong?"

"Wait, what if who is wrong?"

"Inara, Larena, your mother, the other empresses. Everyone. What if the writings are all a little bit right and a little bit wrong?"

He's making no sense.

"Think about it. What if God gave us a gift, special abilities, perfect bodies, but He gave these things to us so that we could protect His children, so that we could maintain peace and prosperity for the whole world?"

"But we didn't protect them. Right?"

"Exactly. We took that gift and we preened and we postured and we squabbled among ourselves and we failed to do the basic task for which we were given the gift in the first place."

"What should we have done, then?"

"Let's take a step back, shall we?" Dad asks. "You asked a question I haven't fully answered. We're nearly out of time for today, but I want you to think about how we can find out, given that we've totally ignored His directions up until this point. We've disregarded what God wants us to do."

My hands clutch the empty book in front of me so tightly that my knuckles go white. "Okay."

"If His most choice servants don't listen to Him, to whom do you think God will speak?"

Humans. "Anyone who does listen?"

Dad nods. "Exactly. And they may disagree on some particulars, but the humans who claim to have talked to God—they have a lot of commonalities. And when you're trying to decipher what path to take, your best tool is to look for the things the world's religions have in common. It's like if you're taking witness statements to determine what happened in a high-pressure situation. All the accounts may differ a bit. Some of the observers might speak a totally different language, or because of their past experience, they may see things from a unique perspective, but when they all describe things the same way. . ."

"Then you know that's probably right."

"Your mother doesn't believe there really is a God, you know. Or at least, if He or She exists, she thinks after making the world, God bowed out, leaving us to manage things on our own."

"You don't believe that?"

"That idea seems awfully convenient. I believe it justifies the narrative that your mother wants to perpetuate."

"So you think God is watching us?"

"I believe God is still at the helm, yes. God's nature is so vast that we can't comprehend it, not without a lot of effort, in any case. I have a lot to tell you, a lot to learn with you, but we have time. You don't have to find all the answers by Friday."

"Thank goodness." I stand up. "But the blank book?"

"I'd like you to start writing down your questions, your thoughts, the things that don't make sense. Write down the evian laws that don't seem right. I'm going to teach you to be better at Sovereignty than any other player, because you're going to look at everything and question the world in every way possible. You may not agree with me, and that's okay. But I want you to at least consider the realm of possibility before arriving upon a conclusion."

"But Sovereignty isn't our main goal."

Dad smiles. "It's not."

"You want to teach me to try and find the path God wants me to take."

"That's exactly what I want you to do. There's a prophecy I overheard your mother mention long ago, something about an empress locating the Garden of Eden and saving the world. I believe that you are going to accomplish that, because you're not the same as everyone else. You're not a typical evian. You're more than that. And I believe my calling is to make sure that when the time comes, you're ready."

"I'm not special." I'm barely acceptable.

"But you are," Dad says. "You're as pure and strong and resilient as every royal with a ferocious mother, and yet you'll learn of God and the value of every life from me. Years ago, I thought your mother and I could change the world. I've long since realized that she has no respect for me. For a depressing stretch, I wondered if I had misunderstood my purpose on earth. But today, oh, Melina. It has become clear to me that I have been walking the correct path all along. *You* will save this world and all the evians in it, but you won't stop there. Your mother and I, we were merely laying the foundation all along."

"The foundation for what?"

"For your footsteps, paving the path as it were, that you will take to save us all."

3

THE PAST: 2000

The first few notes usually call out to me, clear, pure, like the trill of a Kona Nightingale on the early morning breeze. I raise my sword and listen.

Liam's opening notes are deep and staccato. He stands with both feet firmly planted, like he intends to conquer the entire room with only the heft of his broadsword. The ferocity of his scowl and the strength in his rippling shoulders complete the image. I weigh barely more than half what he does, and his reach dwarfs mine.

But I'm not afraid.

I haven't been afraid in the training ring for years. Mother taught me far too well for that. And underneath the opening notes of Liam's song, I hear his fear, like a trembling violin string. It's in the flutter of his eyelashes when I shift. It's in the sweat already gleaming on his brow. I let him make the first move. That will uncover his real melodic line more quickly than anything else. The first line in a novel sets the tone of the narrative. The first glance shared between a couple establishes most great love stories.

The first strike always tells me what my opponent hopes and often what they fear.

He thrusts boldly, shifting his weight to the balls of his feet, but he doesn't commit. He doesn't sink his full weight or his full strength, no matter how much he wants me to believe he does.

I parry without thinking, and ask, "Who do you love more?"

Liam grunts.

"Your mother," I continue, "or your father?"

The end of his sword dips and then lifts again quickly, but I notice he doesn't stumble. He also doesn't answer.

"I prefer my mother, I think." I rain blows down, which he blocks adeptly, his feet moving in a simple half step scale. "But maybe that's because not to love her most is practically treason."

"My father," Liam finally says. "He's around more."

His mother Prudence is gone most of the year—typical security placement. An honest answer. Interesting. His melodic line sharpens marginally, and my desire to destroy him lessens. Time to dig deeper.

"I don't think it's treason to love your father more." Liam blocks a solid swing. "As long as you obey your mother."

I smirk. "It was a joke, Liam."

He frowns and I begin to pick out the harmony that follows his melodic line. It's low and not very subtle.

Luckily, I appreciate forthrightness. It's a rare enough trait among evians. "If you had to choose, would you rather a memorable life?" I ask. "Or a happy one?" I pull a knife from my boot and begin to advance, strike and counter-strike, sliding in between his symphonic form.

He senses that the end is coming, even as he blocks and

strikes with more force. The line of his mouth hardens. "Why would I have to choose?" Liam stumbles back.

"We all have to choose," I say.

"Memorable, then," he says.

That's a lie, but is he lying to impress me? Or does he believe that it's true? Liam doesn't care whether people remember him. He cares only about this moment. He loves his father more because he spends more time with him. He wants to beat me, but he can't decipher why he's losing ground. But most importantly, he only cares to win because defeating me brings him glory, pride, and attention. He wants a happy life, but he lacks either the insight to realize that or the courage to admit it.

I spin, bob under his guard, and sweep his legs. I didn't even need a third question to get a read on Liam. I kick the center of his chest to lay him out and press my sword to his throat.

I ask my final question anyway, because I want to see whether I'm right. "Why do you want to beat me?"

"I don't."

Another lie, but this one is to cover his wounded pride. "You do. I want to know whether you know *why*."

"It would be impressive."

Half true. I lean down and whisper in his ear. "You want to impress your mother so she'll spend more time at home. Until you start to understand what you want, you'll never accomplish it. Know yourself, and listen for others around you. It's true in melodics, it's true in life."

Liam grunts again when I offer him a hand, unwilling to accept help after a defeat. I shrug and step away. It's not my job to improve his attitude or turn him into a better warrior. Balthasar will handle that well enough tomorrow, I imagine. I'm glad I don't have to watch.

"You didn't finish it," Mother says from outside the ring.

My head whips around and my eyes widen. She won't love my obvious agitation either. "I defeated him quickly and efficiently."

"You didn't defeat him at all."

Liam groans softly next to me. He clearly appreciates that I didn't finish in the way Mother means. I can't fault him for not wanting a severed spine.

"So we'll go another round," I say. Mother usually isn't happy until the arena floor is slick with blood. I should have gotten in a few good slices at the very least.

"No, you won't. Liam, report to Balthasar. Now."

Liam ducks under the side rope and hops out, fleeing with a burst of speed he didn't exhibit during our match. Coward.

No one climbs over the ropes surrounding the ring gracefully. It's an awkward process, rising and ducking, then swinging through. And yet, Mother does it. She barely even seems to bend. It's almost as if the ropes move out of her way, which I recognize is scientifically impossible.

"Today you'll fight me to first major, without any of your usual chatty interrogations. You learn what you need to know from your preparation and my movement. Nothing more."

I suppress a scowl. She mustn't know how annoyed and embarrassed her public reprimand makes me. More importantly, the gathered crowd cannot know. I hate that so many Alamecha citizens come to watch my morning training. Mother moved my sparring into this public arena on my twentieth birthday, but it still bothers me, even after several weeks. She insists that it brings our people together and strengthens their faith in the future.

I think she does it to put me off my game and prepare me for the crowds at the Millennial Games.

"Fine." I try my hardest not to sound sulky. "Let's get it over with."

Mother's smile reveals shiny teeth and the barest hint of pink gums, and her eyes sparkle with anticipation. I might love fighting in front of an audience as much as she does if everyone worshipped me. But I'm under a social microscope, on display to *inspire confidence*.

I pick up the notes of Mother's familiar melody quickly. She's bold and confident, and today she's also *molto vivace*. When she's this pleased with herself, her movements are sure and energetic. She strikes with quick, sharp blows. I block with my dagger as often as possible to leave my sword arm free for attacking.

"I can't ask you any questions at all?" I lift my eyebrows. I get my best information out of her during training sessions.

"You shouldn't have the energy for questions. It means I'm not working you hard enough." Mother redoubles her efforts and I back away from her, block and shift, block and spin. I shouldn't have baited her. I'm an idiot. You can predict overall movements from the melody, but the finer shifts, the far future attack strategy requires comprehension of the opponent's harmonic line.

But in nearly twenty years of fighting my mother and watching her fight others, I've never been able to piece together a whisper of anything beyond her basic melody. I can't predict her moves, so I never win. Mother can read me like a book, but I can't pierce the veil around her motivations. What does she want? Does she just push me to preserve her legacy?

"Why do we fight with real swords?" she asks softly.

"I thought we weren't talking." Sometimes a touch of petulance escapes.

Mother's mouth turns up slightly. "I'm barely working at all. I figure a little conversation might keep me from getting bored."

Great. I push harder, and then throw my dagger, lodging it in the meaty part of her shoulder. "We use bladed weapons instead of wooden or blunted practice swords because it helps us learn how to fight through the pain. Also, we learn to heal while fighting."

She dances away from me, yanks the dagger from her shoulder, and tosses it out of the ring. "Partially correct. We use actual weapons to raise the stakes as high as possible, to prepare you as much as we possibly can for the day your fight isn't to first major. Eventually the person you're fighting will want you dead."

I stumble a little at the thought. "You fought your first bladed challenge when you were eleven years old." I press my slight advantage while she might still be healing, raining blows down on her injured side.

Mother laughs. "I thought I was ready, but I nearly died." She's favoring her injured arm. I must have landed a better hit than I thought.

I don't gloat, but I do press harder. The tempo of her melodic line increases, but she's still not fighting at full strength. It's now or never. I might actually defeat her. I step forward dramatically, quickly, into her personal space, and bring my sword around, arcing toward her body. Her sword is angled away. She can't block me. I doubt she can even spin out of the way.

Mother slides a dagger underneath my ribs, punching through my liver and spearing my spinal column. I should have paid more attention. My fingers involuntarily release their hold on my sword inches before it would have connected with Mother's hip. Pain radiates through my lower body, so I know Mother hasn't severed my spinal cord—yet.

"Your problem isn't that you don't hear my harmony," Mother whispers. "It's that you're not ready to do what needs to be done. You shy away from harming others, even when that harm isn't permanent. It's time to shed the training wheels and *fight*."

She shoves her hand forward, driving her blade home. My legs give out, but the pain also drops off dramatically. My body collapses to the blood-spattered mat, my head turning sideways. My eyes meet Dad's stormy ones. His mouth is taut, his shoulders tense. I plead with my eyes. *Please don't say anything. Leave it alone.*

He either doesn't notice, or he doesn't care. "If you just eviscerate her a few more times, publicly whenever possible, I'm sure you'll completely rewire her so that she'll become exactly like you. Since you're clearly on the right path here, you should lean in." Dad only uses such a droll tone when he's livid.

"I thought we agreed you'd act less insane in public." Mother's hiss is so soft it barely reaches me. Her face looks pleasant, proud of herself. But it's clear from her tone that she'd like to slice Dad open like she just gutted me.

Dad flinches.

"It's just a lesson," I say, hoping he'll let it go.

"Melina doesn't need this particular lesson. She does what needs to be done and nothing more. Which is perfectly acceptable. Her personality is unique among evians in that she doesn't gravitate toward destruction, devastation, and subjugation."

My spine finally heals, and I regain feeling in my feet. I shift into a seated position and ignore the sharp, silent screams from the muscles in my torso that haven't yet knit together. The gush of blood down the side of my body isn't ideal. But none of it hurts as much as watching my parents tear into one another while our people watch with bated breath. At least Mother spoke softly.

"I'm fine, see?" I force myself to my feet. "And I'm paying attention, Mother. I really am. I'll take it to first major next time, I promise, and I won't hesitate."

"You're all dismissed," Mother says loudly.

The onlookers hear the command in her tone and filter out quickly.

Mother tries to force a smile. It looks more like a grimace. At least she's not perfect at everything. After the last citizen is gone, she spins on Dad so fast I worry she's actually going to knife him. "You will never criticize me in public again."

"Or what?" Dad asks. "You'll gut me? Or were you thinking of a more permanent solution?"

"The idea has crossed my mind," Mother says. "One little beheading would spare me a lot of trouble."

"You're too hard on her. She doesn't have to be *you* to succeed."

"I'm preparing her," Mother says. "The Millennial Games are less than a month away, and she's still not ready."

"Funny. I'm training her for the same thing," Dad says. "And I haven't stabbed her once."

Mother wipes her blade on the bottom of her shirt carefully. The dark crimson of my blood contrasts sharply with the white cotton fabric. "You're teaching her to play a board game. I'm training her to compete in Weaponry. I hardly think it's a fitting comparison."

"She needs to win both," Dad says. "We're on the same team."

One of Mother's eyebrows lifts incrementally. Something has shifted. Mother still looks angry, but there's something else in her expression. Something that makes the hair on my arms rise.

They say the opposite of love isn't hate. It's apathy. Maybe I should be pleased that they aren't apathetic toward one another, but the way Dad jumps into the ring has me sliding across the floor, slipping over my own bloody spots, and practically sprinting for the exit. I don't turn around to confirm, but they don't seem to notice my departure.

Once I make it through the doors, I lean against the wall and close my eyes. I breathe in and out a few times, trying to reset the image of Dad staring at Mother like he might slap her. Or kiss her. Mother's lip curls and her hand clenches against the hilt of her sword. I shudder.

"You're smearing blood everywhere. What a disgrace."

My eyes fly open.

Gideon's arms are crossed over his chest, but he doesn't bother hiding his smirk. His eyes lighten to the color of hammered gold when he's happy, like he is now. He's always in his element making fun of me. I pretend not to mind, but I hate it. Because I want him to look at me the way he looks at Inara. Like the world begins and ends with her.

As usual, my older sister is beside him, totally relaxed, her foot tapping. "You really are making a mess."

"What do you care?" I ask. "It's not like you have to clean it up."

Inara shakes her head. "Let's get you back to your room before this becomes an all-hands-on-deck situation."

I rocket off the wall, suddenly desperate for a shower. "I don't need help."

"Of course you don't," Gideon says. "Didn't you hear?"

I pause in front of my door. "Hear what?"

"You're Alamecha's greatest hope," he says. "Entering not one, but *two* categories, and favored to take both."

"Favored by who?" I frown.

"By whom." Inara winks.

I want to scream at her sometimes. "Do people really expect me to win?"

"Mother's been telling everyone you're the best fighter she has seen in centuries," Inara says. "I'm busy trying to pretend that one doesn't sting."

"The best fighter trained in melodics," I hedge. "You were trained in sladius."

"Have I mentioned how much I love being a guinea pig?" Inara pushes past me and into my room. "I mean, Alora wins the Games, and then Mother decides to hop on the bandwagon and try the new big fad with her very next heir. Really? And then, after me, she goes *back* to melodics. Ouch."

Complaining, for Inara, is like a finely developed art form. It's how I know she's happy, like a cat purring and clawing a blanket. I'm glad she's in a good mood, but I'm irritable, filthy, and a little stressed. "Are you two planning on helping me shower, or did one of you need to use the toilet?"

Gideon salutes me with exaggerated formality. "I'll wait outside." He takes up a position to the left of my door, jostling one of my guards aside to make a spot.

I stalk inside after Inara and slam the door behind us.

As soon as it closes, Inara's face falls. Her voice is soft when she asks, "Are you really okay?"

"I will be." I walk across the room and perch on the tile floor in the doorway to the bathroom. "Once these dumb games have come and gone. It's not fun to have them both bickering all the time. I feel like they're getting worse. I wish they got along."

"Mother's worried. She's aging, and she wants our people to accept you and our enemies to fear you." Inara sits down on the carpet a few feet away from me. Somehow, even sitting cross-legged on the floor, she looks regal. The only other person I know who could pull that off is Mother. I suppose it's fitting that they're practically identical in appearance.

"It's a lot of pressure," I say.

"The Millennial Games are rare. This will be the only one you or I see, and the only one Mother ever sees, too. She wants the family to win for honor and all that, but it's better if Alamecha's *Heir* wins. It sets the precedent for the next thousand years. I think she sees it as symbolic, that we'll stay on top."

"Wow, not making me feel better."

"Lying wouldn't really help," Inara says. "Facing the truth is the only way. Always."

"What do you suggest, then?"

"Win." Inara beams at me then. "Or had that not occurred to you?"

I stand up. "I'm going to shower."

"I know it's hard getting it from both of them, for different reasons and in different ways. Keeping them both happy is stressful, I'm sure," Inara says.

"I think they want me to succeed for the same reasons." Or at least, publicly that's Dad's position.

"Oh please. Your father wants you to win so that you'll be poised to do God's will."

My jaw drops.

The corner of my big sister's mouth turns up. "You thought I didn't know about Eamon's plans?" She swats my leg and then stands up. "I met your dad before Mother did."

"You know what he believes about. . ." I'm not even

sure how to broach the topic. For a decade, Dad's been teaching me about God and prophecies and our calling to right the ship—in secret. I had no idea *anyone* else knew.

"Eamon has become more circumspect," Inara says. "But that's a recent development. I know he thinks big things are coming at the end of this year, and I suspect he believes you'll be involved. It stands to reason he wants the other families to look to you with respect."

I nod. "He does, yes."

"I haven't ever won at the games." Inara steps closer. "So I don't have a lot of advice to offer. But." She leans closer until her forehead meets mine. "I believe in you, goose. You can do this. You're Enora's daughter, and you're Eamon's daughter, and you're strong. You're smart. You're tenacious and you won't crumple when the hammer hits the anvil. The antagonism between Mother and your father might have actually helped temper you."

"You really believe that?" I whisper.

She embraces me then, and it's exactly what I need.

"I don't think Eamon's right." Inara releases me. "I don't believe the world is standing on the precipice of destruction. But I believe we all hold the keys to our future, and we use them today to unlock tomorrow. You have no idea how much easier your rule will be if you gain the approval, respect, and faith of the evian people."

My sister squeezes my shoulder and walks toward the door. "I know you've got a lot of training to do and you're running short on time, so I won't make you late. But I want you to consider something. You're looking at all of this as an unfortunate coincidence—that you happen to be born in 1980, just before these Millennial Games. You're only twenty, and you'll be fighting warriors with hundreds of years more skill."

"Is there something inspiring hiding under this demoralizing summary?"

Inara laughs. "Maybe it's not an unfortunate coincidence."

"You think it's destiny?" She sounds like Dad.

She shakes her head. "No, not quite. But I think it might be a *fortunate* circumstance. Mother may not live much longer. Less than seventy-five years, probably. Alamecha's enemies will circle like starving wolves when she dies, unless her successor proves herself to be just as capable and just as fierce. You have the opportunity to do just that."

"No pressure."

"A thousand tons of pressure," Inara says. "But also the opportunity for greatness. It's pressure that changes the world, you know."

"Accept the world as it is," I say.

"Or." Inara opens the door. "Do something to change it."

✯ 4 ✯

THE PAST: 2000

I finally get a break from training, but only because we're hosting the pre-game summit for the Six. The first day went fairly well, if you don't count the snarly squabble between a very pregnant Melamecha and Analessa. Luckily Analessa was in a good mood—after she cut off Melamecha's finger, she let the whole thing go.

Today hasn't been quite as smooth. Adika raised the very motion Mother expected, requesting a modification to the rules governing bloodlines for determining evian Royal Families. She even presented a pretty compelling case.

"I see no reason to relax the rules," Mother says. "It's genetic inflation of the worst kind."

"Of course you think that," Adika says. "You're sixth generation and your older sister and older daughters have had an unbelievable number of children. But for the rest of us, the numbers of our royals have been dwindling dangerously for nearly a century."

"Many of us feel that the line should be shifted," Ranana says. Her mother smiles at her and nods in approval.

"The determining line for what constitutes a Royal has been set at tenth generation for two-thousand years," Mother says. "My mother refused to acquiesce to this exact motion a thousand years ago, and I'm inclined to refuse now. Modifying something this significant shouldn't be done lightly. We should evaluate the total number of individuals this would impact and make an informed decision after a thorough investigation has been conducted."

"Royal evians receive a number of perquisites," Analessa says, "many of which create additional headaches for us. I don't believe we should bestow that title indiscriminately."

Melamecha opens her mouth to argue.

"But." Analessa raises her voice, clearly unwilling to cede the floor. "As you mentioned, Enora, it has been *two thousand years* since the threshold was modified. It's past time. As you're currently the only one opposing this motion, and you're only doing it to maintain your stranglehold as the only sixth generation monarch, we request you bow to what's best for our people. Soon enough, one of your daughters will rule, and she'll be seventh generation, like the rest of us."

"Melisania is eighth generation, and Adika is ninth." Mother's finger taps on the end of the armrest on her throne. Everyone else sits in large wooden chairs. As if they needed any other reminders that she's more powerful, has better lineage, or holds the power here.

"Are you going to approve our request, or not?" Melisania snaps.

Mother's eyes practically sparkle. Melisania is acting like a supplicant and an angry child at the same time—deferring to my mother's power, but unhappy about it. Mother probably dreams of moments like this every night. "I haven't decided yet. Until we know the extent of the impact, we won't be equipped to determine how far to modify it—if indeed we should at all."

"We expected you to balk," Melisania says. "And we did our homework." She waves one hand toward the door. "David, bring the reports." Her Warlord brings her briefcase. She withdraws packets of paper and bids David distribute them, one copy for each empress and one for each Heir. "As you can see, we've prepared actual costs and numbers for every single family."

I scan the numbers along with Mother, and they're right. Their numbers are very close to the figures we arrived upon last month. We benefit from the measure too, in spite of not needing it as desperately. More royals means our reach extends more easily. The royals are also the largest supporters of Mother's rule. Expanding their numbers is an obvious move—Mother has known it was coming for decades, but these votes only take place at the Summit, a meeting of Empresses held once every thousand years.

"As you mentioned, the numbers for Alamecha are estimated." Mother makes no mention of the fact that we've run our own figures on the costs of adding royals versus the infrastructure benefits.

"We didn't have access to your database," Melisania says. "However, I'm sure the estimates will be quite close. You'll see that for each family, the benefits far outweigh the costs, and in fact, the families will quickly approach instability without this shift: less than fifty years for the rest of us, and within two centuries for Alamecha."

Mother looks like a hawk about to tear into a juicy rabbit. "Again, the other families might suffer, but Alamecha maintains its position of strength. I see no reason to yield."

In order to hold a position of strength, you must be able to walk away. Mother's the only one who can, and they all know it.

"The vote must be unanimous." Lainina bares her teeth in a smile-scowl. "What do you want in exchange for your agreement, oh great and mighty ruler of Alamecha?"

Mother shrugs. "I would be doing my people a disservice if I were to agree to something that is better for every family. . . other than ours."

"This doesn't harm your family. Quite the opposite," Analessa points out. "You'd be petty indeed if you refused to do something that benefits the entire evian race."

"I agree," I say.

Every head in the room swivels in my direction.

"If it's better for our people," I say, "it's better for us all."

"Preserving our bloodline has always been one of our primary objectives," Mother says, going on as though I didn't say a word. "My Heir is seventh generation, and as she pointed out, what's better for the Alamecha people is best for our entire family."

Oh no. Everyone is looking at me. They all know that's not what I meant, but I don't have the guts to speak against her a second time.

Mother continues, unflappable. "Many of your children are ninth and tenth generation. Which means your grandchildren will not be royal at all, and will therefore be ineligible to rule."

Check mate for Alamecha.

Because another empress would need to step in for each of those families unless the law changes. The air goes out of my lungs. Is Mother really threatening to refuse to vote. . . so Alamecha can take over the families one-by-one over the next thousand years, as their empresses die or are killed and their children move beyond tenth generation?

It's brilliant.

And it's awful.

I'm an idiot because I didn't consider the end of the line ramifications of Mother's bluff until she spelled it out in a threat to the others. It occurs to me for the first time to wonder whether this *is* a bluff. If she refuses to vote for this measure, we will likely be at war.

With all five of the other families.

Adika leaps to her feet. "There are no statistically significant genetic deletions until after the twentieth generation, and nothing truly significant until the hundredth. This is an unadulterated power play."

"And yet, if we decide to follow your *scientific* method, then why not make any evian above fiftieth generation Royal?" Mother asks. "Oh wait, I know the answer to that one. Because that kind of power inflation impacts the rest of you. It undermines your importance and your strength in the same way what you're proposing undermines mine. Speaking of, why don't we share all the *scientific data* we have accumulated on the fact that there isn't much of a difference between say, sixteenth generation and nineteenth?" Mother shifts in her chair, seemingly uninterested in the entire debate. "Oh, right. We can't convincingly pretend we're all better than everyone else, if they know that the data doesn't back that up." Mother leans forward, her eyes flashing. "Your data is garbage. I could defeat any of you in the ring, and my daughter will defeat your children in a short time. Because we are *superior to the rest of you*. So don't try and convince me with claims that the actual numbers don't matter. They do, which is precisely why you're here, entreating me to have mercy. Mercy has always been and always will be a boon for the weak."

"You haven't had time to read our full proposal or review the accompanying data yet," Melisania says, "but we also want to shift the bar for citizenship—to the point that the data does support. One hundred and twenty-five generations out would now be considered full evian instead of one hundred. There is a statistically significant break there. Beyond that point, there's a steep cliff—illness occurs, shortened lifetimes, dramatically reduced response times, healing that approaches human levels. Solid data we could release."

Mother stands up, her eyes flashing. "Wonderful. Perhaps next Summit, we can expand our numbers to include all the half-evians. And what comes after that?"

"I doubt it will come to recruiting half-evians, but our numbers are waning," Melamecha says. "A hundred and twenty-five generations isn't significantly different, and it would reflect that another thousand years have passed—it will allow the evians to maintain our purity while remaining strong."

Mother's eyes flash. "Again, Alamecha is strong now. I am disinclined to vote for this proposal."

Adika crosses her lean arms and her nostrils flare. "Gibón, bring the offer." One of her guards brings her a folder and she hands it to Mother. "We expected you to balk. We're willing to offer you the following trade incentives and grants of land if you will change your position."

Mother purses her lips and peruses the document. Finally, she looks up, meeting the eye of each of the other empresses one by one. "I'll have a counter proposal ready for you in an hour." She stands up and marches out of the room, leaving me to scramble after her. She doesn't slow until we've reached her chambers. Gideon is standing outside Mother's room.

He cocks one eyebrow at me, clearly asking whether

things went well, and I shake my head. He pats my arm as I pass, but I wonder whether he'll be supportive once Mother rips into me for opposing her.

Inara's pacing in Mother's study.

"Exactly as we anticipated?"

Mother nods.

"And their initial offer?"

Mother shrugs. "Ten percent higher than we predicted."

"And our counter?"

"Why are we arguing about this at all?" I ask. "It really is better for us too, although we aren't quite as desperate. You can counter with a hundred and ten generations, as we planned, and the entire thing is done."

Mother's lip curls.

"What am I missing?" Inara asks.

"My Heir, in front of everyone present, expressed her concurrence with the other empresses. She said she agreed that expanding the royal and citizenship pools was a good idea."

I open my mouth to defend myself, but I can't think what to say.

Inara closes her eyes and sighs.

"Why are we arguing over it?" I ask. "They've offered to compensate us for something that is better all around. Let's just take it and be done."

Mother's brow furrows. "I am concerned."

"About?" I sit on one of Mother's office wingbacks.

"Your father has been handling your Sovereignty training in the hopes that you would learn another viewpoint. I believed that you might take what I teach you and augment it with his vastly different perspective."

That's not what I expected her to say. "What?"

"I now believe that was a tremendous blunder. You've

been watching me for twenty years, and you're asking why we wouldn't simply take a first offer?"

I stand up. "No, I know that we negotiate everything to make sure we obtain the best possible deal, but the offer is already ten percent higher than you expected. Why not simply take it? Think about the goodwill you could generate in doing so. How gracious you could appear, and how much positive energy that might pour into the rest of the summit, and the coming millennium. Do we always have to fight about every single thing?"

Mother's face flushes.

Inara throws her hands up in the air toward Mother as if to say, 'I've got this one,' and turns to address me. "It means we didn't realize how strong our position was, but we can't let on, or we'll lose ground."

"We don't lose anything," I say. "Did you hear what I said about goodwill?"

"Goodwill is a myth made up by people who have nothing better to bargain with. If we don't wrest every single thing from them that we're able, then we're losing our *power*," Mother says. "Power is the only real commodity. They all need something that I can do without. That's the textbook definition of power. Alamecha hasn't been the first family for six thousand years by doing *the kind thing*, or by trying to keep the other families *happy*."

"You threatened to steal all their crowns."

Inara's eyes widen infinitesimally.

Mother's smile is broad. "Not at all. I reminded them that I'm the only ruler whose family is currently poised to rule by right for the next thousand years, without watering down the requirements for rule. I'm not wrong, you know. And by right, every one of their staridium stones should be mine. Alamecha was the youngest of Mahalesh's daughters. We should have been ruling everything from the start."

I don't even know how to respond to that, because I don't even want to rule Alamecha. "Do you really want more than we have?"

Mother frowns. "Do you not? The more we extend our reach, the safer our people are."

And by our people, she means the evians who meet her standards.

She clears her throat. "I'll be taking over your final Sovereignty lessons. Clearly you're learning nothing from him." Mother drops the offer on the table and begins to flip through it with Inara.

I hate this. All of it. The constant fight for control. Amassing more money, more power, more land, more resources than the other families. Considering a *war* with the other five empresses, and why? It's not because we need more of anything. It's not to create better conditions for the evians, and it's certainly not to improve the lot of the humans.

Dad's right—we have gone astray. We've lost our purpose. Mother's only concern is that she improves our position relative to everyone else's, and her rivals aren't even surprised that it's all that matters to her. They expected it. Except, I doubt Dad would be impressed to learn that I don't want to rally the troops and fix any of it. I don't want to save everyone. I may have opened my mouth to express my sentiments, but it wasn't because of a burning desire to right the wrongs of our world.

More than anything else, I want to escape.

But I can't, so I go through the motions, even pointing out a few areas where we could reasonably ask for more. Mother beams at me before she writes down her list of demands and flings the door open, ready to head back into the fray.

Dad is standing next to Gideon, laughing, unaware that

I've ruined everything for him with my ill-timed remark. Our training sessions together are done, thanks to my big, fat mouth.

I've loved learning from Dad over the past ten years. I've gotten to know him in ways I never did before. We've analyzed nearly every religious text in existence, discussed his ideas for God's plan, and even begun to explore some of mine. We've talked strategy, and we've talked about his childhood. He told me funny stories and sad ones, too.

But I've never seen him laugh. Not like he's laughing now, with his head thrown back, his eyes alight with merriment. At first, I can't figure out why this looks so different. But then I isolate the difference, and I'm not sure what to make of it.

My dad is happy.

"She really did that?" Dad asks.

"Who did what?" Inara asks.

Gideon's eyes meet Inara's guiltily. "Nothing. Have you worked up a counter offer?"

Inara crosses her arms and the way she's looking at Gideon tells me she'll press him for details later.

Mother, however, does not look amused. I assume she's angry with Dad and worry she'll eviscerate him. But she's not glaring at Dad. She's glaring at Gideon. She looks like she'd happily string Inara's head guard up by his toes. But without saying a word to Gideon or her consort, Mother storms down the hall and re-enters the throne room. She demands twenty percent above what we planned in her room.

And she gets it.

When I finally climb into bed, I'm sick to death of everything to do with evian politics. The anger, the jealousy, the tension, and the greed have zapped my energy. The vying, the maneuvering, and the favors have killed my love for life. Dad taught me to read body language, and Mother made sure I can interpret people's desires and emotions, but none of what I read or interpreted today seemed worthwhile. I wish I could delete all of that information from my brain and quit my life.

Dad has been quite clear that we can't even begin to try and make any changes until after Mother has died. That thought is depressing enough, but I'm beginning to wonder whether I can do what he wants, even then. Not that I should worry about any of this right now. I have more pressing concerns.

Only five days until the commencement of the Millennial Games.

I've just closed my eyes when I hear a quiet tap at my door. I sit up in bed. Who could it be? Inara, perhaps? Mother? I slide out of the bed and cross to the door, listening. Nothing. No whispered explanation, and no more knocks.

"Who is it?" I ask.

"Open the door, angel."

A familiar, if unexpected, voice. I flip on the light and crack the door. Dad's smiling face surprises me, but I widen the gap so he can come inside. "What's wrong?"

He shakes his head and pushes the door closed behind him. "Your mother shared the news with me earlier."

Huh? "About the negotiation?"

Dad wraps his arm around me. "I've been fired."

Oh. Right. "At least you only had a few days left."

Dad crosses my room and sits on the edge of my rumpled bed.

I follow him over and sit next to him. "I'm sorry I blurted that out. I'm sick of saying nothing while she pushes everyone around."

He ruffles my hair. "It's not your fault. I've been asking

you to do a very hard thing, to learn all my grand plans and thoughts and keep them secret from your mother. It probably wasn't healthy for you, and I know it wasn't fair. I'm the one who should be saying I'm sorry."

"It's okay," I whisper.

"It wasn't," Dad says. "But I didn't know what else to do."

"Mother thinks I'm doomed."

Dad laughs. "You might be."

That stings.

"But that's why I came. I wanted to apologize, of course. And I needed to tell you something, by way of explanation."

"Why does it feel like you're about to tell me that something awful is imminent?"

"You know that I don't believe any of the religions have a good handle on timelines. I've always said this. Hundreds, no, thousands of prophesied deadlines have passed without any kind of ramifications."

I nod.

"But this might be different."

"Okay," I say. "How?"

"There are some really heavy hitters who have predicted things will go haywire this year. Nostradamus says a giant asteroid will hit earth this fall. Confucius predicts a solar flare this summer, right around now. And of course the Biblical prophecies, many of them, fall at the two thousand year mark."

"I don't see how that impacts the games at all."

"You're going to be up against the toughest negotiators, the most experienced strategists, and the cleverest players on earth in a few days. Most of them will be ten times your age and have at least that much more experience and training."

"This is a swell pep talk," I say. "Really. Now that you won't be stuck training me, you should become a motivational speaker."

Dad rolls his eyes. "I've known our odds for the past ten years."

"Maybe you could have prepared me for my looming demise a little better." I can't quite keep the edge of bitterness out of my tone. "Or, I don't know, spent more time on strategy and less time on religion and philosophy."

"I think you have a strong chance of winning, and I had a method to my madness. Truly."

"But you just said—"

Dad grins. "You'll be up against a lot of people, all of whom are extremely intelligent. But you're extremely intelligent too. All of your opponents have been well trained. But you've been well trained. And all of them are devious, but I've taught you to be devious. Your mother may not approve of your good heart, but I have taken great care not to alter that. For a specific purpose."

"I don't understand."

"You're *good*, nugget, and that's something rare among evians. It's not preserved, valued, or respected, being good I mean. Your enemies won't expect it, they won't understand it, and they won't know what to do with it."

"You're saying I might win. . . because I'm *nice?*"

Dad shakes his head. "I'm saying you might win because, unlike other players, you still have mercy in your heart. You have care for others, and you don't slash and burn for the fun of it. If you play as well as you can, but also act as the person you are, your opponents will see that, and you might be surprised how it works in your favor. So when you train with your mother, be as fierce, as greedy, and as unyielding as you know she wants you to be. Show her that I've taught you all the strategies and all the underhanded moves. But when you play for real, remember what I said when you're forming alliances. Don't do anything that will destroy your position, but don't squash others with total abandon either."

"Like Mother would."

Dad doesn't meet my eye.

"You don't want me to be like her, and she wants me to learn from her example." I fold my hands in my lap.

"We've made it impossible for you to please us both." Dad finally turns to face me, his eyes dark, his lips slightly open. Vulnerable. He looks like I could gut him, but he trusts me not to do it. "And I'm going to entrust you with one other thing. It's an excuse, in a way. It's my explanation for the terrible position I've placed you in, but it's also critical that you understand what's riding on your performance. You're twenty years old—quite young. And yet, Enora was only twenty-two when her mother died, and she became Empress of Alamecha. Six months from now, January 1, 2001 marks the first day of a new millennium. It might mean nothing, or it might be significant. We don't know. But if it is significant, we need to be ready. We must be poised to take advantage of the opportunities in front of us. I have worked with you so you'll be prepared to save the world, and all the children of Eve. Not only the ones your mother and others like her deem worthy."

"I get it, Dad. Winning the Games will make you both happy, and it might be even more critical than that. If I lose, people might not trust me, either my own citizens or my enemies."

Dad places his hand over both of mine. "It's a lot of pressure, but know this: I also believe God will guide our path. I have faith in you, but He has more. You will win the day if you place your trust in Him, whether you win at Sovereignty and Weaponry or not."

I wish I had his faith or my mother's burning ambition. As it is, I'm afraid I'll fail everyone. But if I have to choose, I'd rather please my dad than my mother.

And it would horrify him to hear it, but if it came down to it, I think I'd rather please my dad than God.

5

THE PAST: 2000

Winter in Rio de Janeiro is cooler than I expected, likely due to the coastal breeze, or perhaps the nearby Sugarloaf and Corcovado mountains. I'm surprised Mother didn't grill me on my knowledge of the climate and geography before we left.

Then again, there are only so many seconds in a day. Even if she's Mahalesh's rightful heir, Mother can't change that. Upon discovering my Sovereignty deficiencies, everything else collapsed to the bottom in the hierarchy of desperation. Even now, with only a single day to settle in, Mother won't let up.

"We must make an appearance," she says. "But you won't prolong any of it. We'll go directly to the Alamecha beach house. We have time for two more rounds tonight."

I don't grit my teeth. I don't argue. It won't do any more good than her frenetic last minute shoveling of strategy into my brain. "Yes, Mother."

She narrows her eyes. "You think this is overkill."

I shrug. "It's a little late to be trying to show me new approaches, but you never know what might stick."

"Exactly."

Inara catches my eye a few steps behind Mother and winks. It's a good thing she and Gideon are lagging back, because Mother wouldn't appreciate the wink or Gideon's smirk.

"I know you hate Suburbans," Balthasar tells Mother up ahead, "but they're better than vans." He points to the edge of the runway where three Suburbans are idling. "And even though we sent several Alamecha planes ahead, we still have quite a hefty contingent from our two jets."

Two jets, because the Heir and Empress never take the same one. Unsafe, even en route to the Games, apparently.

Mother doesn't comment, but her mood certainly won't improve during the ride in a vehicle she once described as 'one step above mass transit.' Balthasar and Frederick accompany Mother into the first SUV, along with half a dozen other guards. Gideon and Inara climb into the second vehicle, and Dad follows them. If he tried to ride with me, Mother would probably flip out. I haven't heard them speak a word to one another since Mother fired him from training me.

We all have to take separate vehicles to mitigate the risk of attack on the way to the reception, and then to our 'beach house,' which I suspect will more closely resemble a fortress. Since this is a formal event, I'm flanked by the head of my personal guard, Lucas, and his second in command, Douglas. The Heir isn't required to use the males purchased by the Empress for her guard, but it's traditional. Also, I haven't found anyone else I prefer. By default, my guard is exclusively male.

I tried telling Mother I didn't need a full complement of watchdogs, especially as a contestant. She's not known for being yielding though, so here I am. Eight guards surround me as I motor along toward the reception that kicks off the single biggest event of my life.

"Are you nervous?" Lucas asks softly. But of course, everyone else can still hear.

"Not really," I say. "I either have the skill to win, or I don't. It's not like I'm risking my life."

Lucas' eyes meet mine and then quickly look away, but he doesn't point out the obvious. Losing isn't the greatest risk. If I don't at least perform well, since I'm the Heir, it won't put Alamecha in a good position going into the next thousand years. But telling him I'm so nervous my stomach is consuming its own lining won't help either of us rest easier. Besides, some of the other guards might believe my lie.

I force myself to look out the window as much as possible from the center seat. Rio de Janeiro is a beautiful city, perched on the edge of the water as it is, framed by mountains. "There aren't nearly as many old buildings as I expected," I say.

"There was a lot of renovation in the early 1900s," Douglas says. "They tore down or gutted a lot of the old buildings."

"How far is the Palácio Laranjeiras?" I ask. "I hear it's beautiful."

"It's fine," Douglas says. "But it could have been maintained a little better."

"How do you know so much about Brazil?" I ask.

"He was stationed here for six months." Lucas jabs me. "You should pay better attention."

I really should, and not only to Douglas. I'm supposed to be evaluating my guards for suitability as a future consort. I have twenty-three options. It's not the most any heir has had, but it's not a bad number. Unfortunately, not a single one makes my heart beat faster. I suppose that's not really a *requirement* for a consort, but I'd really like to be attracted to my future spouse.

I should be carefully considering Lucas. He's the most obvious choice, but I've never been interested in him. It's not Lucas's fault, of course. He's tall with broad shoulders, shiny black hair, and a strong nose. I even like strong noses, generally speaking. I'm aware that he's textbook perfect, but other than a clinical acknowledgement of his beauty and an appreciation of his competency, I don't ever miss him when he's gone. I never need to suppress a smile when he says something funny or clever. I don't ever seek his opinion, except perhaps on finalizing my guard rotation.

Thankfully, Inara set the precedent with Mother that taking some time is acceptable. She didn't choose a consort, not for the hundred and sixty years she spent as Heir. People may tease her—just marry Gideon already— but she never pays them any attention. Actually, she might be drawing fire away from my lack of interest. It's ridiculous when you think about it. Mother may have met the love of her life when she was sixteen, but we live for a thousand years. Expecting me to make a decision about who to spend my life with after knowing them for what amounts to two percent of that time is ludicrous.

And I won't choose someone rashly. I've seen how that turns out.

We pass through the entrance easily enough, Melisania's guards waving the Suburbans past on sight. The grounds look exactly like the images provided in the security briefing. A large, stately building with an impressive front staircase. The entire palace is surrounded by greenery yet located in the middle of the city. Balthasar's probably breathing a sigh of relief. Or, he would be if anything was ever a relief to him. And if he knew how to sigh.

Melisania is waiting at the top of the stairs when we pull to a stop in the circular drive. Her hair has been piled on her head in a large shining nest, like always. She's wearing a different crown today than at the Summit, this one replete with pink Brazilian imperial topaz and Columbian emeralds. I don't care for gems like she does, but I prefer this to the boring Venezuelan diamonds she wore last time, even if they were worth more. She color-matched her eyes to the emeralds, which was a nice touch, but the green and pink sheath dress might be overkill.

Once we have all exited the vehicles and are ascending the stairs, she spreads her arms wide. "Welcome to the Millennial Games! Lenora is delighted to host."

Mother inclines her head. "This is a breathtaking venue. We appreciate your hospitality, as well as the resources and time involved in planning such an event."

"Oh please," Melisania says. "Alamecha hosts more events for the Six than any other family by a factor of ten. I should probably have asked your advice."

"Where should our people park the vehicles?" Balthasar asks.

"My security team will take care of all that." Melisania waves her hand and men in navy blue walk toward the Suburbans. "Please, follow me."

Mother leads, with Frederick and Balthasar falling in on either side of her. I trail along, my guards surrounding me in the same way. Dad hangs back with Inara and Gideon as we weave through the center of the palace. We emerge from solid wooden doors into the middle of a courtyard, which I know from the security briefing bisects the two buildings that shoot off the main palace. More evians than I have ever seen in one place are gathered behind us, sitting on rows and rows of benches. They fall silent when we walk through the doors.

We follow Lenora's Empress to the seating prepared for Alamecha, the first dais for the first family. Everyone else is already here—I should have known Mother would be the last to arrive, forcing everyone else to wait on us. She doesn't wave as she walks up to her makeshift throne, but she does acknowledge the gathered crowd with a tilt of her head. She could be sitting on a boulder, for all the difference her seat makes. The evians gathered respond to her presence and reputation, not the setup.

Melisania walks to the podium in the center of the temporary stage. "As you know, the number of evians who would like to attend these games far exceeds the number of seats available. Even so, we have tried to line up a venue for each of the six competitions that will accommodate as many viewers as possible. If you're here today for the Commencement, it's because you or a direct family member are participating in the Games this year. Each family may select only eleven participants for each category, so congratulations! Being selected to participate is quite the honor, both for you and for your family. You're literally the best the world has to offer."

Melisania steps back and gestures toward the six pedestals set up behind her. "You all belong to one of the six families of Eve. Your bloodlines are among the purest on earth, and we watch eagerly to see who emerges as champion in each of the six disciplines: Sovereignty, Weaponry, Military, Vitality, Tenacity, and Monetary."

I know the nominees from Alamecha for each of the contests, but only representatives from Lenora know the nominations from all the other families. I lean forward in my seat right along with everyone else, eager to learn the identity of my competition.

"Before I read the names for each discipline, I wanted to note something unique. There's no rule that prohibits participants from competing in more than one category, but it's rare because each family is limited to only eleven contestants in each event. Also, with the overlap, you can't compete in the two events that take place simultaneously. Even so, quite a few ambitious individuals have managed to secure a spot in more than one discipline over the years. I combed through Lenora's records dating back to the very first Games. As you know, the Games take place every hundred years. We celebrate slightly more with the Millennial Games, since they come only once every thousand years. Including both Centennial and Millennial Games, I've found only thirty-one instances of individuals competing in more than one event. Thirty-one, over a period of six thousand years."

Mother cuts her gaze toward me and widens her eyes, her mouth turning up slightly.

"None of those individuals were a current empress or consort, of course, as we're prohibited from competing."

Mother smiles now, even showing teeth.

"This year, there are only two individuals in more than one event, and both of those hail from Alamecha. Unsurprisingly, Balthasar is competing in both Weaponry and as a Military commander again. He has even won both in the past. Twice. But the other—well. For the first time ever, an Heir has entered more than one category." Melisania turns sideways and gestures at me. "I'd like to commend Melina Alamecha for her boldness in competing in both Weaponry and Sovereignty, and I'm sure you'll all join me in wishing her the best of luck. Especially since she's only just turned twenty years old."

Mother's going to kill me, because when the eyes of the entire gathering turn toward me, I can't quite keep heat from rising in my cheeks.

"And now, without further ado, I'm delighted to

announce the participants in our first event, Sovereignty."
Melisania begins with Shenoah, which means she reads
Alamecha last, saving my name for the very end. It almost
feels like the applause is for me.

Because I needed more pressure.

I am surprised by the Alamecha list for Weaponry. I
knew that Balthasar was going to be one of the participants
against whom I might be matched, but the last time I saw
the list, Alora's name wasn't on it. I've always admired my
big sister, and I know she won the Games in 1800, but I
hardly ever see her. I refuse to scan the audience for her
face, or glare at Mother for not preparing me, but I feel
Inara's gaze.

I turn toward her.

"It's fine. You've got this," she mouths.

I'll have to interrogate Inara about Alora later. Alora
trained in melodics as well, which means if she knows more
about me than I know about her, I'm at a big disadvantage.
Now that the lists of my competition have been read, I'm
ready to go. I have some research to do about my competitors, and I'm excited to start. I stand up to try and hurry
things along.

"I need to speak with Melamecha briefly." Mother rises.
"We'll leave directly after that."

I want to groan so badly. Nothing with Melamecha is
ever short. It's not even short-adjacent.

"There's a practice match starting over there," Inara
says. "Let's go watch while we wait. Frederick, come and
grab us when she's done."

Frederick shrugs, so I fall in with Inara, Gideon, and
Lucas. The rest of my guards trail behind.

"How exciting to have Melisania make sure all eyes are
on you," Inara says.

My nostrils flare. "Right? What's her problem?"

Inara laughs. "Her heir is thirteen years old. That means she's too young to have any hope of winning—which means she has no opportunity for upside here. But if she can draw attention to any mistakes you make, or better yet, force you into errors by stressing you out, she mitigates her rival's progress, which is nearly as good."

"Evians suck," I say. "I mean, really. Why can't we be less. . ." I don't even know how to finish that.

"Less like a pack of wolves in the middle of winter, ready to eat a wounded packmate?" She laughs. "Because, it's a kill or be killed world, goose. That's how it works."

"I don't want to kill," I whisper. "I hate this world." I've never said that out loud to anyone, not even to Dad.

We've just reached the edge of the field where two teams are currently practicing for their battles tomorrow. Swords clang, sweat beads on their skin, and shouts ring out. Inara glances at Gideon and tosses her head slightly. He backs off, and Lucas and my contingent follow suit, giving us space. "I'm sorry to hear that."

A knife to my heart. Even Inara is disappointed that I'm not like everyone else. Which means that only Dad understands me.

"But not for the reasons you probably imagine."

"What?" I meet her eyes.

"I've noticed that you don't seem to enjoy fighting."

I shake my head and tears threaten behind my eyes.

"I hoped maybe I was imagining it."

"No."

"You hate the negotiations. You hate asking for more and more and more."

I nod.

"You hate the heart of who we are."

One lone tear escapes and I duck before anyone can see it. But Inara saw.

She can't hug me, not here, but she takes my hand in hers and squeezes. "You can always abdicate, you know. There's no reason to spend your entire life hating the core of who you are. The rest of the world isn't like this. I've thought about leaving a million times."

"Why didn't you?" I ask.

Inara's cerulean eyes bore into mine. "I think you know why," she says. "You freed me, and you shackled me, too. I love you, Melina, like a sister should. Like none of mine ever did. I stayed to help you. Mother isn't. . . the most effusive parent."

"But you could have children of your own," I say. "So why haven't you?" It's as close as I've ever come to asking her why she has never married.

Inara pulls me against her then, apparently unconcerned by who might see. "You're as much a daughter to me as any blood child ever could be, and it kills me to see you miserable."

"Mother would be furious if I abdicated."

"So wait to do it until she dies," Inara says.

I stiffen. I can't help it. It sounds almost threatening.

Inara laughs and releases me. "I don't mean *kill her*, goose. I love Mother as much as I love you. But here's my promise to you. The second she dies, I'll be there to hug you, to wipe your tears, and to step into your place. You don't have to do this if you don't want to. You can escape all of it, I promise."

A weight lifts from my heart and for the first time, I imagine a future full of light instead of darkness. I wish I wasn't standing in the middle of a million starving wolves. I'd love to sing at the top of my lungs and then hug Inara properly. I'd love to express the depth of relief I feel at her offer, but I have to settle for a quiet, "Thank you."

Until I remember that Mother isn't the only one who expects great things from me. Dad's far younger, and I doubt he'll consider Inara a suitable replacement. It may not be my solution, but for the first time, I wonder whether there might *be* a solution, and that calms my frayed nerves.

The ferocity of the fighters in front of us intensifies. I try to identify the combatants. Gerald leads a team from Malessa, but I don't know his troops. He did quite well at the last Games, from what I hear, but he's not a favorite. Or at least, Balthasar isn't worried about him. The opposing team is led by Rakira, Melisania's recently displaced heir, but I only know one of her troops—Hanna is a permanent member of her guard. Of the original teams of ten, Rakira is down, four troops to Gerald's six.

Gerald severs Hanna's spine, below T10, as I watch. A significant blow, and a bold move for the commander to make, striking troops down himself in a training match. Then again, the world is already watching. Gerald's troops are quick to press Rakira on opposing sides.

If they take her out, Malessa's team wins, or they would if this wasn't a practice. Defeating the commander wins it all, but it's not like Rakira's other troops are in a wonderful position to assist her. The last two Lenora fighters stand back to back, facing off against three of Gerald's troops. They fight as a team, shifting forward and back together, ducking and blocking and striking completely in sync. They're both using the facão, a Brazilian machete.

At a cry from Rakira, some kind of exchange takes place between the two warriors. One of them springs almost impossibly high in the air, flipping over the head of one of the attackers and sprinting across the field to save his leader. I should be watching him, since that's where the win or loss comes.

But my eyes don't leave the warrior who's now facing off against three of Gerald's attackers alone. His job is nearly as important: to occupy all of these men long enough that they don't join the press on Rakira. The man who flipped and ran might prevent a loss, but Rakira wins or loses on the skill of this lone fighter. A smile spreads across his face and his eyes spark. He shakes his free hand and I notice a small flash that tells me he's using the capoeira razor blade. The three Malessa fighters advance together, but this warrior is perfectly trained. He drops onto his hands and spins to the left, changing their advance and forcing them to shift. Now he can take them one at a time.

And he does.

It's one of the most glorious things I've ever seen. The cry from Rakira doesn't even distract me. His team may have lost, but he's not going down without a fight. His facão blade is black and sports three holes near the widened end, and it moves in a never-ending whirl, blood flying from the end in all directions as he moves steadily nearer to where I'm standing. Finally he stops moving, and I wait.

None of his attackers rise.

Clearly the wrong fighter was dispatched to save Rakira, who is still down on the other end of the field, attended even now by the warrior who left to defend her.

"Melina," Frederick says. "Your mother is ready to leave."

But I can't look away. I need to see his face, meet his eye. For the first time in twenty years, I'm completely transfixed by someone. The way he moves, the beautifully corded muscle across his back. He finally turns and when I see his face, I stumble back, nearly knocking Frederick to the ground.

He's. . . not a he. The warrior who just defeated three other fighters alone in one of the most stunning displays I've ever seen is a woman. And she's the most gorgeous evian I've ever clapped eyes on.

❧ 6 ❧

THE PAST: 2000

I'm still staring dumbly at Rakira's warrior, wondering how I missed the fact that she was a. . . well. . . a female, when Frederick grabs my arm. "Are you alright?" His voice is low, urgent.

It snaps me out of my fog. "Yes, I'm fine. I'm sorry about that. You startled me, that's all."

"It was quite a match out there, from what I hear," Frederick says.

"Absolutely it was," Inara says. "And I know Mother's waiting, but I'd like the chance to meet Rakira's twin fighters, if you think she won't be too upset."

"Enora was reviewing the lists and discussing strategy with Balthasar in the Suburban when I left. She won't know how long it took me to locate you." I love Frederick. He's always been the best of Mother's guards.

"Well then, shall we?" Inara lifts her eyebrows and glances toward the battlefield.

Absolutely.

We climb the fence at the same time, our guards realizing our plan and vocally objecting.

"Have you lost your mind?" Gideon asks. "What are you doing?"

"It's not a real match," Inara says. "And I have got to learn how he managed so much height on that backflip."

Gideon is already scrambling over after us, but Lucas has crossed his arms and is scowling at me. "You can't go chasing after other warriors. It's not proper."

I shrug. "You've known me for twenty years and you still think I care whether I'm proper?" No wonder Lucas isn't the guy for me.

"Careful there," a low female voice calls. "I dropped my navalha."

I focus on the ground in front of me, scanning for a razor—and notice it a few feet in front of me. I crouch and reach. In the split second before my fingers touch it, another hand shoots out and snatches the thin, dark metal strip from the thatch of sod where it's lodged. I jump back.

"Sorry for startling you. It's sharper than people expect, so frequently someone who isn't used to the navalha will slice their hand open." The warrior from the field is standing less than a foot away from me.

I straighten, unsure what to say.

"Melina Alamecha probably wouldn't even notice the wound," a man behind her says.

I shift to see who's talking and realize he's the man Inara called my warrior's twin. Does Inara know them? Or was she guessing because they look similar?

"You know my name," I say. "But I don't know yours."

"And we are dying to ask you to demonstrate that amazing back flip," Inara says. "I'm Inara—"

"Neither of you needs an introduction," the woman says. "And we're happy to demonstrate anything you'd like. This monstrous show-off is my older brother, Paolo. And my name is Aline. We're Francisca and Vitor's children."

Francisca? I can't think of a Francisca, and I know ten generations out in each family. For some reason, it disappoints me that they aren't royal.

Or maybe, with the extension, they now are. Not that it matters.

"Wonderful to meet you," I say. "And even if you didn't win, that was quite the fight."

"Inara! Melina!" Balthasar's bellow hits me like a slug to the ears, even from fifty yards away.

"Frederick might have been mistaken," Inara mutters.

"We need to go," I say. "But if you see me in the next few days, be sure to come by and say hello."

"Rakira is throwing a party tonight," Paolo says. "Why don't you come? I'm happy to do a demonstration of my modified macaco lateral. It's supposed to be low, but I've found a few uses for launching high."

"I'd say so," Inara says.

Paolo smiles at me, his teeth gleaming brightly against deliciously dark skin. "The gathering will be here, behind the courtyard, at the long pool. Maybe bring a swimsuit."

"Have you two gone deaf?" Balthasar practically growls from the edge of the field. "Your mother and I have been *waiting*."

"I doubt we can make it—" Inara says.

At the same instant, I say, "We'll try."

Aline smiles at me and ducks her head and I *need* to figure out a way to return for the party.

"If we don't see you," Gideon says, "good luck tomorrow."

"Thanks, but I'd rather if you do see us." Paolo winks at me, and my mouth goes dry.

Balthasar doesn't climb over the fence, but I'm worried he's thinking about it when we finally turn around and head back toward the waiting Suburbans. Mother arches an eyebrow, but she doesn't reprimand us. Even so, no one speaks as we pile into our respective vehicles.

Once we're on the road, Douglas clears his throat. "I might have read this wrong, but you seemed curious about the Lenora siblings, Paolo and Aline."

"I am, yes," I say. "And from here on out, if any of you know anything about anyone we encounter, I'd like you to share it with me. Even small things might help." Which is totally true, but also hopefully will distract them from the unnaturally high level of attention I paid to two insignificant and otherwise unimportant fighters.

"Good to know," Douglas says. "Their mother is the third daughter of Heloisa, and her mother is Bianca, eighth daughter of Mayara, who is the second daughter of Leamarta."

As he finishes his explanation, the iconic Christ the Redeemer statue appears on the horizon. It fills my view, distracting me from his words and my musings, but I can't decide whether it's beautiful or garish. What would Christ think of an enormous representation of himself? I wish I knew. I'm curious what Dad thinks about it, but there's no good way for me to ask him with all these people around, not if I want an honest answer, and I do. A hundred feet tall, with arms spread wide—almost as wide as it is tall. Does it help people remember God's laws and perhaps God's forgiveness? Or is it merely a representation of how religious they want the world to believe they are?

"Melina? Did you hear me?" Douglas glances back.

"Sorry, I was distracted."

"Which is natural," Lucas says. "I mean, look at that thing."

It's clear what he thinks about it. Sometimes I miss the days where the whole world seemed black and white. Right and wrong. Dad wanted to teach me morality in ways

Mother never did, but now everywhere I look, I see shades of gray.

"Was that what you wanted to know?" Douglas asks.

He basically told me that Aline and Paolo are twelfth generation and only newly royal. Barely acceptable companions, and only thanks to the recent mandate. Mother would never approve of anything more than polite acquaintance, but it's better than it would have been prior to the summit. "Yes, it's what I wanted to know. Although, if any of you have more insight, either on the siblings, or on Rakira or Gerald, I'm interested. Feel free to share any time."

I'm almost disappointed when no one else offers any more thoughts or information. The rest of the ride is quiet, and when we pull up in front of the house Mother bought on Leblon beach, I smile a little. I wasn't wrong. It's definitely fortified, but the beauty of the view surprises me. Clearly Dad selected the house, and Balthasar took over from there.

The second I walk inside, the conflicting aromas of braised beef and meringue and fresh strawberries surround me. Clearly Angel arrived before us, and thank goodness for her. Plus, Mother's always in a better mood after she's had something decent to eat. I'll wait to ask her about the party until after dinner. I race into the kitchen to lend a hand.

Angel grills me about the contestants I'll be up against. "Francisco is the strongest fighter from Lenora," she says, "but you can take him, I think. Capoeira draws heavily on melodics forms, so as long as you get your information straight, you'll be able to defeat them."

"Speaking of," I say. "I just got an invite to a party Rakira's throwing tonight. Might be a good chance to find out what I can about Francisco."

Angels eyes widen. "Do you know who else will be in attendance?"

I laugh. "Yes, when the warriors I met extended the invite, I asked them for an embossed guest list. I'm sure it'll arrive any moment."

"You are far too saucy." She thumps a watermelon and tosses it in the trash.

"You can't possibly know that's no good from the sound alone."

Angel cocks a hip and points. "Try it."

I salvage the watermelon from the trash bin and slice it in half with one clean stroke. It's mealy.

"How?" I ask. "How could you know from one tap?"

Her grin isn't disguised at all, which is one of the reasons I love Angel. For a spymaster, she's remarkably forthright. "You can hear the texture easily, child. It's the flavor that takes more investigation."

"Oh?" I ask.

"Yes, you need to smell the melon." She leans down and inhales. "This one has good flavor, but the texture made it trash. But even if you can't smell the sugar, you can look for more obvious cues. Pollination markings, the color of the spot on which the watermelon rested—it should be yellow, not white, if it was picked ripe and not early—the list goes on and on."

"Watermelons are like people," I say. "You can discover a lot from small clues."

"Even so." She tosses the pieces of the melon in the trash for a second time.

"But less complex, clearly."

"When you open your eyes to see, you'll be shocked how many things will become clear."

"My eyes have been open for twenty years," I say. "I'm basically a walking sponge."

"Oh, Melina. Your eyes may be open, but you can still fail to see. Too many people notice only what they expect to notice. They allow their beliefs, and their wants, and their prejudices to color the world around them. They interpret facts in the way they choose. Do not waste your time on those people. They will never *see,* not really."

"How can I know whether I'm letting my own view color the truth?"

"The fact that you're asking me," she says, "is a wonderful start. But listen to your friends and your family, and pay attention to the advice of those you trust. Ask them when you aren't sure. Often they'll set you back on the right path, if you're willing to let them."

I think about meeting the two warriors today. "How do you know when you're in love?"

Angel drops the knife she was holding and it free falls, landing blade first onto her foot. She swears under her breath and yanks it out. "I really liked those boots."

"Sorry," I say.

"You should give me some warning before springing that kind of question on me, child."

"Sorry," I repeat.

She turns then and places her knife-free hand on my arm. "You won't know until you know. It's not something I can explain. But if I could offer you any worthwhile advice on that topic, it's that love isn't just a feeling."

"Excuse me?" I ask.

Angel lowers her voice so low that it barely qualifies as a whisper. "You've seen your parents."

"They're not in love," I whisper back. "Anyone could tell you that."

"They might have been," Angel says. "There was genuine passion between them. I think there still is. But it's buried under actions that smother and poison any love that might grow."

"Grow?" I ask.

"Grow," she says emphatically. "Love is an action, or more specifically, a sequence of actions. You may be inspired to act by a feeling, by attraction, but love is something you *do*. When it's reciprocated, when you find someone who loves you, and shows you with their actions, not only their words, it becomes something spectacular."

"Words matter." I think about the words Mother hurls at Dad and the way he responds.

"They do—they can wound quickly, but alone? Words are cheap, useless, and fleeting. No, if you find someone who will sacrifice for you, and for whom you'll do the same, over and over, that's real love."

Uh, okay.

Angel laughs. "You don't understand, but you will. One day. And then you'll call me and you'll say, 'Angel, you're a goddess. How were you so wise?' "

I definitely think she's wise an hour later, when I'm eating the meal she prepared in a strange place. And then, once we've all finished eating, she does me a huge favor.

"What do you think Melina should wear to this party tonight?" Angel asks.

"I'm sorry." Enora dabs at her mouth. "I must have misheard you. Did you ask me what Melina's wearing to a party?"

"You told her to go, right?" Angel rests both her hands on the table and stares at Mother with wide eyes. "I mean, this is a wonderful opportunity for her to observe some of her opponents and talk to others. I assumed you'd have already come up with a list. I have, if you're not sure who she should target."

Mother's hand comes down hard on the solid oak table-top, her napkin crushed between her fingers. "What are you talking about?" She pins me with a stare.

"Rakira invited me to a party at the palace tonight," I say. "But I didn't think you'd be keen on sending me out on our first night here."

"We do have a lot of things to discuss," Mother says. "But certainly a few hours could be spared, especially if you can find out some information on the less known individuals." She turns to Angel. "Who's on your list? I imagine we should focus on Weaponry opponents, since that's the first event."

Inara cuts her eyes toward me and then throws me a thumbs up under the table.

"Rakira invited Inara, too," I blurt.

"Even better," Angel says. "I'll give her my list, and you compile one for Melina."

Which is how, less than an hour later, I'm wearing my favorite pair of black pants and a new, blousy yellow top as Inara and I head for the front door of the urban palace. Gideon walks next to Inara, matching her stride perfectly. Lucas tries to do the same, but keeps bumping my hip and banging my elbow. I don't roll my eyes. Not while he can see, anyway. When we reach the door, Henry, Douglas, and Caden all step around me, taking up every last inch of space on a very wide entry step.

"Do they really all need to come in with us?" I ask.

"You're lucky I'm only insisting on four," Lucas says. "Don't push it."

Inara knocks.

A man in an intricately designed black tux answers the door. His gaze slides over us one by one, his left eyebrow rising and his lips pursing. If he weren't so short, he'd definitely be looking down his nose at us. "Are you expected?"

"Uh, we were invited to a party Rakira—"

"That party is around back." He frowns before slamming the door. I'm standing close enough that the air from the dismissal blows across my nose.

"I'm going to punch that guy tomorrow," Lucas says, "and pretend it's an accident."

Inara laughs. "Let's go."

As we march around the back, in the dark, I realize that I've never in my life felt more like an errant child. But when we round the corner and pass the courtyard where we gathered earlier today, I hear evidence of a much nicer party. The steady samba rhythm washes over me, more like the pre-1920s samba. Less melody, more beat. My hips begin to sway and my feet fall into step naturally.

A hazard of melodics training.

I mentally review my homework in my head. Mother and Angel hashed out a short list of only eleven people I'm supposed to gather intel on tonight. Magnar, Stara, Klaxon, Antoine—

"I'm so glad you came." Aline emerges from the crowd in front of us as if she teleported there. Her dark hair is loose around her shoulders, and she exchanged the leather bands for a fitted white tank top. She's also wearing dark eye shadow and thick eye liner, and her golden eyes shimmer in the warm tea lights. I have no idea how I ever mistook her for a man.

The entire list evaporates into a fog inside my brain.

"Of course," Inara says. "I couldn't let your brother's kind offer expire."

Paolo spins a woman in a blue dress out of the way and steps out of the crowd, right next to his sister. "Did I forget to explain the payment required?" His face boasts the same boyish grin from before, but it's more compelling somehow, maybe because of the music and dim light.

"Payment?" A thrill runs through me. What will he ask us to do?

He holds out his hand. "One dance."

Inara groans and reaches for him. "Oh fine. You boys are so insistent."

Gideon snatches her hand away. "You aren't so old that you can't tell who's asking you and who's asking your sister."

The glint in Inara's eyes tells me Gideon was right. She was teasing. But when I step toward Paolo, Lucas keeps pace.

"Easy boy," Aline says. "No guard dogs required. She's utterly safe here, I promise."

"Oh," Lucas says. "You promise?" His chest swells. "Well in that case, I'll just go take a nap."

"Why don't you dance with me, instead?" Aline says. "Then you'll be within inches of her if my brother tries anything. . . untoward."

Lucas glances from Aline to Paolo and back, and then he nods. "That would be acceptable."

"Acceptable?" Aline laughs and I feel it all the way down to my toes. "Excellent. I'm delighted to hear that my proposition finds favor with his excellency."

"You're mocking me." Lucas frowns.

"Come on, Señor Importante." Aline takes Lucas' hand in hers and begins to sway and bounce, her low-slung pants shifting as she gyrates.

Lucas stumbles along behind her, and Paolo takes my hand. I follow him, absently noting that Gideon and Inara are already dancing. Looks like she's making as much progress as I am on the reconnaissance that scored us the night off in the first place. My guilt about our truancy evaporates as Paolo guides my steps, his hand on my hip and his weight shifting in the quick, quick, slow pattern.

A new song has just begun, and luckily Paolo is patient. I've heard the samba before and even used its patterns as a melodics cue, but I haven't actually danced it with a partner. I stumble when he does a kick change, but he braces me and acts as though I never made a misstep. When my timing on the side step is wrong, he pulls me closer, showing me with his feet, his ankles, and his knees, how to follow. I finally settle in enough that I can take a breath to look for it—the spark I felt earlier.

Paolo's hands at my waist are sure. They're steady. They're strong. His smile is beautiful and genuine. His eyes are open and earnest, and he's clearly having a good time, even while teaching me the steps. But am I? I reach for it, the feeling from earlier, my excitement about coming tonight. I know Angel said love isn't a feeling, but I'm craving the one I felt before, for probably the first time in my life.

Only, I can't find it. The intensity of my desperation is deeper with the memory of that zing, that thrill, that electric current like a live wire so fresh in my brain.

The music builds until I hear the climax approaching. At least I know what to do when it arrives. When the music washes over me, I fling my hands wide and toss my head outward. It's hardly a surprise that my hand comes into contact with someone else's, as close as we're all standing.

But at that moment, when I turn to look at who I've struck, I feel it. It starts in my hand and runs from my right palm down to my heart and from there throughout my entire body. A thrill. A pulse I can't define or explain. My heart races, my blood ignites.

Aline's hand tightens on mine, her eyes sparking like she feels the exact same thing as me.

But love is not a feeling.

And even if it was, I would certainly not feel anything for a woman.

I yank my hand away and swallow hard, redirecting my attention to Paolo. The guy who did a leaping back flip. The amazing dancer. The reason I was excited to come tonight.

Only, even I don't believe it, so I can't hope to convince anyone else.

"I need to find the restroom." I race away, edging around the dancers who are already hopping to another song.

Douglas follows me. "Is everything okay?" He looks ready to draw his sword and cut Paolo to ribbons, which would probably spark some kind of war.

I shake my head. "I need to find a bathroom. That's all."

He searches my face for a moment, but finally his shoulders relax. He points behind me. "There."

I flee into the safety of the women's restroom and collapse on the toilet seat in one of the stalls. My heart races, and thoughts buzz around in my head too quickly to be heard, much less interpreted. But one thing is absolutely sure.

I am not gay.

No matter what I may have felt, no matter how thinking of Aline may cause my heart to pound, I would never fall in love with a woman. Some new evidence seems to indicate that being gay isn't caused by a genetic deletion, but it's not normal. It's anomalous, at a baseline. The Heir of Alamecha cannot be gay. Mother tries to turn a blind eye among her people, but technically the law demands that she execute gay evians—to purify the bloodline.

Not that gay people have many kids.

I've always assumed that I haven't been interested in

any of the men Mother bought for me because none of them were the right match, but what if. . .

Unbidden, Inara's offer to step in for me rises in my mind.

I shake my head and calm my heart. Mother would never allow it. Dad would be heartbroken. Everything in my world would wither away.

Besides, it's not true. In fact, only today Angel was telling me that love isn't a feeling. It's not a zing, it's not something fleeting, something outside of our control. It's action, it's sacrifice. Perhaps God placed her in my path so that I would learn this lesson at this opportune time.

"Hey are you okay?" Aline's voice is the last thing I want to hear.

And I'm simultaneously desperate for even one more word.

"I'm fine. I'll be out in a minute."

"I'll wait. You looked pretty shocked out there. I should have been paying more attention to where I was flinging my fingers."

She sounds so normal, so calm, so uninterested. Maybe I imagined it, that connection. Maybe I'm so stressed about the upcoming events that my brain has short-circuited. That actually sounds more likely than the alternative.

I stand up and open the door.

Aline's standing in front of me, her blouse a little skewed so that her right shoulder is bare. I can't look away from the corded muscle exposed by that errant shirt. Her perfect, shining shoulder.

"So you're fine, then?" she asks.

My eyes fly up to her face. "Oh yes, totally fine. I drank too much water on the way over, that's all."

"Right." Aline nods. "Of course you did. Adjusting to a

new climate, I'm sure."

"Yeah, that's probably why."

Aline reaches her hand toward my face and I flinch. She tucks a strand of hair behind my ear and it shoots through me again. The same electric feeling, the same longing. When she drops her hand to her side, I want to snatch it back and press it to my cheek. I want her fingers threaded through my hair.

"Are you sure you're okay?" She leans closer.

I back up a step, my rear bumping into the sink. "I almost forgot to wash." I spin around and pump soap onto my hands, and then run them under the water, even though I didn't actually use the toilet.

Behind me, her heart is beating faster than it should. She steps closer still and my knees wobble. I grab the edge of the sink as the heat from her body radiates toward me. She's going to touch me again, I know it. Aline's going to reach out and put her hand on my shoulder or my back, and I'm going to melt into a puddle on the floor and run down through the drain. I'll utterly disappear.

Or worse, I won't.

Because the other option is that when she touches me, I'll burn. If that happens, I already know that I'll never put out this fire.

"I'm nervous," I say, hoping the truth will protect me.

She freezes, her heartbeat accelerating again, but her position holds steady.

I'm in agony. What is she thinking? I pull a towel out of the holder on the wall and dry my hands.

"About what?"

I spin around and words tumble out, helter skelter. "Mother sent me here with a list of names. I'm supposed to see what I can discover about them. I've made zero progress, and I don't even know where to begin."

Aline's eyes lighten and a smile curls up the edges of her wide mouth. "Maybe I can help. Who's on the list?"

I gulp. "Why would you do that?"

She meets my gaze for a long moment, and then looks down, releasing me. Like a cat playing with a mouse, but deciding it's not time to pounce, not yet anyway. "I think you know why."

I can't breathe. I can't talk. I can't form words. I shake my head very slightly.

"My mother was recently made royal, and Paolo and me by extension, I suppose. But we've never been treated as anything but a tool before. I don't expect that will change. Plus, Melisania deserves to lose after that nonsense she pulled today."

"Nonsense?"

"You're twenty years old," Aline says. "I'm five years older than you, but I've learned a lot about life during that time. And even now, I can't imagine being held up in front of every single combatant and waved like a red flag before a herd of angry bulls. She as good as painted a target on your back."

Nothing she said is untrue, but it's also nothing new. I've had a target painted on my back since birth. Today's not much different than every other day of my life.

"Tell me who's on your list, and I'll tell you everything I know." She beams at me. "And then we'll ask Paolo. He'll help too, I know he will."

"It's a long list."

"Well, I'm sure Francisco's on there, but Magnar should be too. Everyone favors Francisco, but Magnar's the stronger fighter. And let me tell you, I know all about him."

I'm torn then, between relief that thanks to her willingness to help me, the moment is gone, and horror at how depressed I am about the very same thing.

❧ 7 ❧

THE PAST: 2000

I don't tell Mother how I acquired all the information at Rakira's party, an omission which is hardly surprising. But I don't tell Inara either. I try not to spend much time thinking about that, which hasn't been too hard. The last two days have been spent right here, in a never-ending strategy session with Balthasar and Mother's guards, Inara and Gideon, my guards, and even Angel and Dad. We've spent every minute researching my opponents in Weaponry and Sovereignty and strategizing the best methods of defeating them.

I could really have used some time alone in my room to try and figure out what's going on in my brain, but here I am instead, dutifully preparing.

"They release the first pairings in an hour," Mother says. "Do you feel ready?"

In two hours, I stand up for my very first match, the first time in my life that any fight of mine really matters. To first major, single elimination. I should be a basket case, and I am, but not for the reasons I would have expected last week. I catch myself staring at Mother's guard,

Heather, again and force myself to look away before she notices. She's as classically beautiful as all evians, and yet, I feel nothing for her.

I turn toward Lucas again, probably the best looking of my guards, and evaluate him in the same way. He's tall, broad shouldered, and his hair practically glows, it's so shiny. He crops it short, but he could grow it longer. I imagine it falling forward, and how it would look when he brushes it from his eyes. Nothing. Still. I recognize beauty, but I don't feel drawn to anything in particular. Which hopefully means I'm not. . . I can't even bring myself to think the word.

I'm losing my mind.

"Melina?" Mother asks.

She's going to figure out something is wrong if I don't stop obsessing. "I don't feel like I really understand Alora," I say. "In spite of what you've told me."

"You don't need to worry about her," Mother says.

"I agree. Her win two hundred years ago was a fluke," Balthasar says. "I was off my game."

"She *accidentally* won six rounds against the world's top fighters?" I ask. "That's a pretty long string of luck. Where do I sign up?"

He rolls his eyes.

"Maybe I should be talking to her instead," I say. "I could ask her how she defeated you. Melodics expert, sladius expert, Warlord for Alamecha for eight hundred years, and six-time winner of Weaponry."

"I doubt your sister Alora will have a lot to offer."

"Maybe she could answer the one question I really have about you." I fold my arms.

"What's that?" Balthasar cocks one eyebrow.

"Why are you fighting?" I ask. "With both Alora and

me competing and nothing left to prove, what's your motivation?"

He smiles. "You're like a dog with a bone. My motivation." He laughs. "You never know what may happen, your highness. If someone should eliminate you, for any odd reason, I'll be there to step up and defend Alamecha's honor."

So basically he's Mother's fall back when I lose. Very comforting.

"What do you want to know about Alora?" Inara asks. "Mother's not the only one who knows her."

"Well, Mother said she fell in love with a human," I say. "But he must have died long ago."

"You're wondering why she never moved back?" Inara asks.

I shrug.

"She did, actually." Mother frowns.

"Alora left Benjamin when Mother demanded it," Inara says. "But she never got over it, even after he died. Not even after their child died."

Their child? I swallow.

"She's hiding in New York, even now." Inara stands up and begins pacing. "I have no idea what prompted her to participate out of the blue. The fact that she's not staying here with us tells you something, too."

Mother sighs. "She only asked to be included last week, and I had my doubts that she would even show. But when a child of mine requests permission to enter the games. . ." Mother shakes her head. "She has a solid chance of winning, and I won't deny her the chance to return to a more active role if she wants that."

Maybe Alora hasn't forgiven Mother, but Mother mourns her separation. That much is clear.

I don't have long left to fret, at least. We load up and

drive over to the Copacabana Palace a few moments later. It's not really a palace, but it is one of Lenora's nicest hotels, and frankly, it's more impressive than the palace where Melisania held the opening reception.

Shortly after we arrive, the first match is posted and it's time to change and head down for my fight. My opponent is Arinya, from Adora. She's tenth gen, and the file we had on her is extensive, but none of the information gave me a great feel for who she was or why she's here. Lainina, the current ruler of Adora, is her great grandmother, but her grandmother was displaced long ago. She's still on the Council for Adora, and Lainina relies heavily on her counsel. If Arinya was Darika's daughter, I'd understand her selection as a combatant. She'd have been trained at court, probably by their Warlord.

But Darika's daughter, Apinya, left court and went into economic infrastructure. She manages half of the assets of Adora in Thailand. Everyone expected her daughter, my opponent Arinya, to follow her mother's lead and focus on business.

When Arinya founded her own gym in Hua Hin instead, training evians, half-evians, and humans alike, it caused quite the uproar. Her mother disowned her. That was more than fifty years ago, and the gym is still going strong. I'm actually a little sad to compete against her. If I have to lose to someone, it would be nice for her to be the one to do it.

Dad adores her.

No one expects me to struggle to defeat someone who's three generations lower and trains regularly against half-evians, which means losing to her would look pretty bad. Mother might never talk to me again.

I take up my position in the front ring of the Crystal room. Chandeliers, decorated marble columns, parquet floors, they all look extremely out of place to me. Once the blood begins to spray, the disconnect will only increase. At least our training room at home is set up with very little panache. I focus instead on the weight of the familiar sword in my right hand, the heft of the dagger against my left forearm, the solid yet springy mat beneath my feet. No matter the setting, no matter the opulence, this is familiar. I am prepared.

Melisania counts down methodically, and all six matches taking place in this room begin at the same time. The faces gathered around the enclosure, the cameras broadcasting this fight around the globe, Mother's hopes, Dad's dreams, a mountain of distractions—none of that matters. It all blurs together until the only thing I see is Arinya's face, her twin scimitars held at an angle with the left out front.

She's left-handed. That wasn't in the intelligence, and it probably should have been. Both swords are weighted the same, which means she'll fight at an angle the entire time— or she risks my blocking both her swords with one stroke. Interesting. But she's had fifty years with fighting as her profession, so I mustn't discount her.

She begins with a feint to my right side, and I hear her opening notes. Discordant, angry. She's been overlooked her entire life. Everyone assumes things about her. Things that aren't true, and some that are. Those true assumptions hurt the most, because they impact her value of herself. I wonder what price she paid to be selected as one of her family's eleven participants. I'm glad not to know how exactly she'll suffer when I defeat her.

"I'm sorry," I say.

She begins to spin, falling into a practiced pattern, and her notes emerge even more clearly. Anger, frustration, and burning ambition. "Sorry for what?" she spits. "You owe me nothing."

"I'm sorry you drew me for your first match," I say.

She lunges toward me, and I realize how condescending I sound, which only increases my regret. I pull back a bit, and let her tag me once on my thigh. Again on my forearm. Small slices, tiny victories. They're only delaying the inevitable, but she'll replay this fight for years to come, rehearsing her failure. It's only fitting that she has something positive to remember.

I don't immediately heal the wounds. No reason to invalidate her attempts.

The hardest fights in life are the ones we can't win. Often we know we can't win them, but because of who we are, we must fight them anyway. Why would God send her here? Shouldn't He care enough to spare us these fights, the ones we've lost before the opening marks? And yet, He doesn't spare us. He sends us to our inevitable defeat.

I drag it out as long as I can, but false hope is as mean as finishing her too quickly. So when she steps too far left, I move right and slice her right arm. She tries to buy herself some time by launching a quick offensive while I'm within reach of her left arm.

I let her gash my leg, and then I drive my sword up under her ribs and through her spine. I lower her to the ground slowly. "I really am sorry," I whisper. "And I wish you the best. Never quit fighting."

From the way her eyes flash at my words, it's clear that Arinya would remove my head from my neck, given half a chance. I wish I could tell her how much her work impresses me, but there's a time for everything, and now is not the time to stroll out on a limb. I could bring the whole tree down in my haste. If Dad has taught me anything, it's that I must employ patience on things that matter.

When I stand up, my eyes meet Aline's golden ones, and she beams at me. I'm happy she came to watch, but I shake my head, unable to celebrate this win. She glances down at Arinya and back up at me, and I know that she understands. It's not exciting to crush someone's hopes, especially someone who began at a disadvantage.

A few feet away from Aline, Inara's smile cannot be contained. "On to round two." She gestures for me to climb down.

I reluctantly do, walking past Aline as though we've never met. It's as much for her safety as mine. If Melisania knew what she shared with me. . . she wouldn't be pleased.

"Good luck on the next," she whispers. "I'll be watching."

A shot of adrenaline I didn't even experience during the fight burns its way through my blood.

"Melina," Dad says, "this way. We've prepared food and a place to change and rest."

The hour of rest between matches ends too soon, but true to her word, Aline is watching again. Everyone else's face is a blur, but every time I spin, strike, and block, I see her sharp features, paying rapt attention. I don't even realize Paolo is standing next to her until after I slice Alexander's carotid.

It's the messiest way to win, and I practically slide out of the ring to wait for my last fight of the day. I insist on showering during my break, and I don't wait to hear who I've drawn for my next match. When I come out of the bathroom in my third outfit of the day, it's clear Mother has called in the heavy cavalry. That's not a good sign.

"You're doing very, very well," Mother says.

Effusive praise from my mother. Another very bad sign.

"One 'very' would have been perfectly adequate," Dad jokes. "But two? You might give my little nugget a heart attack." Mother should scowl at him for using that nickname. She hates it.

She doesn't.

If they're getting along, something bad has happened. Something very bad. "Who did I draw?"

"Magnar," Mother says. "So it's a good thing you finagled an invite to his mother's party. We knew next to nothing about him before you met him that night. He has done extremely well in his last two matches."

"The first to finish on both," Balthasar says grudgingly. Balthasar hasn't bothered to shower. I wish he'd at least wipe the dried blood off his face. I suppress a shudder and focus on my next match up.

Melisania's grandson. Rakira's son. And every scrap of information I 'gathered' came from Aline—who says she knows him well. But she's on Rakira's military team, and she's a royal with Lenora. If I told Mother where I procured the information, or if I even confessed the truth to Inara, they'd tell me Aline made it all up to screw with me, knowing I was trained in melodics.

Angel says love is founded on actions, on sacrifice, and I imagine she'd add trust to that list.

Not that I love Aline, obviously. I don't even know her. But my gut says I should believe her. She gave me two compelling reasons she offered aid—she felt Melisania was unfair to me, and she hasn't been treated very well by her own family. Not that I know what that means, exactly.

"Magnar's mother Rakira stayed with her mother after a new heir was born," Inara says. "Just as I did. She continues to advise her mother and support her sister. Also like us, Melisania has a new Consort, which means Marde and Rakira don't share a father."

"No one knows the identity of Magnar's father. Rakira has refused to share that information," Mother says. "Her refusal made him ineligible for sale."

I didn't share this, but Aline told me that Magnar's

father is another empress's Consort. Revealing his name would get Magnar killed, and likely his father as well. Magnar knows the truth, but he can't share for the same reasons. He's grown up amidst constant speculation and jokes. Rakira remains unmarried, which is acceptable among evian royals, but it's unusual for royals over a hundred years old.

"He's Rakira's only child."

Also not true, according to Aline. She told me Rakira has two half-human children she gave up at birth. For obvious reasons, Melisania has kept that under wraps. Aline says Magnar sees them periodically, his brother and his sister.

"And you recently found out that he's been their most promising fighter for thirty years, but he doesn't enjoy it." Lucas snorts. "He would rather be in a boardroom negotiating trade deals."

"But he goes where the family needs him," Mother says. "So he obviously has a strong sense of responsibility."

Aline said I'd be doing him a favor to defeat him—so he can quit all this and do what he wants to do. "And he's in love with the daughter of Melisania's Operations Manager, which is why he *loves* negotiating deals. It's a way to prove himself to his girlfriend's father."

"It's lucky you heard that gossip at the party," Mother says. "You might have a career with Angel, if you weren't Heir." She offers me a half smile.

"I saw him that night too. He's tall," I say. "And strong. His reach is better than mine, and he fights with a massive broadsword."

"He's Balthasar lite," Mother says. "Luckily, you know how to fight Balthasar."

"Speed and a thousand small jabs." It's good this is my

last fight of the day, because that's an exhausting strategy. Hopefully he's a little worn down already.

"If you let him inside your guard, he'll gut you," Lucas says.

Mother scowls at him, but I prefer honesty to forced cheer.

"That's true." And if Aline's information is wrong, I could miss his harmony entirely, and he'll squash me anyway.

"It's time," Dad says. "You can do this."

I grab my sword and my dagger and head for the door. I hope he's right.

Aline's on the second row, Paolo at her side. I wonder how her boss perceives her watching all three of my matches. She probably hasn't noticed, since Magnar has been fighting too. Surely Rakira was ringside at each. When I meet her eye this time, she doesn't smile.

Did she set me up? Does she feel guilty?

Paolo's gaze skates right over mine as though we've never met. And Rakira, right next to them, scowls at me. Ah, perhaps they can't acknowledge they know me at all. Not right in front of her. Duh.

Could the whole thing have been planned? I climb into the ring, replaying the moment I saw Aline and Paolo on the field, weapons flashing. How Inara and I lingered, and they invited us to the party.

The moment in the bathroom.

Magnar is already waiting on me. He's even bigger than Balthasar, his reach several inches longer than mine. I can't focus on fear, just like I can't focus on doubt. Instead, I contemplate my purpose today.

It's not fame. It's not accolades. It's not even Mother's approval, though that would be nice. I'm here today so that I can fulfill the destiny Dad believes lies before me. I destroyed Arinya so that I could step into the fray and fight the battle she's already waging—a battle to redirect our entire people, our purpose, and our future.

For the first time in my life, I feel a true swelling in my chest, like God is with me. This is my purpose, and I am on the right path. My heart burns. When Melisania counts down, I'm ready.

Magnar's first blow isn't skilled or well timed or particularly innovative. But it packs a wallop I haven't ever encountered. He's like a blowtorch when I'm accustomed to matches.

I block, but I stumble back anyway. Not a promising start, but I hear his melody, trumpets loud and clear. It's accompanied by the beating of strong timpani drums. That's okay. I have plans in place for this. So I pivot. He slams, and I deflect, spin, and slash back.

Slowly, I piece together his harmony. He's frustrated with being forced here. He's mad at his mother, for putting him in this place. He's furious with his father, even if he can't do anything about it.

Then it hits me. Wouldn't his father want to watch? I scan the crowd, looking. My answers might actually be outside the ring in this particular fight. Aline wasn't sure whether he knew who his father was. "Is he here?" I whisper.

Magnar pauses and swallows. Then his face flushes red.

I've made him mad. Whoops.

There are three Consorts watching. Melisania's standing between her Consort and Rakira. Adika's Consort is present, but he may be scouting me and Magnar for the next round. Dad's standing between Mother and Gideon. I'm sure it's not Dad, not that it matters. But it matters to Magnar, and now he thinks I'm taunting him.

I listen to him again, trying to filter out the harmonic

line I've been hearing. I'm missing something, but I can't figure out what. I expect him to slam me with another stroke, but he sweeps me instead.

Something utterly unexpected.

I crash to the mat, barely rolling to the left in time to avoid being skewered. My eyes land on an attractive blonde in the front row, her hand at her throat. She's not a passive onlooker—she's vested in the outcome, and I don't know her. Which means she's here for Magnar.

I scramble to my feet and lift my sword in time to block Magnar's next strike, but it knocks me to my knees and he's still coming. My mind spins frantically, grasping at straws in the absence of a plan of attack. Next to the girl stands a tall, severe man. In a suit. Her father?

I've been assuming Magnar wants to lose and escape this life. But what if his future father-in-law is impressed by his brute strength? What if he has agreed to allow Magnar to marry his daughter only if he wins? Finally the last piece clicks into place and I hear it—the fury, the frustration at all the injustice, and the element I missed before.

The desperate hope.

If Magnar beats me, he releases the anchor that has been dragging him into the deep. He's finally free to marry the girl he loves. Oh how I want that for him! He has fought, he has struggled, and all to try and win that fresh-faced girl's hand.

So he bangs away at me, one dogged blow at a time.

Now that I hear it, I know what's coming. I'm on my knees. Moments ago, I'd have been expecting another huge blow to crush me further, but now I know. He's going to go for the kill shot. He wants to end this. He'll have a dagger, or some other blade he's kept hidden in the last two rounds.

He's going to hit me again, and then using his other

hand, sever my spine with something nasty and unexpected. I could let him. I hate all of this as much as he does, but winning doesn't free me. It sets me up for more. And more. And more.

It will never end for me.

But I think about the peace I felt, the burning feeling, the surety that I am where I need to be, and I know. As much as I'd love to let Magnar win, I can't hand this to him. Dad tasked me to lay the groundwork, and I must do it. I've got my own concealed dagger.

I whip my wrist to release it and throw it straight up, lodging it in his throat. His eyes widen. He gurgles. And it's time. My sword slides up, angles between his ribs and spears straight through his heart.

Major injury sustained. I might never have gotten there without Aline's information, which was all accurate. It's a significant victory to reach on the second day. Even so, I drop to my knees and inhale and exhale repeatedly, trying to slow my heart, trying to assuage my guilt at shattering all his hopes and dreams.

I look up and meet Aline's eyes, not wanting to draw attention to the fact that I know her, but not being able to help myself. She doesn't smile, but her eyes sparkle.

Mother clears her throat on the front row a few feet over and I drag my gaze sideways to meet hers. She's watching me carefully, and I wonder what she's seen. Actually, that's not quite accurate.

I fear what she might guess.

A short burst of laughter beside her draws my attention, thankfully, and I watch Dad, laughing at something Inara said. But he's not looking at Inara. He's staring at Gideon.

Dad's always staring at Gideon. He's always laughing with Gideon.

A quick glance back at Mother reveals that she's scowling at Dad, too.

I should have seen it before. Inara and Gideon have been best friends for nearly two hundred years—practically inseparable. And yet they've never married. Mother told me Dad was flawed. She doesn't respect him, she doesn't trust him. She granted him severely limited time with me, and I never knew why. They don't agree, sure. He values humans and she doesn't.

But now I wonder whether it's more than that.

Because while Dad never looks happy around Mother, he always looks joyful when he's near Gideon. What if Dad's gay? And worse, what if Job's latest research is wrong?

What if he passed it on to me?

❧ 8 ❧

THE PAST: 2000

As I stand in the Crystal room, waiting for them to post my next match, I can't help but review the numbers. Eight people remain, and three of us are from Alamecha. Balthasar, Alora, and me.

"No other family has won Weaponry in seven hundred years," Mother says.

As if I didn't already know that. "At least if I lose, we've still got a good chance of maintaining our streak."

Mother frowns.

A few seconds later, the next match is posted, and Mother's frown lines deepen.

I'm fighting Balthasar.

I shouldn't have been dreading this. I mean, by the time you reach the very end, every single fighter is the best of the best. Fighting Alora would have been nearly as scary. She beat him the one time they fought, for heaven's sake. But the next Games, he won again. Because he was *made* for this.

And I am a baby, comparatively.

A baby waving a sword around, and Balthasar is going to

slap me down. What do I know about him? He's old. Like, eight years older than Mother. He's been her Warlord since the beginning. And his brother was her Consort. He's from Shamecha but long since stopped identifying with them in any way. He would chop Melamecha into potpourri and then slice off both his hands if Mother asked him to, and I doubt he'd even blink about doing it.

Although, once he sliced off one hand, he probably couldn't really slice off the other without help.

Boy, my mind is spinning.

Balthasar has never married, has no hobbies, and runs both the Security and Military branches within our family. That's uncommon. So he's obsessed, and he is scary, and he's pretty much indestructible. But he's old. Maybe there's something there.

Balthasar strides toward us, his head held high. His russet hair shines. His back is straight and strong. His shoulders are broad, massive even, but it's lean muscle. He's one of the strongest men I've met, but he doesn't sacrifice speed for strength.

I'm definitely going to lose.

"I've just spoken to Melisania," he says. "And I wanted to let you know my decision before it's announced."

"What?" I ask. "What decision?"

Balthasar's smile is apologetic. "I've conceded. It's not that I believe you wouldn't defeat me, but after fighting Alora years ago, I resolved never again to fight the Heir. It was a lose-lose."

Panic evacuates my body in a whoosh. "So. Wait. You can do that?"

"Of course. You can always concede." He smiles.

"I appreciate your sacrifice," Enora says. "More than you know."

He bows deeply. "I live to serve."

"You always have," Enora says softly, her eyes never leaving his.

"I may go to watch Alora's fight," I say.

"Wonderful idea." Mother finally looks away from Balthasar. "You need to listen for her melodic line. See if you can piece it out."

Dad steps a little closer. "Did I hear correctly? Did Balthasar concede, and you're going to watch Alora's next match?"

I nod.

"I'll follow you over." Dad offers me his arm and I take it.

"Her fight is in the Gallery Room," I say.

As the matches progress, fewer and fewer rings are needed, but the number of people who want to watch also grows. Consequently, the last four matches are still spread across four rooms. The walk to the Gallery Room isn't a long one, but if we want a good view, we'd better hurry.

Inara shows up a moment after we arrive, Gideon on her heels. Dad's whole face lights up when they reach us. "You're watching too?"

I wish Dad's joy didn't cause me so much distress.

"I still can't believe Balthasar conceded," Inara says. "That's totally unlike him. Alora will be furious to hear it, I imagine. Fighting him was one of the hardest things she has ever done."

"At least she won't need to do it again," I say.

"That's true," Gideon says. "Maybe she'll be pleased."

"Maybe," Inara says.

Alora walks out and climbs into the ring, the Alamecha crest emblazoned on the front of her white shirt. Thorny vines surrounding the sun. Light in the face of adversity. It's always on the front of my uniform, but I haven't really thought about it much lately. Actually, other than pondering Mother and Dad fighting, I haven't thought about adversity much in my life at all.

Alora uses a single sword, so thin, so lightweight, that it looks more like a ribbon than a blade. She doesn't speak, and she never drops her eyes from her opponent. She moves so fluidly, she nearly matches her blade. Smooth, light, effervescent even, flowing from one form to the next.

Arias. Arabesques. Progressive chords. And then she strikes. So early on, without settling in, without listening for the line of Ginnefer's attack. It's almost as though she already knew her opponent's harmony before the match began.

She slices Ginnefer's hamstring and never gives her a chance to recover. She's not playing with her, she's not cruel, or bored, or angry. She's respectful, effective, and accurate.

And she's going to destroy me unless I can figure out why she's here and what she wants. It's my only hope. So the second she climbs out of the ring, I approach her, only a little distracted by the blood spatter on her cheek. "Alora! That was masterfully executed."

Her eyebrows rise. "Melina. I assumed you'd still be fighting."

"I finished my match in under a minute." And then sprinted here, all without a speck of blood or sweat reaching any part of my body. Yeah, right.

"Against Balthasar?" Her eyebrows rocket up her forehead.

I grin. "I'm kidding. He conceded, so I decided to come and cheer you on." And wet myself, for good measure.

"Balthasar *conceded*?"

"Mother thought you might be surprised. Frankly, I was shocked, too. He's not really the kind of person who gives up on fights. Ever. Over anything."

A tall man with ink-black hair wraps an arm around her shoulder. "Brilliantly executed, again." His voice is deep, silky, and steady. He gently wipes a smear of blood from Alora's forehead and turns toward me. Flawless features, deep brown eyes, and full lips all scream evian, but it's the confidence that clinches it. I heard Alora lived among the humans and had a human husband. Apparently, I was misinformed. "I'm Isamu, your sister's husband."

"You're. . . I didn't realize. . ."

"That he's evian?" Alora laughs. "I knew Mother would press me to move home if she knew, but we love New York, and we both love our autonomy. I figured we could tell her here and hopefully convince her to leave us alone."

Does Alora even want to win?

"I'm happy to help in any way I can, but as you likely already know, Mother does what she wants without regard for what I think."

Alora says, "She hasn't changed at all, then."

"Probably not," I say. "But I'm not like her in that regard and I've been dying to see you for a long time. Tell me all about how you two met."

"Oh, that's a good story," Isamu says. "But your sister tells it much better than I do."

"But it takes some time." Alora leans against his chest. "Maybe we could meet for dinner and then you and I won't be so pressed for time."

"Will you still be keen on dinner, after you've either decimated me or I've defeated you?"

Alora laughs. "I should have come home more often. The last time I saw you, you didn't reach my shoulder. You're much funnier now. And yes, I think I can assure you that no matter today's outcome, I'll be happy to have dinner with you tonight."

"If Mother allows it," I say, "I'd love to see you then."

Alora leans close. "Good luck today. I mean that."

"Since you're both done," Inara says from behind me. "Gideon and I are going to watch the sprints on the live feed in the Noble room."

"I think I'm going to try and rest for a moment in our room upstairs," I say. "Angel's up there, and a few others, maybe." I hope not many of our people are up there, or our rest rooms will be awfully crowded.

"I'll go with you," Dad says. "I could use a break too."

"Oh, great," I say. "Okay."

Dad and I walk quietly to the elevator together.

I key in the right floor and the elevator doors close before anyone else enters.

"You're doing extremely well," Dad says.

"Would you say I'm doing very, very well?" I ask.

Dad laughs. "Your mother was trying to help. I told her you respond well to encouragement."

All I want to do is ask him about Gideon, but I can't do that. Not without being a little surer of his answer.

"Is something on your mind?" Dad asks. "You've looked. . . apprehensive this morning."

I stop, unable to help myself, and ask without meeting his eyes. "What happened between you and Mother?" Angel's words run through my head on repeat, that my parents never loved each other. But I can't make sense of it. Why would they have gotten married in the first place? I want to pretend it's not true. I badly wish to believe that they love each other, but they simply don't get along very well anymore.

But the way he was looking at Gideon, not just yesterday, but for years. Sometimes evian recall is a real curse. I need to know what it all means.

And I'm dying to ask whether I'm alone, or whether, possibly, he might understand how I'm feeling.

"That's a complicated question," Dad says. "And I'm not sure I can answer it before your next match begins, nor am I positive this is the best use of your time."

"Do you love Mother?"

He frowns.

"It's a simple question," I press. "I know you fight because you disagree fundamentally on so many things, but something drew you to her at the beginning. Did you love her then? Are you glad you married her?"

Dad flinches.

"Or."

Dad grits his teeth. "Or what?"

"Do you love someone else?"

The color drains from his face and I glance around, relieved the elevator is still closed. As if my thought prompts it, the doors ding and roll open. I don't move.

He finally says, "I—" and then he coughs.

I step off the elevator into the empty hallway.

Dad sighs like he's just escaped execution.

But I'm not letting him off that easily. "I'm asking you, because maybe I do, too."

"Excuse me?" Dad's mouth hangs open a little. I've never seen him look dopier in my life.

"I might care for someone I shouldn't. . ."

His entire face softens. "Oh, Melina. I'm sorry."

He's sorry. Which means I'm right. He does love Gideon, and he understands exactly how I feel right now. Lost, confused, scared.

Maybe even flawed.

Which means I'm not alone. Dad will surely have advice on what to do and how to handle this. Maybe he'll be able to tell me what he would do if he could do everything over again. "I don't know what to do, Dad. Do you regret marrying Mother?"

Dad gulps. "I made a conscious decision to marry Enora. I did it knowingly, and I did it after a lot of thought and consideration. I can't always control my feelings, but I can control my choices."

He holds my gaze until I nod, and I realize that I've gotten my answer, but somehow, I'm sadder for it. I trudge down the hall and through the door to our rooms, not paying attention to anyone else. I hide in the middle of my bed for a few moments, trying to find a peaceful center without any success. My thoughts careen through my mind like pinballs on uppers. Normally I'd pray, but it feels disrespectful to ask God to help me with something He likely doesn't approve of, judging by the 'most religions of the world' criterion.

Finally, I emerge.

"Omelet?" Angel holds out a plate.

"I didn't even fight my first round," I say. "I doubt I need—"

"Of course you do," Angel says. "Time has passed, and we need you in top condition."

I take the plate and force myself to chew and swallow. "Thanks," I mumble.

The elevator in the hall outside dings. Angel, Dad, and I all turn toward the door to the hallway. Inara barrels through, her eyes bright with excitement. "Mediation time is over, tiny sis. They just posted the next match."

"And?" Dad asks.

"It's Kirabo." Inara crosses the hall and opens the door. "Mother's on her way. We don't have much time to prepare."

Not that there's a lot to be done at this point. We've been over all the candidates a million times. But once my next match is announced, it feels so much more immediate.

I'm not even surprised when Mother marches through

the door like a general preparing for battle. "She's lazy from what I hear, and engages in excesses of every kind." Mother clenches her hands so tightly on the back of the carved dining chair that I'm worried she'll shatter the wood.

My mother isn't the friendliest person. She's not on the best of terms with the other five empresses, and I'm pretty sure Melamecha wouldn't offer her a rope if she were drowning. But she absolutely despises Adika, and the feeling is more than mutual. To say she'll want me to defeat Adika's daughter Kirabo would be a major understatement. I had been hoping Balthasar would knock her out. I should have considered that with him conceding, Kirabo would advance to the semi-finals.

"I'm not sure that's precisely the kind of information I should be focusing on," I say. "I was thinking less about her foibles and rumors of her excess and more—"

"Hopes, dreams, yada yada." Mother inhales deeply. "I'm the one who taught you all this."

"And I appreciate it," I say. "But maybe we need to bring in someone a little more emotionally distanced on this one."

"Kirabo was displaced by a baby sister ten years ago," Inara says. "I know a little about how that feels, but you might need to imagine."

Mother breaks in. "Then you should also imagine that your monarch is a sadistic, clinically insane—"

"If you're going to rant," Inara snaps, "then please do it on the patio so we can continue to work in here."

She doesn't leave, but she does plop onto a sofa and begin squeezing a throw pillow instead of the back of that poor chair.

"Think about what you might want in her place," Inara says. "She could be relieved."

Mother snorts.

Inara continues as though Mother isn't behaving like a toddler. "Or she could be angry. Or jealous, or most likely, some combination of those. She did leave court for several years, but she returned and has a place on her mother's council as her Warlord."

"But she chose Weaponry instead of Military," I say. "I wonder why."

"I hear she prefers not to rely on the ineptitude of others," Dad says. "She's not big on team building, or trust either, apparently."

"We should go down," Gideon says. "It's ten minutes until the match."

I grab my sword and head for the elevator. Dad stands right by me and squeezes my arm. "You've got this."

When the elevator doors open, I don't wait for any more pep talks, and I don't hang back for reassurance. I practically sprint into the hall and around the corner to the Crystal Room. Of course Paolo and his sister are waiting in the front row, both smiling.

I make a *choice* not to make eye contact and clamber into the ring, but it doesn't feel right. Kirabo follows my lead and swings into the ring as well. I can't help facing her and making my own evaluation. Alamecha always wears white—and we claim to be the true heir of the entire earth —Alamecha was the youngest daughter of Eve's youngest daughter Mahalesh. That has pitted us directly against Shenoah from the start. The youngest daughter of Mahalesh's older sister.

We rule by right—that has been an unalterable truth taught to me since my birth.

But for the first time ever, it occurs to me that Shenoah rules because of love. Mahalesh loved her sister so much that she gave her a portion that would have otherwise gone to one of her older daughters. Mahalesh loved Shenoah as much as she loved her children. Which means, if we chose, we could extend the same love our great ancestress had, instead of expending all our energy bemoaning that we were robbed.

I wonder what Mother would say to that. If love exists in *actions*, Mahalesh should have shown her love by giving everything to Alamecha. Only she didn't do that—she split control of the earth six ways. I know the world needs leaders, but sometimes it feels like our people have chosen the worst way to select them.

Melisania begins counting, and I shake myself. No time for philosophical musings, not right now. Kirabo's eyes practically glow at me from her dark face. Her hair surrounds her head in a halo, curls springing outward in all directions. Both her hands grip her enormous sword, the kind of sword most women don't wield, and there's a short spear strapped to her back. Two blades each, the rules say, no specification of what form they can take.

But I've never heard of anyone else bringing a spear.

As always, I let her mount the first attack, listening for her melody. It's surprisingly quick, staccato even. With a broadsword, I usually expect long, sweeping notes, and clean, even strokes. She almost pokes with it, like it's a spear with a very long blade, but I can hear the rhythm now.

And I understand. She's happy in this role. She's found a place for herself. She's known for a long time that she wouldn't be her mother's heir. After all, her mother's only five hundred years old. No, she's not jealous, or angry, or even relieved. At least, not anymore.

She sought her equilibrium, and she has found it. She has a purpose, she has a plan, and she knows who she is. Her blade spins toward me and I barely evade it, but I'm not expecting the spear in my back.

The blade slices deep, but before I can hop away, taking her weapon with me as payback for the injury, she yanks it backward. Blood gushes down my back and my entire right side goes numb. My sword point dips.

Kirabo knows this is her chance. She drops her spear and brings her broadsword down with both hands, her spear clattering against the ground as her sword meets the tiny blade of my blocking dagger. My entire body shudders with the blow, and blood pours down my arm and onto the mat, splattering the discarded spear.

I kick the spear upward with the edge of my foot and catch the blade, slicing my palm open in the process. I should drive the spear through Kirabo's chest. I should end this right now. I see the kill strike in my mind—her widened eyes, her exhalation of pain.

But suddenly, I hear my own harmony, for the first time in my life, and it's nothing like Kirabo's. It's not sure, it's not at peace, and it's not established or happy. It's lost, haunting, confused. I'm only fighting this brilliant, shining warrior because Mother wants me to win and Dad asked me to do it.

My purpose crumbles and I drop the spear and meet Kirabo's eyes. She twists her blade, releasing it from my dagger and bringing it under my ribcage. When it pierces my heart, I finally understand the phrase heartbroken.

Because the spear cleaving my heart in two? It's not nearly as bad as when my dad told me he chooses to be with my mother every day, even though he doesn't love her.

And he expects me to do the same. . . for the next thousand years.

❧ 9 ❧

THE PAST: 2000

When Mother opens the door, her back is to me, but her voice carries fine. "For the first time in seven centuries, Alamecha did not win Weaponry. You're brave, Alora, coming to dinner tonight."

Alora doesn't miss a beat. "It's wonderful to see you too, and I'm quite proud of making it to the final round, even if Kirabo defeated me." She pushes past Mother, dragging Isamu with her. "I'm also proud of Melina. We were defeated by the same warrior, but we both did an excellent job at the Millennial Games."

"Balthasar shouldn't have conceded," Mother says.

"Perhaps not," Alora says, "but there's no way to know."

Mother's face blanks. "You're right, and I apologize. For my bad mood and for my terrible manners. It is wonderful that you came to the Games, and you did an excellent job. Second best in the world isn't too bad." It's clear the words are acid on Mother's tongue, but she says them.

At least she's trying.

"Neither is tied for third," Alora says. "Especially for someone who's only twenty years old."

"And whom did you bring with you?" Dad asks. "Did I hear earlier that he's your husband?"

Mother's eyes widen. "You've remarried? Again? You're just like your grandmother."

Alora laughs. "Cainina had eighteen husbands. Isamu is my fourth. I hardly think that's comparable."

"My mother lived nearly nine-hundred years," Mother says. "Give it time. You might catch her."

"We all need goals." Alora wraps an arm around Isamu's waist.

"If you'd marry more durable men, they might last a little longer," Balthasar says.

"A joke," Alora says. "Are you growing soft in your old age? Is that why you conceded?"

Balthasar grunts.

Angel pops her head through the door. "Dinner is ready."

"Thank goodness," Inara mutters.

"Before we sit down," Isamu says, "Alora needs to explain something. I'd hate to stay under false pretenses."

Mother's eyebrows rise.

Balthasar's hand goes to the hilt of his sword.

Frederick's shoulders stiffen.

I can't see Lucas or any of my other guards, but I'm guessing they're bristling, too.

"I was sent to New York City as a spy by Lainina." Isamu holds his hands out in front of him, palms face up.

"I flipped him," Alora says. "And we fell in love during the process."

"Only the Empress may grant him admission into the family." Mother's eyes flash.

"Which is why we are here, above board." Alora meets Mother's gaze.

"You should have requested a pardon before marrying." Mother crosses her arms. "But you gambled and married first. And then you came to compete in the Games, an activity you have long eschewed as pointless, in order to remind me that you still have a skillset I might find useful. That's quite a lot of effort to ensure that I don't remove your shiny new husband's head from his broad and serviceable shoulders."

"Even so," Alora says. "I thought bringing it up in this room—the very first time I've seen you in person, as the law requires—might be a better idea than flying into Ni'ihau and sitting through an exhausting hearing."

"But you lost." Mother scowls.

Alora laughs. "You're every bit as awful as I remember."

A bomb shelter might not be enough cover, but I'd dive behind the sofa if I didn't think Mother would be drawn to the movement. Anything to spare myself from the imminent blood spatter.

But Mother doesn't behead Alora, or throw her to the wolves either. I would never have predicted her response, not in a hundred years.

Mother throws her head back and laughs. When she finally stops, a tear rolls down her cheek. She swipes at it absently and crosses the room to hug Alora. She whispers, "I've missed you so much it physically pains me."

"So you grant him admission?" Balthasar asks. "Or should I draw my sword?" He strokes the hilt of his blade. "Maybe we could mount his head in the arena as a warning."

"Did you make two jokes in the same ten minute period?" Alora beams. "Balthasar, I'm worried you're stroking out."

"Isamu may keep his beautiful face for now," Mother says. "I'll instruct Larena to include him on the rolls for Alamecha. It's about time you married an evian."

"You didn't even ask his generation." Alora beams. "I'm so impressed with your restraint, but I know it's killing you. He's twelfth, but he's not on the records."

"Which was legal, because he wasn't royal until last week," Dad says. "Brilliant for someone going into intelligence."

Isamu shrugs. "It seemed prudent, but now I hope it doesn't impede my future with Alora."

"Your old family doesn't matter," Mother says. "As long as you're dedicated to your new one."

He bows. "I am, Your Majesty. I'll gladly swear my oaths to you at any point."

"After dinner, I hope," Angel says. "I time these things carefully, you know. Thanks to Alora's theatrics, the soup is cold and the prime rib will be overcooked. Any longer delays and the soufflés will go flat."

"And nothing is quite as tragic as a flat soufflé," I say.

Angel winks at me. "At least someone understands me."

By the end of dinner, after hearing the story of Alora's first meeting with Isamu and the way she discovered him, thanks to a jar of grape jelly no less, Mother isn't nearly as disappointed with my loss. But when Alora leaves, and everyone else heads to their rooms, I can see it in her eyes.

She may have forgiven Alora, but I'm a different matter. I didn't just let her down. I let the entire family down. But tomorrow is another day, and I'm back in the saddle for another event. I square my shoulders and stand up to go to bed, too.

Mother grabs my arm. "I saw you pause."

My heart skips a beat.

"I may not have been part of that fight, but I heard her,

and I heard you."

"That's not possible."

Melodics is a song made by the two combatants. You can't hear it from the outside, not the same way. Your perspective warps it.

"You're my daughter, child of my womb. I know your song—I've heard it for two decades now. You were in that fight, and you heard her too. Why did you hand her the win?"

She told me before that my weakness is in my hesitation, my reluctance to harm others. She was right. I chose not to win, knowing it would harm her, harm the family, and harm myself. But I placed our harm below the harm it would do to Kirabo in that moment—probably because of my own issues.

With a little space, it's clear that I made the wrong choice.

I put my own desires above what the family needed. For the first time, I understand what Dad meant. I can choose every day. I can do what needs to be done, like Mother has for hundreds of years. Like Dad has done since marrying her. Like I am expected to do every day.

Or I can make the easy choice, the one that feels good. Mother's right. The hard choice is the right one. I can't deny her accusation, because she would hear the lie. "I'm sorry, Mother."

"Spare me the apologies. Don't ever do that again. Hesitation is always cowardice."

"I understand."

"Your father has his own agenda. I ignore it, but I won't ignore it if it weakens this family and my heir. Do you understand?"

Is she threatening him? My heartrate accelerates and I blink several times.

"Get some sleep. You have a big day tomorrow."

I spend most of the night reviewing past events and wondering whether to warn Dad. Ultimately, I decide that it's not like she said she would harm him. Just that she wouldn't ignore his agenda anymore. I finally fall asleep, but I'm not sure at what time.

The next morning, Inara and Angel wake me up and present me with a tall glass on a tray.

I rub my eyes. "What's that?"

"You don't look very good," Inara says. "Did you sleep at all?"

"Good morning to you, too," I say.

"You have actual bags under your eyes," Angel says. "I'd tell you to go back to sleep, but that's not an option. You're due in less than an hour, and they're locking the room down. If you're late, you'll miss it."

I force myself to swing my legs out of bed and hold out my hand for whatever concoction they've worked up. The first sip is surprisingly good. "What is this?"

Inara bites her lip.

"Do you like it?" Angel asks.

"It's an energy blend," Inara says. "Something new called goji berries, and a handful of other fruits. Plus some protein powder."

I slurp up the rest, energy buzzing through my body as the fuel hits my bloodstream. "That's not all that's in there, or you'd have just said 'it's a smoothie.'"

"It might have raw eggs," Angel says. "You know how much your mother loves them. She insisted."

Raw eggs? Blech. At least I couldn't taste them. "I do feel better."

"Color's returning to your face. Thank heavens for good genetics," Inara says. "I imagine I'd be a little stressed after a huge loss too."

Uh. "Thanks."

"I don't mean it like that." Inara sits next to me. "I mean, I get it. Today's scary. By the end of the day, you'll be done, and it's going to be an intense twelve hours."

"Timed moves, forced alliances, constant maneuvering." Angel shakes her head. "In some ways, it's worse than real life."

"But at least no one actually dies if I choose wrong," I say.

"That's true enough," Inara says. "But your win today could help prevent war in the future."

"I've heard that already." I yank some clothing out of my suitcase and march toward the bathroom. "I'll be sure to put on my most peaceful blouse."

Mother provides nearly as much support as Inara and Angel. She walks me to the door to check in and stops me with a hand on my wrist. "Remember."

"Failure is a choice," I say. Mother's personal motto, but in light of my loss last night, and my hesitation, it's especially fitting.

"Make sure you choose right today." Mother releases my wrist.

"I will."

Dad throws me a double thumbs up from behind Mother, but he's not fooling me. He cares as much as she does.

Luckily, the first match-up always includes one contestant from each family. I'm not even surprised that I've been placed on the third level. It's the selection least likely to win the match, strictly from a probability perspective, but I like working my way up. The view is always the best from the bottom. There's nowhere to go but the right direction.

After a decade of preparing, the first match is almost a disappointment. I play conservatively and wait for my opponents to make a blunder. After being forced to read the hopes and dreams of opponents who are swinging blades at me, watching for flinches, blanches, and heart-stutters is a little anti-climactic. It only takes me two dozen moves to eliminate the Analessa competitor on the third level with me and ascend to level two.

By the time I do, Shenoah's candidate has already decimated Adora's. I take his king, thank you very much Hubert from Shenoah, and create an heir for myself in the process. Two queens on the board is the only thing better than one.

It allows me to sacrifice one after destroying Hubert while ascending to level one. That level presents the first real issue. Somehow, in all this time, the two top level competitors have accomplished relatively little. They both still have a handful of pieces, and they're pretty evenly matched.

Which tells me they're nervous that the wolf is coming for them. So I do something strange and ascend the throne the very second I'm able. They eliminate six of my pieces in the process, but neither of them is eligible to rise, which means they'll have to keep trying to kill one another in order to pursue me, and I'll be left fighting only one of them from above.

The congratulations start before the last few moves finalize it.

Now if only the next two matches could be completed this simply. . . It takes nearly an hour for the other ten games to conclude. Of sixty-six initial contestants selected for Sovereignty, only eleven players move to round two. Each of us destroyed all five competitors in round one.

And all of them are hoping to shred me in the same way.

It takes the judges half an hour to determine the configuration for the second round. They finally post the lineup, and I'm as eager to see it as everyone else. Eleven competitors remain, which is enough for two games. One including five players, and one including six. I've been assigned to the full set, along with five others:

Alwina of Malessa

Catherine of Alamecha

Casimer of Adora

Pershing of Shamecha

Yetta of Malessa

Catherine is one of Mother's security officers. She runs the European contingent, so I don't often see her, but it's strange they would pair two competitors from Malessa and two from Alamecha.

I glance at the list for the other match. Another set of Malessa, and both Richter and Ian from Alamecha. That explains it—Alamecha and Malessa are dominating this year. It makes Catherine an obvious ally, which means they'll likely put us together from the outset.

I'm not at all surprised when I reach the proper table to discover that Malessa's two competitors begin on level three, and Catherine and I are both assigned to face off on level two. Catherine's wearing black pants and a grey shirt —typical security issue fatigues. Her hair is pulled back into a simple ponytail. Everything about her screams no nonsense.

But she smiles at me the second we sit down. "It's an honor, your highness."

"We have a few options," I say.

She advances her first piece boldly, offering a sacrifice. "You may eliminate me without resistance."

It's the strongest move I could make—clearing the board with the least troop loss—and it's also what Alwina and Yetta are already doing just below us. Alwina's gobbling up Yetta's pieces with compete abandon, coming at me with an heir already created. Consuming Catherine is my lowest risk move. If I send Catherine up and she botches the play, I'll lose my advantage. Or if she turns on me, I'll go down in flames.

Catherine's deep brown eyes hold no malice, and she's clearly used to taking directions. I trust that she's both loyal and competent.

Up it is.

"They won't expect me to send you ahead." I shift my piece out of the way.

The side of her mouth curls. "An advance attack to carve a path."

"Kamikaze style."

"It leaves you to defend against a full strength assault from below," Catherine says.

"I can handle them." I split my forces around Catherine's advancing armies. "But." I glance at Casimer and Pershing. Both male, both tight-lipped, both fierce. "You need to choose a target."

"Which?" Catherine asks.

She's asking me to choose the player who will come in second place. The last to be eliminated advances to the third round with a harder position. Do I choose the weakest, or the strongest competitor?

Everyone always chooses the weakest. After all, they could lose to them in the next round. Analessa winners regularly finish in the top at Sovereignty. They're brilliant strategists, and they're skilled at negotiating. I could forge an alliance with Alwina that would carry me through the first part of the next game.

It's what Mother would do. She'd leverage a joint attack on level one in exchange for passage through level two. If I allow Catherine to do a lot of damage and fall back just in time, I could get the best of both worlds. Eliminate her, granting me access to the throne and softening the resistance from above.

But I'm not my mother. Dad warned me against just this.

Shamecha hasn't won Sovereignty in a thousand years. Pershing is tenth generation, son of Melamecha's oldest daughter. Which means he's also my second cousin through my dad.

"Take out Casimer."

Catherine doesn't hesitate. And while I have my hands full with Alwina, I keep an eye on her moves as well. Pershing immediately realizes what we're doing, and he smiles at me, broadly. It takes me two pieces more than I expect to eliminate Alwina, and Pershing has defeated Catherine and already ascended to the throne by the time I reach level one.

Unfortunately, he's strung out his position in the process. I could decimate his troops and eliminate his king if I chose, shoving him squarely into second place. Again, it's what Mother would do. She'd show him, in no uncertain terms, that she's the stronger player. She'd go into the final round in first place and secure the best position from the outset.

But I've always liked the sideways plays. I used one to defeat Mother at chess that first time, with the Grob. I've used it on multiple occasions with Dad, and I'll try it today. Be who I am, Dad said to me the night before we left. So I allow Pershing to shepherd his pieces up and I ascend behind him.

Firmly in second place.

"Thank you," he whispers.

I chose well. He knows I could have destroyed him at the

end, and I didn't. It's exactly what Dad wants me to do—I'm already Heir. I have a position, a family, fame and support. Pershing has none of that. He's been attacking from below his entire life. If I had chosen to drive through, straight to the top, Casimer and Alwina would have destroyed him together.

No one ever gives Pershing a leg up, not in Sovereignty, not in life. Except I did, and he's unlikely to forget it. I could do worse than going into the final round with a friend at my back.

There's no break between games, which is part of the difficulty. Since our game was the last to finish, it's time to begin the last round almost immediately. My stomach growls with displeasure and my hands shake. They'll bring me a drink if I ask for one, but then I'll need to go to the bathroom and that's no better.

Melisania steps through the door and holds her hands out, gesturing wildly. "You four have advanced to the final round. Congratulations. You've brought honor to your families. But it's time to determine our winner. The board is being set right now. From the first match, Pershing from Shamecha advances into position on level one, and Melina Alamecha advances onto board two. From the second game our level one candidate is my niece, Omelia of Lenora, and advancing to level two is Claude of Analessa. Best of luck to you all." She glances over her shoulder. "The boards are set, so please take your seats."

A wave of exhaustion crashes over me. I wish I could do a dozen jumping jacks, but that would alert the other players to my state. Instead, I bite a chunk out of the inside of my lip, blood flooding my mouth.

Yep, that did it.

I swallow several times, careful not to gag when I swallow the chunk of my own flesh. Once I'm sure there won't be blood in my teeth, I introduce myself. "I'm Melina of Alamecha. It's an honor to play against you all."

"The honor is all mine," Claude says. "I've already far exceeded my mother's expectations."

"Commence play," Melisania says.

I expect Omelia and Pershing to immediately attack one another, but as though they had a plan in place, they both attack down.

Both targeting me.

Three on one? Impossible to recover from that, if that's what is happening. My only hope is that the über polite Claude isn't in on it. I ignore him and defend against both sides at once, leaving my king wide open to Claude.

In some kind of miracle, Claude attacks Omelia instead of ending me. When I glance his way in shock, he shrugs. "She stole the last round. It pissed me off."

With Claude's help, we drive them both back up. Then he and I begin to maneuver, both of us with one eye on the fighting above us. But Claude's short game isn't as strong as mine. When I take his king, I bite my lip.

"It's fine," he says. "That was a good game. I was lucky to play against you. Good luck."

But as it happens, I don't need it. Omelia took a bigger beating in their attempt to destroy me, and Pershing finished her off quickly. I might have regretted taking him out, if he had taken more than three seconds to double team me. But as it is, I push my queen and heir on opposite sides, stalking him like a pack of cheetahs would to take out a wounded gazelle.

I could have ascended the throne and attacked from above, but I'm too angry for that. No, I track his troops down one by one, eliminating each one in turn. Then my queen takes out his king while his queen is stuck in the corner by my heir. My heir takes his queen down, even though it's unnecessary. When I ascend the throne, there's no one left on the board to oppose it.

"You surprised me," I say. "I didn't expect you to team up with Omelia."

"Fear is a great motivator," he says. "We both figured that was our only shot."

"It would have worked," I say.

"Except Claude came to your defense," he says.

"He could have taken me down," I say. "And with an heir, he might have defeated both of you on level two."

"Honor," Pershing says, "is a funny thing. He should have done that."

Somehow, even though I won, I wish I'd lost like Claude. I felt better after my last round than I do winning the entire thing. Of course, once they open the doors, that sentiment shifts a little.

"You won!" Mother smiles broadly at me. "It was brilliant, every single move. I'm extremely proud of you." She hugs me.

Mother is gushing. She's hugging me. She never gushes and hugs.

The second she releases me, Dad swings me into his arms. "Flawless, darling. Absolutely flawless. You've redeemed yourself in every way."

Inara, Gideon, Angel, and Lucas. Everyone babbles with joy and pride. Everyone is delighted. It's the exact opposite of how I felt yesterday, when I didn't make the decision everyone demanded of me, and I lost. Maybe Dad's on to something. Maybe life is about choices, and we have the power to make choices that are selfish or choices that will bring joy to everyone around us.

Which is why, when I notice Aline standing at the back of the room, smiling coyly, I meet her eyes and then I pointedly walk away.

❧ 10 ❧

THE PAST: 2000

I collapse into my bed the second we reach our beach house and sleep until the following morning. The next day I watch with everyone else as Lucas and Balthasar go on to win first place in Military. Balthasar's an excellent Commander, and his troops know it. They listen to every word and react immediately.

I'm not sure when Rakira's team is eliminated, but Aline and Paolo aren't competing the second day at all. I know, because every time I turn around, she's there. She doesn't smile at me again, but I can't seem to get away from her.

I wish I didn't need to—the hurt look in her eyes eats at me.

We're about to leave for the airport when Paolo walks toward me in the hall. He slips a note into my hand as he passes. I'm tempted to throw it in the trash, but I can't quite bring myself to do it. Mother's discussing last minute details with Frederick while Lucas and Balthasar run through protocols with the guards. I glance down at the note, spreading it across my palm.

Don't you need to pee?

That's the message? Paolo wants to know whether I've gone to the bathroom?

But of course the note isn't from him at all. It's from Aline. And the only time we've been even somewhat honest with one another was in the bathroom.

My heart rate spikes, which someone is bound to notice. I have to get out of here, and the bathroom is only a dozen feet ahead of me. "I'll be out in a moment." I point at the restroom.

"Sure," Lucas says, barely pausing to acknowledge me. "Caden, wait outside the door." He turns back to Balthasar and asks him something about the route and traffic.

I practically race toward the doorway, and Caden smirks at me. He's my favorite guard for a reason. He's got a sense of humor. I shrug and duck inside, my heart hammering against my ribs.

I'm actually disappointed when there's no one else around. I push my way into a stall and close the door to give my heart a second to slow. Why would she send me in here? Is it the wrong bathroom?

The sound of the door startles me and I nearly fall into the toilet bowl. If I came out soaking wet—Mother's face. I can't quite help my laugh.

"Having a good time in there?"

Her voice is the same as I remember from last time. Husky. Droll. I stand up and walk out. Again, I'm facing her in a bathroom after hiding in a stall, and again, I don't need to wash my hands, but I feel compelled. I don't want her thinking I'm dirty.

Plus, it gives me something to do. I walk past her, ignoring the pounding of my own heart to listen for hers.

It sounds exactly the same—she's nervous too.

"We don't have much time." I turn on the water. "Mother's waiting."

"I saw her," Aline says. "And I understand."

"What do you want?" I spin around, my eyes wide.

"Nothing," Aline says. "I don't want anything from you. But I couldn't let you leave without saying something. With as shocked as you looked when our hands touched at the party, I'm guessing you've never felt this way before."

"Have you?" My eyes widen.

Aline steps toward me then and I can't breathe. I can't think. I can't do anything but blink and blink.

"I've never felt, around *anyone else,* the way I feel when I look at you." Her eyes burn. "But I've known I was gay for years. I'm guessing that's the difference."

I open my mouth, but no words emerge.

"You're Heir—I get it. But if anything ever changes." Aline steps so close that only inches separate us. "Melisania is very progressive. It's not illegal to be who I am within Lenora. I know the idea of leaving Alamecha seems impossible to you, but if that ever changes, I'd be very curious to see where this might lead. Somewhere good, based on the chemistry between us. My brother, Paolo, he understands and he supports me. You might be surprised who could accept you, the real you."

The real me.

I close my eyes. Her breath on my face and the smell of salty air and coconut. Every cell in my body hums. I'll never forget this feeling.

But I've already chosen, and I will choose every single day, just like Dad. My path isn't strewn with dancing and coconuts and stolen kisses. I'm the Heir of Alamecha. I'm Dad's daughter, and he has a purpose for my life, a plan that I understand the importance of—rerouting the course of the evians—redirecting all the children of Eve. I can't do that if I run away and hide. I am more defined by my parents and my calling than by the yearnings of my heart.

I inhale one last time and then I shake my entire body, as if I can dislodge this part of myself and leave it in Brazil.

"I can't," I say.

Aline's lips tremble, but she bobs her head. "I understand. I really do, and I'll be cheering for you."

My knees don't give out, and my heart beats slow and steady when I walk out of the bathroom with clean hands and a clear conscience.

The trip home blurs together, and I feel a little adrift. I've been aimed at the Millennial Games for so long, like a torpedo sent to destroy Mother's enemies, that I'm not sure what to do now that they're over.

I'm not even sure who I am anymore.

The day after our return, I report to the courtyard outside Mother's room for training before breakfast, like always. Only, she's not there. The door to her room is unlocked and I tap before entering as a courtesy.

"Mother?" I ask. "Am I early?" I know I'm not.

"Oh, I'm sorry." She's sitting at her desk, chewing.

"You're eating? Aren't we training today?"

She nods. "Of course. I forgot to tell you that Balthasar will be taking over for a while. He had some suggestions for improving your technique."

I lift one eyebrow. "One loss and you're giving up on melodics?"

"It was a significant loss," she says. "A loss I blame on your soft heart. Sladius doesn't rely on your understanding of the opponent. It relies on agility, skill, ferocity. It might have kept your weakness from blocking your success."

I drop into the chair next to her without asking permission. "What's going on?"

Mother shrugs.

I listen for her heart. Is she nervous? Agitated? It's a little faster than usual, but. . .

"Wait. What is that?" I ask.

Mother taps her fingers on the table.

I slam my hand down over hers and still the noise. "You're trying to mask it."

She yanks her hand away. "Excuse me?"

"It's faint. It's barely there, but it's . . . it's a heartbeat."

Mother smiles. "Impressive attention to detail. Someone trained you well."

"When were you going to tell me that you're pregnant?" Hope soars inside of me. A little sister would free me. I could leave here, and Mother would have another child to torture in my place. I spare a moment of pity for that little girl, but I don't know her. I don't owe her anything.

Aline.

No, I can't think like that. I've chosen to walk this path.

"It's probably a boy," Mother says. "For some reason, of the eighty-one children I've given birth to, only twelve have been female."

But if it's not.

Mother leans forward and takes my hand. "Melina, you don't need to worry. I'm sure it's a boy."

"Have you already had an ultrasound?" I ask.

She shakes her head. "They'll do one in another week or so. It's early yet."

"Right." I bob my head. "Are you—" I choke. "Are you happy about it?"

Her hand shifts to her belly and her eyes are unfocused. "I am. A baby is always a blessing."

"I'm delighted, then," I say. "I'm not nervous at all. And if it's a girl, that's fine too."

"Thank you." Mother glances at the clock. "You

shouldn't be late for your first day of a new training regimen."

Right. I stand up and walk toward the door to the hall, my sneakers sinking into her thick carpet. "Wait." I turn around. "Does Dad know?"

"Not yet," she says. "He's coming to breakfast so I can tell him."

"I'm the first one to know?"

She grins. "You are. Your first sibling."

"Oh? And what's Inara? And the other eighty? Chopped liver?"

Mother laughs. It's rare, but the sound brings me joy. "Your first full sibling."

"I hope it's a girl," I say.

Her eyes widen. "You do?"

"So that I actually get to know her. I won't spend any time at all with a boy."

Mother stands up and begins to pace.

"What's going on?"

She spins on her heel, her hair flying out behind her. "I've been considering something. It's allowed, but it's not common."

"What?" I ask.

"I've been thinking that if it is a boy. . ."

"Yes?"

"I might keep him."

"Senah kept her last son," I say.

Mother frowns. "Yes, that worked out well."

"Edam's a sweet boy, Mother. You're not upset that he was older when you bought him, right?"

"I'd rather not keep this boy, if it is a boy, and then wonder whether you'll sell him when I die."

I laugh. "I'm nothing like Analessa. I'd never sell my sibling."

She stiffens. "I'm not saying you shouldn't have sold your other sons. I know you did it for me and your other daughters, so the other families would sell you theirs and we'd have choices."

"Speaking of choices."

A knot forms in my stomach.

"Do you have a preference for any of them?"

I shake my head.

"Balthasar adores Lucas."

I think about my 'guards,' the men Mother purchased so she could raise a cadre of men who are loyal to our family, acceptably well bred, and genetically pure. None of them particularly appeal to me.

"I think worrying about my future consort can wait until we find out whether I even need one," I say.

A knock at the door lets me know Dad's here.

"I better go," I say.

"Or maybe you should stay," Mother says. "It's your family, too. It might be good to have us all together for this."

I open the door and Dad's shocked face makes me smile.

"Is everything okay?" he asks, still standing in the doorway.

"Come in," Mother says. "We have some news."

Dad glances from me to Mother and back again. "What did I miss?"

"Would you like to tell him?" Mother asks.

"Tell me what?" Dad frowns.

"It's good news." I beam. "We're having a baby."

Dad's face contorts. "I'm going to kill him, whoever he is. I will cut his throat. You're only twenty."

"Excuse me?" I wave my arms at him. "Mother is pregnant, not me."

His mouth drops open and he turns toward Mother. I'm not sure what to expect, not after that dramatic misunderstanding. But as comprehension dawns, his mouth turns upward into the biggest smile I've ever seen on his face. Then he whoops.

In the middle of the palace.

Huge, energetic shouts continuously erupt from his mouth. "I hope she has your eyes," he finally says. "And my nose." He picks up Mother and swings her around and around, and I don't think I've ever been so happy.

I've certainly never seen them this happy, not in more than two decades.

Dad finally releases Mother, and he reaches out his hand for mine. He's hugging me tightly when Mother drops her second bomb.

"I've been thinking about it, and Melina agrees with me. If it's a boy, we'd like to keep him."

Why is she dragging me into this? Then it hits me. She's not sure how he'll react, and she's worried. I'm her shield.

"Oh yes, we'll keep it." Dad whoops again, even louder this time.

And for the first time in years, I hope that things between my parents might be reparable. Maybe love really is an action, a decision, or in this case, a divine gift.

❧ 11 ❧

THE PAST: 2001

I hate training with Balthasar. He's not bad, of course, but I miss melodics. Without listening for what motivates your opponent, we're basically just hacking at people and healing the damage as fast as we can so we can whack at them more.

Other than enduring my daily training, my life has never been better.

Mother goes for daily runs with Dad, and they come back smiling. I was disappointed when the ultrasound revealed that the baby is a boy, but they don't seem to care. In fact, Dad might have been happier. He kept squeezing my hand and saying, "Nothing needs to change."

My stallion Splash and I are only a few paces behind Inara and her high strung mare, Savannah, their hooves pounding against the sand on the north shore, when Lucas sprints out of the shrubbery into our path.

"It's time," he shouts.

I yank the reins so hard that poor Splash nearly rears back. "Let's go, boy. I've got a brother to meet." He wheels around and takes off even faster toward the palace. Sometimes I forget how blessed I am. Mother and Father both love me, I live in a beautiful home, I have an absolutely fabulous horse, and I spend most of my time with a sister who would cut off her arm to keep me safe.

I beat Inara home, but I don't even stop to gloat. I throw the reins to a groom. "Cool him down for a long time, okay? Then give him a fistful of the apple treats. They're his favorite."

Poor Splash's sides heave in and out, and sweat coats his neck and belly. I rub his nose for a moment before rushing to the infirmary. It's always empty—hello, evians don't need much help—but not today. Mother's finally having my little brother, and I can't wait to meet him.

Dad meets me at the door to Mother's room holding a baby in his arms.

"Whoa," I say.

"Is that what you said to Splash?" Dad asks.

"What?"

"I figured maybe you told him to slow down, and that's what took you so long to get here."

My mouth falls as my eyes meet my tiny little brother's for the very first time. "I raced here as quickly as I could."

"With evian deliveries, if you blink, you miss it," Dad says. "Trust me, nugget. I've seen a human one, and you'll be glad of that eventually."

"Can I hold him?" I ask.

Dad passes the tiny bundle off to me carefully. "Support his neck," he says. "He could heal the damage, but I figure we'll give him a few weeks before we start the training on that."

"No kidding." My little brother smiles at me. The completely toothless grin should freak me out, but for some reason the shiny pink gums and doughy cheeks are the perfect combination to inspire pure, unadulterated bliss. "I could squeeze him forever."

His smile goes on and on.

Until, in the span between one second and the next, it shifts. Into a wail. "Oh no," I say. "I think I broke it."

I pass him back to my dad, the horrible mewling sound like nails on a chalkboard. No, worse. Like someone running a razor blade across my brain. "Make it stop." I begin pacing. "How do we make it stop?"

Dad laughs. "He's just hungry. Your mother should be recovered enough to feed him by now."

"She wasn't healing?" I hate the note of fear in my voice. Having a baby isn't scary, not to us, but for some reason I'm nervous anyway.

"She healed up immediately, what little healing she needed. But then she wanted to take a shower before people started coming to wish her congratulations."

"Heaven forbid she look a little disheveled or tired," I say. "After having a baby."

Dad laughs. "The day you were born was the happiest day of my life. Right up until this moment."

"Great." I poke the wailing newborn. "I loved you so much, little guy, for five minutes, until you started howling and Dad confessed he already loves you more than me."

"Let's get him to your mother." Dad beams at me. "I know you're kidding, but for the record, today is only better because I have two kids now, instead of one."

I understand completely, and my heart is full. All my dreams are finally coming true. The rest of the day is perfect. Mother nurses him, and then she shows me how to change his diaper.

"Flawless DNA and we haven't come up with a better system than this to deal with baby poo?" Complaining is fun, because my parents both get it.

"You never need to change him, you know," Dad says. "There are plenty of people who will do it."

"No, I want to help." I finish the diaper and swaddle him up, like Mother showed me. And once he's nice and warm again, my little brother smiles at me. "Besides, if you sub-contract all the gross parts, you miss all the best parts. Look at this little face."

Dad coos, but Mother frowns. Uh oh. "What did I say?"

"Nothing." Mother shakes her head and reaches for him.

"What will we call him?" I ask. "Have you two agreed on a name yet?"

"Not quite," Mother says. "Do you have any suggestions?"

"How about Jered?" I ask. "With two Es?"

"I like that," Dad says.

"I don't hate it," Mother says.

"It's our frontrunner, then." Dad sits down next to me on the sofa. "So far, anything I've liked, your mother has hated, and vice versa."

Story of their marriage. If I'd known all they needed was another baby to repair it, I'd have pushed for this long ago. The next few hours are amazing. But eventually Mother looks worn out.

"I may head back to my room and give you two some room to enjoy little Jered."

"So that's the name?" Dad asks.

Mother smiles at me. "I think it is. We may have made him, but he'll have the name his sister gave him."

The next few days go pretty well, too. I spend most days with Mother and Dad and little Jered, and they all seem pretty happy. He's burbling, they're not fighting, and I'm at peace.

"Why are you taking a photo?" Mother asks me, one week after Jered's birth.

"He's a week old today," I say. "I don't want forget what he looks like."

"You can't forget," Mother says. "You're evian."

"Fine," I say. "Then I want to print them out and put them on the wall so I can look at them. I want to be able to flip through photos of him and see how much he has grown each week. That's a reasonable request, I think."

Mother turns away.

"What?" I ask. "What's wrong? You didn't take photos of me?"

"You know that I did."

Dad takes Jered from me. "I think your mother is thinking of other babies for whom she never took photos."

I shrug. "Right, but you can't help being old. I'm sure you painted portraits or something."

I don't recognize the sound at first, because I've never heard my mother cry. Once I realize what's going on, I pass Jered off to Dad and escape. I hope that consoling her will bring them together.

Except it doesn't.

The next few days progressively worsen. Mother loves Jered, that's clear, but she's also mourning the babies she lost. I bring a bouquet of Mother's favorite flowers, plumeria. Before I can walk through the door and hand them to her, I hear the strident voices and freeze.

"You chose to sell them. I hadn't even met you yet." Dad's tone bristles, like the back of an angry cat.

"I didn't have a choice. You know that."

"You're the bloody Empress. You're the only one in the world who can do whatever she wants. Always. And don't I know it."

"It's not that simple. There are consequences to every

action I take. I didn't make up this particular convention, but there are good reasons for it. I did as I was taught, as we must to succeed on the throne."

"What if what you were taught is wrong? You've never been brave enough to say, 'Then I won't do it.' That has always been our problem."

"You think you're the only one who knows right and wrong. Everything is so black and white for you, but the world isn't black and white. It's everything in between, and I have to do what needs to be done to maintain your splotches of truth, to keep order, so you can sit up there on your high horse and judge me safely."

"For someone holding all the power, you sure are a coward."

"Get out," Mother screams. "If you won't even try to understand, then leave."

"What I understand is that you did something terrible, and you have done, over and over, and now you're doing something even worse. You're turning away from your own child, a child you have right here in front of you, because of the way you abused the others."

"If you don't leave this second, I will end you. Do you hear me?"

Dad flies through the doorway without even noticing me.

I should go inside and try to talk some sense into Mother, but she's never listened to me. That's unlikely to change now. I drop the flowers on the tile floor and run back to my room, tears streaming down my face.

How has something so happy turned into something so *wrong?* I give my parents the day to cool down, but the next morning, my arms ache to hold my little brother. If I can just look into his eyes, I'll be okay. After all, Mother fought with Dad my entire childhood, but Inara was always there.

A place of peace in a world of anger. I can do the same for Jered. I want to run to the nursery, but I force myself to walk.

When I arrive, Dad's leaning against the window, staring at the ocean waves.

There's no sign of a baby in the room. "Where's Jered?"

Dad doesn't turn to face me. "Ask your mother."

I want to argue with him. I don't want to track her down. Why won't he just tell me? But something about the slump in his shoulders, the tension in his shoulders, the dejection in his voice, keeps me from pressing.

This time, I don't keep to a reasonable walk. I sprint down the hall to Mother's room and don't wait for anyone's permission to enter. Mother's rocking slowly in a glider when I arrive, but her arms are empty. Her eyes are downcast and unnervingly vacant.

"Where's Jered?" I ask, my voice wobbly this time.

Mother doesn't look up. She doesn't even pause in her rocking.

"Ignoring me won't make me disappear." I take a step toward her. "Where is my brother? He's not in the nursery, and he's not here. Dad told me to ask you."

Mother shakes her head.

This time I scream the words, because I'm beginning to think I already know the answer. "*Where is he?*"

"Jered is gone," Lyssa says from the open doorway. "Your mother sold him. It was too hard for her." Lyssa chokes up.

"His name isn't Jered anymore," Mother whispers. "I told them his name is Moses."

"Because you gave him up?" I ask. "Are you kidding me? The difference is that in the Bible, Jochebed had no choice. She had to hide him, or he would have died. But you have a choice."

"It is done," she says. "And I don't expect you to understand, but I did what I had to do. I can't afford to be a pathetic wretch. I must be strong."

"You didn't spare him," I say. "You spurned him." I spin on my heel and race for the door, dodging Lyssa's arm when she tries to stop me.

But Mother's voice halts me immediately. "You hate me right now, and that's okay. I'll survive. When you think about this, and I'm sure you will think about this moment often, I want you to remember that a thousand years is a very long time to live with your decisions. You don't get do-overs, and some things can't be healed. Consider the price of regret when it's compounded for centuries before you make a big, irreversible decision. Then perhaps, if you're lucky, your own children won't hate you like mine hate me."

THE PAST: 2001

"Why can't we celebrate with a cake and a few friends?" I ask.

"Oh please. This is a small party—she's only turning eight hundred and eighty-one. You should have seen her eight hundredth birthday fête." Inara laughs. "Besides, I can't believe you're complaining about the party, which you don't even have to plan. I'm way more worried about finding a suitable gift. Mother has given me everything I have, and on top of that, what does she not already have that she might possibly want? She's the *worst* person in the world to shop for. Literally."

"I haven't given her a gift in years," I say, "for all of those reasons. And the last time I tried, I painted her a picture. I found it in the trash the following week."

"Why don't I remember this?" Inara scrunches her nose. "Was it a good painting?"

I roll my eyes. "Of course it wasn't, but that's not the point."

"Well I set the bar too high a few decades ago, and now I'm always scrambling to try and clear it. Besides, I can't give her nothing—or I won't remain the daughter she likes best for very long."

That's a little too true to be funny. "I am wearing the horrible dress she chose for me—I consider that a generous gift in and of itself." I stand up and shove the fluffy pink and gold skirt down as much as possible. "Did she forget what year I was born? I'm not eleven. I'm twenty-one years old."

Inara tilts her head sideways. "The embroidery on the bodice is beautiful and the cut is quite flattering, but the skirt." She chokes on a laugh. "It's like the tulle fairy got a stomachache and vomited all over you."

"It's chiffon," I say, "not that it's much better."

Inara smirks. "It really isn't."

"Well you're as doomed as me, although perhaps not as publicly."

"My salvation is that even though the party is today, her actual birthday is two days away. I can still find a decent gift. Tonight, you must listen to everything she says and come up with some ideas for anything that might be unique or special."

"I don't need any more time," I say. "You should paint her a picture."

Inara tries to punch me just as Lucas opens the door. His look of horror makes me laugh.

"It's time to go?" I ask.

Lucas nods. "Guests are beginning to arrive in the ballroom and your mother requests you attend her." He looks askance at Inara. "She was asking after you, too."

"Right," Inara says. "Well, I'd better head to my room and change, then."

"Please, please tell me that you're wearing the same thing as me."

"Absolutely not. Mother knows better." Inara walks

toward the door and turns back for one last jab. "I'd accidentally spill something on that, if I were you."

"Maybe I would, if there was anyone there whose opinion mattered to me."

Lucas frowns, ever so slightly, and I wish for the nine-millionth time that the thought of kissing him didn't make me want to suck on a bar of soap.

I try one last time to smooth down my skirts. No luck. They just spring right back. "I'm ready."

"For what it's worth, I like the dress. It's an amazing color choice for your skin tone." Lucas holds out his arm and I take it.

"Thank you."

"You're welcome."

Lucas's arm is strong and capable. I'm lucky to have an escort who never presses or prods. I wish I could say the same about Mother. Ever since she sold Jered—Moses—she has decided to focus instead on me finding a consort so I can produce little babies of my own. It's beginning to grate.

Mother's already waiting in the ballroom in her similarly designed gown, Dad at her side, both of them smiling and chatting with guests. I wonder what it costs them to behave as a united front to the outside world when they've barely spoken in the past eight months.

"I'm sorry we're late," Lucas says. "I just couldn't get my hair to lie right."

"The shorter the haircut, the harder to style," Dad says. "You could grow it out and pull it back in a ponytail. That wouldn't take long at all."

"Oh please," I say. "You two are both ridiculous."

"You look beautiful," Mother whispers. "Thank you for wearing the dress I chose."

"It's your birthday," I say. "I may not have much in the way of painting skills, but I wear whatever you pick."

"I'm never going to live that down, am I?" Mother asks. "I didn't even throw it away. It was a misunderstanding."

"I don't have many things I can still hold over you." At least, not much that I can discuss without making her murderously angry. "Let me keep this one."

Inara finally arrives, gliding toward us from the opposite end of the room. She's definitely not wearing coordinating colors; her gown is crimson. Whereas our bodices are heavily embroidered with fitted panels, Inara's dress wraps tightly around her neck, entirely covering the front of her body. And it's backless. And clingy.

Mother hates it, which will likely distract her attention from me.

"Where's Gideon?" Dad asks. "You need someone around to appreciate your stunning beauty tonight."

Small spots of red appear on Inara's cheeks. "He had an errand to run for me first."

"Oh good," Mother says. "Melisania has brought Marde *and* Rakira."

"I hope no one slits anyone else's throat tonight," Dad says. "From what I could tell, that blood stain never came out of Melamecha's rug."

I can't help myself. My eyes seek out Rakira, if only because I know Paolo works with her. And Aline. I've avoided thinking about her for months on end, not that it has done much good. She's probably already with someone who isn't afraid to hold her hand, to speak her name, or to meet her eye across the room. Even knowing that people don't wait around forever, I hope she hasn't found someone new.

I'm actually disappointed that only her brother Paolo stands in the circle of guards behind Melisania and Rakira.

"Welcome to Ni'ihau," Mother says. "I hope your flight wasn't too onerous."

"It's a brutal trip," Melisania says. "But we slept most of the way, didn't we?" She turns back toward her daughters.

They both nod.

"We're delighted to be here," Melisania says. "We haven't seen you since we hosted the Games. You haven't been attending birthdays or anything else lately."

"I haven't felt very social." Mother's heart rate is steady and her face looks serene, but there's still sadness in her eyes.

I've blamed her for so long about Jered that I haven't even considered how much it might have hurt her, or how much pain she must have been in to do something so drastic. Something that, for her, was the norm. Oh, Mother.

"Part of that is my fault," I say. "My training was so intense in the decade before the Games that I asked Mother if we could take a few months off of the normal routine to do relaxing things instead."

"But you live in Hawaii," Rakira says. "Is there anywhere more relaxing?"

"Which is why I wanted to stay here for a while," I say.

"Oh," Marde says. "That's good to hear. I heard you had some kind of mental break after your last baby was born—and it was another boy. That would have been hard to deal with."

When Dad's angry, it's almost always directed at my mother, but when he steps toward Marde, his hands clenched at his sides, I worry he's going to strangle her. Not that I'd stop him.

Mother places one hand on his arm and he blinks and swallows hard.

"Nothing like that," I say. "We're all happy and healthy here. And I think that baby is doing well, too. Where did he go, Mother? Shenoah maybe? As you say, with so many sons, it's hard to keep track."

"Your mother has only had three children, all female," Inara says. "Having never had a child myself, I'm not sure I can really understand quite how difficult it is to keep up with all of them." Her words are friendly enough, but her tone is tight, practically vibrating with fury.

If Marde isn't more careful, it won't only be Rakira angling to slit her throat tonight.

"Your parties are always the very best," Melisania says. "I can't wait to see what delightful food your Angel has prepared. Come, children. Let's go find out before the best snacks are gone." Melisania and her retinue turn and walk toward the far end of the room. Paolo shoots me an apologetic look over his shoulder.

"What are the odds that Melisania didn't tell Marde to ask that?" Lucas asks.

He's smarter than I credit him with being.

"Nil," Mother says. "Marde can barely string a dozen words together when I'm close. When I asked her at the Games which contest she liked the most, she dropped her drink. When she saw me the next morning, she squeaked and ran away."

"At least you've gotten through the worst of it," I say. "Which means you can enjoy the rest of the party."

Mother inhales and exhales deeply and meets my eye. "I think you're probably right."

Once we've greeted all the royals, we eat dinner and Mother cuts her cake. Luckily, we don't face any additional outbursts or angry disagreements. When the orchestra begins to play, Lucas asks for the first dance, like always.

But when the waltz ends and Paolo asks for the next, I'm not sure what to say.

"Come now, your highness," he says. "I promise it will be less eventful than the last time we danced, and I vow that I have no nasty innuendos planned." The twinkle in his eye does it. Aline said that he knew and he supported her. Which means she told him what happened after I ran off, and he knows. . . Well. There's not much *to* know. But he knows that Aline liked me, and that maybe I liked her too.

"Sure," I say.

He's an excellent dancer, and true to his word, he sticks to very neutral topics. The last year in Rio, including a fairly exciting mayoral race. We laugh at the humans' concern over who they 'elect,' since we choose the winner anyway—and the elected official is merely a puppet.

"They get so heated over their plans and proposals, and what laws they find acceptable," Paolo says.

"Same in our countries," I say. "Although, Mother goes along with their decisions sometimes."

"As long as it's not something we care about," Paolo says, "we do, too."

"Exactly," I say. "I mean, taxes, government spending, trade agreements. Mother doesn't give on those things. But on the rest? A little freedom can help productivity."

"Like in Vermont," Paolo says.

I stumble and kick his foot, but he acts as though he didn't notice. "What about Vermont?"

"You heard about the civil unions?" he asks. "I'm sure. Your mother didn't stop those."

"She usually lets the states do what they want. Within reason."

The song ends, and Paolo leads me to the edge of the dance floor, on the opposite end of the room from Mother. "Are you thirsty?" he asks.

I shrug.

"I thought you might want to try the Italian sodas," he says. "My little sister loves them. She's been camped out over there all night."

My eyes fly to the edge of the room. Aline's standing near a table against the wall, sipping some kind of drink that's pink on the bottom and whitish near the top. The black gown she's wearing has onyx stones studded along the bodice, and it's slit halfway up her thigh, revealing a ruby-handled dagger. Her hair is pulled into a high ponytail and cascades down her face and neck, highlighting her killer cheekbones.

I can't drag my eyes away.

When she smiles at me, I move toward her as though I'm being towed. At the last second, Paolo grabs my arm and steers me toward the Italian sodas. "You should try the blackberry," he says. "It's the best."

Aline circles around to my other side. "My brother is an idiot. The raspberry is far superior."

The menu lists dozens of options. "I'll have cherry and lime," I say. "Because I'm not going to exacerbate this sibling rivalry."

Thinking about the sibling rivalry I'll never have with my little brother ruins my good mood. With my new drink in hand, I grab a seat near the wall. I take a sip, not sure what to expect. "This is pretty good," I say. "It might be better than either of yours."

"You do have good taste." Paolo sits across from me, leaving only the seat next to me open. "I've known that since the day we met."

"It's true." I look at Aline. "I really do."

She sits down and holds out her free hand. "Mind if I check it? I like to keep an open mind."

When I hand her my glass, our fingers brush and the feeling is exactly as I recalled. A shiver of electricity, a spark of excitement, a thrill of delight. I watch the muscles in her neck ripple as she swallows the cherry lime.

"You might be right," she says. "The combination of flavors is even better than one alone."

We talk about nonsense for the next half hour, but then Paolo stands up. "Too many beautiful women aren't dancing. I need to do something about that."

"It's a difficult burden to shoulder," Aline says, "but I think you'll survive it."

He bows and walks away, and suddenly I'm four years old and too nervous to ask for an extra bowl of ice cream. Without Paolo, the stakes are higher, somehow, for reasons I can't explain.

"I was wrong before," Aline says.

"W-what?"

"I made it seem like the only terms on which I wanted to be in your life was as your—" She clears her throat. "I should have been more flexible. Given the reality of our positions, I wish I had the chance to get to know you better. From the outside looking in, it appears the last few months may have been difficult ones for your family."

I nod, still unable to form coherent words.

"If you want to talk about it, I'd be honored." She rattles off the numbers that dial her cell phone. "Or texting is the new thing, I hear. I'd be fine with that, too."

"Friends," I say.

Her smile nearly knocks me over. "Friends, yes."

"Melina?" Inara asks. "What are you doing over here?"

Before I can answer, she waves me over. "Mother's receiving her gifts, which means this ghastly event is nearly over."

I stand by Mother's side while she expresses faux gratitude for the many things she doesn't need or want. I smile and nod and make small talk, but the entire time, the numbers of Aline's phone run through my mind over and over. When the last gift is unwrapped and the guests begin to filter out, I breathe a quiet sigh of relief.

"I know this was hard," Mother whispers. "It was for me as well."

"It had to happen sometime," I say. "But it feels a little like we're coming out of mourning."

"That's not a horrible analogy," Mother says. "It has felt like that every time, but this is the worst."

"But, what comes after the darkest part of the night?" I ask.

Mother wraps an arm around my shoulders. "You're right. And I sincerely hope it's a gorgeous dawn."

When I get back to my room, I send Aline a text message. One word, two letters: HI.

She replies within seconds. HEY YOU.

For the first time since the morning I woke up and Jered was gone, there's light in my life and warmth in my heart.

❧ 13 ❧

THE PAST: 2001

"**B**althasar says your mother wants you to report to her courtyard for training this morning." Lucas hands me a granola bar and a bottle of water.

"Really?" I take a bite. "That's great news."

"I thought you'd be pleased." Lucas leans against the doorframe. "You've been a little mopey with Balthasar."

"I haven't." I chew and swallow and take another bite, even bigger than the last. "But I miss melodics."

"It's obvious." Lucas beams at me. "I told Douglas to follow you over."

"Oh good." I put my hand over my heart in mock relief. "I was really worried I might be attacked between here and Mother's courtyard."

"It's a hundred yards, I know. But there are rules for a reason."

"You're doing your job, which I appreciate." I scarf down the last third of the granola bar and hand him the wrapper. Then I chug the water bottle and toss it to Lucas as well.

"You're so stunning when you eat, like a ballerina

working on a stage made of food. Have I ever told you that?" Lucas lifts one eyebrow.

"I wish I had that bottle back." I slide my arm sheath into place and tighten it around my forearm.

"Oh?"

"So I could throw it at your head." I slide my scabbard over my shoulder. "I'm not sure I can justify throwing either my sword or this dagger at you for being a brat. But a water bottle? Absolutely."

I jog around the back side of my courtyard and through the gate where Douglas is waiting with a smile on his face.

"Good morning?" he asks.

I bob my head. "I think it is, yes."

"It's about time." Douglas knows the drill. When we reach the gate to Mother's, he halts and assumes a position outside.

I bounce on through, my scabbard bumping against my back. And I pull up short. My jaw drops, and I blink to make sure I'm not seeing things. But no, it's definitely Mother, inside the circle of Frederick's embrace, her head leaned against his shoulder, tears on her cheeks.

I stumble backward, my boot hitting the gate. It clicks into place and Mother leaps away from Frederick like he burned her. She meets my eye and her lips part. She inhales quickly and Frederick bows and exits through the door that opens into the hallway.

She's fully dressed in training gear. Maybe it was nothing. But why does she look so guilty? And since when has Mother hugged *anyone*, including me? The closest I ever get is an awkward shoulder squeeze. I've never seen her hug Dad, that's for sure.

I shake my head. It's not my business. Or, at least, there's nothing I can do about it.

"Lucas said. . ."

Mother brushes off her spotless white pants. "Of course. I thought you might like to do a little sparring."

"Right," I say. "No, I mean, yes, I do."

She looks pointedly at my sword. "I was thinking hand-to-hand."

I whip the sword off and set it by the gate. "Sounds great."

And if I hit her a little harder than normal, well, I doubt she notices. We go a few rounds, enough that I've worked off most of my anxiety. "I thought we might begin again with hand-to-hand three days a week."

It's not like before, but it's better than it has been. "Sure." I almost ask her about Frederick, but if she wanted to explain anything, she'd already have done it.

When I saddle up Splash for a ride that afternoon, I expect Inara to join me, and maybe Gideon too. I don't expect Dad. He doesn't trust horses—never has.

He clears his throat and glances at Splash, who's dancing around far more than he should. "Care for some company?"

"Uh sure," I say. "Although, I suppose we could go for a jog instead."

Dad laughs. "I'm the one stealing your free time. I can muddle through a ride, and if one of these hooved demons throws me, well, at least I'll heal from the broken neck. Why humans think it's a good idea to pull a rope through these beasts' teeth and try to steer them, as fragile as they are, I will never understand."

Splash tosses his head as if to emphasize his point. "He can tell you don't like him. That's why you have a bad time on horses. You expect a bad time, so they deliver."

Dad waves to Nora. "Bring me the most docile cart pony in here."

Nora puts one hand on her hip.

"Denver will be fine," I say. "He won't like Dad, but he won't throw him, either. And he's lazy enough that he won't take off without being told."

Once we're walking along the beach, about half the speed Splash and I usually prefer, Splash skittering sideways occasionally, waiting for me to give him the go-ahead to run, I can't wait any more. "Why are you riding with me today, and why is Mother calling me in for training?"

"We realized last night that we've been neglecting you because of. . ." His knuckles are white.

My heart contracts a little bit. "We've all been doing whatever we could to hang on. It's fine."

"It's not fine." Dad squares his shoulders. "And I miss having time to talk to you."

We spend the next hour discussing the most notable differences between the Old Testament and the Koran. The more animated Dad becomes, the less he stresses and the more Denver settles. By the time we're rounding the bend to the stables, Denver has worked up a sweat, and so has Splash.

"That was fun," I say.

"I'm sorry it took me so long to come back up for air," Dad says.

I'm sorry it took him so long too, but he doesn't waste any more time, which I appreciate.

The next six months are much better than the last. I still think about Jered every day, but the ache isn't as raw. I train with Mother and Balthasar, ride and talk religion with Dad, attend to boring governance and political issues with Inara, and in between my duties, I talk to Aline, who is quickly becoming my best friend. If we're a little flirty and I dream about kissing her, well, dreaming isn't doing.

With the time zone difference, sometimes Aline forgets and texts me in the middle of the night. And sometimes I can't sleep and call her, delighted to hear her voice when there's no risk of someone interrupting a call. But that's how I'm awake at four a.m. on September first, with nothing to do for an hour and a half.

I stare at the ceiling for a bit, until my stomach complains. When I open the door, Douglas's eyes fly wide and I realize he was asleep. Lucas would kill him. I can't help a very unladylike snort.

"I feel very safe, thanks."

Douglas gulps.

"I'm not going to hand you in, dummy."

He salutes me. As if I've ever had them salute me a day in my life. I can't help bursting into actual laughter.

"You'll wake up the entire palace."

I rein it in. "I woke up, and now I can't go back to sleep. And I'm starving."

Douglas holds his hands out. "I don't have—"

I slap his hand away. "Duh. I know you don't have food. You're dopey when you first wake up." I grin. "I'm heading to the kitchen."

"I can grab you whatever—"

I roll my eyes. "I don't know what I want yet. Do me a favor and stay here. I'll be right back."

Douglas cringes.

"Oh fine, follow me over."

And he does, practically bowling me over when I stop in front of the half open kitchen door. Light streams through the doorway, which means I won't even stub my toe. "Thank you for protecting me from the dangerous early morning cockroaches, but I think I've got it from here. You can take a nap in the hallway until I'm done."

"There aren't cockroaches anywhere near my kitchen." Angel yanks the door open all the way. "And why in the world would he take a nap?"

Douglas's heart hammers in his chest.

"It was a joke." I push past Angel and into the kitchen, trying to identify exactly what I'm smelling. "Is that. . . rye bread or pumpernickel? Or both?"

"I'm baking all of them," she says. "Or did you think everything you eat comes frozen in a bag from a factory, like it does for city-dwelling humans?"

"I knew someone had to make it," I say. "But it never occurred to me that the head of the palace's entire kitchen would be here making. . . blueberry muffins?" My eyelids flutter. "That's the smell I couldn't place. Oh, please say that's what it is."

Angel folds her arms over her chest and cocks one hip. "And what if it is?"

"You know you're already my favorite, so I have nothing to offer you."

"You can eat as many as you want, if you help me knead the bread for the rolls. I got a late start, and Margaret has the day off."

"Deal," I say.

An hour and a dozen blueberry muffins later, I jog down the hall with a fresh loaf of cinnamon swirl bread and Douglas on my heels like a Labrador retriever. Cinnamon bread, Mother's favorite. Frederick is at the door, but he doesn't even try to stop me. I tap once before barging through.

"Mother," I say. "Look what I made."

She's sitting at her desk, reading some kind of letter. I race over and set the platter down in front of her. She covers her nose and mouth with her hand and turns away.

"Angel helped, I swear. There's nothing wrong with it."

She shakes her head. "It's not that. I'm sure you did a wonderful job."

I drop to one knee. "What then?"

Mother stands up and walks toward her bed, apparently needing to put some space between me and her. She sits on the edge of her bed and closes her eyes. I want to demand an explanation, but I decide on patience. I'm not convinced it's a virtue, but neither is making Mother angry.

"I wasn't going to tell you yet."

"Tell me what?" I stand up and take a step closer, fear worming its way into my heart. "You're okay, right? You're not like. . ." I gulp. She's not even nine hundred yet.

"I'm not sick, no."

"Then what?"

"I want you to know that this wasn't planned. I know it hasn't been very long." She closes her eyes. "But I'm pregnant. Again."

Jered. His tiny hands, his perfect smile, his little pink gums. His teensy toes. It's like a knife in my heart, like a blinding light in my eyes.

"Melina?"

I don't know what to say. I want to be happy, but I don't know if I can go through all of it again. Maybe it'll be easier the second time.

"It might be a girl."

"What?"

"I'm usually food averse when I'm having a girl."

"What does that mean?" I ask. "You don't want to eat cinnamon bread. . . because the baby is a girl?"

"It's not science," she says, "but it has been my experience, yes. When I no longer enjoy the things I usually eat, and I want things like mashed potatoes on honey toast, yes. That usually means I'm having a girl."

"How long?" I ask. "Do you know when you'll have him or her?"

"It should be March of next year, I believe. Maybe early April. Now that you know, I should warn your father. I believe in another few weeks, we can schedule an ultrasound. I used to have to wait until the birth to find out the gender, you know. This early knowledge is quite a luxury."

"Right."

"Melina?"

"Yes?" I turn to face her.

"Do you mind removing the bread?"

"I'm sorry," I say. "Right, of course." I snatch the loaf from the table and rush out of the room, unsure where to go next. We were supposed to be training. My feet start toward my room—force of habit, I suppose. I walk inside and shut the door. My phone screen is lit up. I've stopped carrying it with me, since I don't want anyone to notice I'm always texting and ask with whom.

YOU THERE?

YES, SORRY, I text back. I'M HERE. STRANGE MORNING.

GOOD STRANGE? she asks.

I DON'T KNOW YET.

FINGERS CROSSED.

She never pries. I love that about her. I'll tell her when I'm ready, and until then she won't bug me. Because she's perfect for me. I've been ignoring that, pretending that I haven't fallen madly in love with her over the past six months.

The reality of Mother's news this morning crashes over me, and I can't breathe. This is it, my lifeline. This could save me. I've never loved this life—stuck on a throne I never asked for, judging people, ruling on things, negotiating and threatening and glowering at everyone.

I hate it all.

And I love Aline. If only I were free, I could leave it all and never look back. Inara offered to step in when Mother dies, but that doesn't help me now. Mother will live another hundred years. The thought of hiding who I am and what I want for a century is the most stifling prospect I've ever imagined.

But if Mother's having a girl. . .

Dad says God loves me. Dad says he has a plan for me, and that's why he married Mother. He's chosen over and over to follow this path, but no one even asked me. What if there's another child to pick up his torch, to accomplish God's will, to fight the fights that humans need, to set the earth to rights? What if I can escape forever? Does a desperate desire for that make me wicked? Does it make me selfish? Do I care if it does?

I drop to my knees.

"Dear God, I know I don't pray as often as I should. I haven't been your best creation. I'm not totally sure what kind of prayers you really like, or how to go about asking you for something so big. I know I'm supposed to start with gratitude, and believe me. I am grateful."

I take a deep breath and try to listen like Dad taught me. I think I feel something. Or maybe I'm so drunk on hope that I can't tell what I feel.

"I know I'm one of the luckiest people alive. Firstly, I have all this." I gesture around. "I live on an island and I have everything I could ever want. I have amazing things I don't even want. And I have a healthy, strong, gorgeous body you gave me. But more than any of those, you created someone else. Someone perfect and beautiful. Someone supportive and strong. I can't imagine Aline came from anyone but you, and I love her, God. I really do. I want to spend my life with her, and I can't do that here, in this place, with this job."

A tear rolls down my cheek.

"I haven't ever asked you for anything. Not when Mother and Dad fought, or when I was desperate to win the Games. Not when my brother disappeared and I was lost and alone and in pain. I probably should have asked for help then, but I didn't. But now I'm standing at the end of a long hallway, facing the same exact trial ,and I can't do it again. So I'm asking you now. No, that's not right. I'm not asking. I'm begging you. Please, please, please. If you love me, if you are okay with me taking the path *I want to take*, send me a sign. Release me from my duties here."

It occurs to me that God might have preferred it if I had actually gone to Him in prayer when things were hard before. I can't change that, though. So I shake it off and continue.

"Please, God, please let Mother's baby be a girl. I promise I'll do anything you need. I'll give whatever I need to give, if you can do this one thing. Free me, spare Mother and Dad the pain of another boy, and bring a strong healthy girl into this world to rule Alamecha. Let her bear the weight of setting the wrongs right, and I will help her, and I will guide her, and I will do whatever she needs."

I wipe away the tears rolling down my cheeks, but I stay on the floor for a long time before I stand up. The heavens don't open up. No angels speak. I have no idea whether God even heard me.

But I hope He did. I really, really hope He did.

❧ 14 ❧

THE PAST: 2001

The world doesn't know Mother is pregnant—even Inara doesn't know yet. Life carries on as always, and we still have to hear petitions, as usual, the second Monday of the month. Mother's heart rate is as steady as the ticking of a clock, no matter how obnoxious the request, no matter how grating the complaint. Even though I know it's likely there, I can't hear the baby's heartbeat yet.

I wish I could. Then we could do an ultrasound and my agonizing wait would end.

But Mother and I are stuck. No ultrasound yet, and life marches along while we wait and hope. Bizarrely, Inara doesn't have to come to hear petitions, but she comes anyway. And she doesn't even look bored. Her eyes are alert, her head is tilted in thought. Almost like. . . she enjoys it.

Mother rules on the final complaint, and I lean back in my chair. Finished at last.

"We have an item that wasn't submitted in advance," Balthasar says. "Your Majesty."

Mother turns slightly to look back at him. "We do?"

"There has been a formal complaint filed, which means it must be addressed." He hands her a sheet of ivory parchment, his mouth set in a grim line.

Mother holds it a little nearer to me than its strictly necessary, so I read over her shoulder.

Violation of the law. . . Demand the utmost punishment allowed. . . Removal from position. . . Inappropriate relationship with another of the same gender.

I close my eyes and inhale deeply. This particular law hasn't been enforced in twenty years. But technically, the practice of homosexuality demands the death penalty.

"It has been quite some time since any charges such as these have been made." Mother stands up and reads the basic allegation. "But Gareth, son of Honoraria has been charged with homosexual conduct and his brother Lionel demands his execution. Presumably so that he can take Gareth's position as director of their family company."

Lionel, son of Honoraria, stands. "Yes, Your Majesty, that is my request. I have ample evidence, including several witnesses."

Mother's nose wrinkles. "And does your brother contest the charges? Is it necessary to hear evidence?"

Gareth stands up at the very back of the room. His voice trembles when he says, "No, Your Majesty, I do not contest the charges."

Mother sighs.

It's wrong. It's unfair for him to be executed. His brother should be ashamed of himself, using Mother to steal from his own family. Before I know it, I've hopped to my feet. "Before you rule, I would like to request an amendment to the law, and I invoke the Heir's Request to Reconsider."

Mother's hand drops to her side, the parchment crinkling in her fingers. "Excuse me?"

Dad's training to help me change the world was meant for real emergencies. I doubt he'd classify this as one, but to me, it qualifies. "There has been a law in place for thousands of years, since Meridalena's time, that allows an Heir to request the monarch reconsider a law in light of the current state of the world. It is meant to allow an Heir to participate in the governance and help the ruling monarch to see when perhaps the law might need a change. This particular law isn't part of the Charter, so it's a simple thing to modify."

Mother raises her eyebrow. "And you believe we should make this modification? This law exists for good reason. The existence of 'gay' individuals among us is evidence of a genetic flaw—one that must be eradicated or our entire species could falter. If all of us were to be gay, for instance, we'd die off."

"If all of us were to be female, we would die off as well," I say. "It doesn't mean that being female is a problem. And I'm not at all sure that being 'gay' means there's a flaw. There hasn't been any solid evidence of that, has there, Job? In fact, I believe you're finding evidence to contradict that belief."

Job's eyes widen and he splutters.

"I'll take that as a confirmation," I say. "And I think that in light of our imperfect knowledge on the subject, we consider an amendment."

"And what change would you recommend?" Inara asks. "Banishment?"

I shake my head. "Why lose good evian workers, good evian soldiers, and good evian managers and innovators?"

Mother laughs. "If you're saying that we shouldn't lose them, what about their children? If this *is* a flaw, we should cull it. If it's not a flaw, as you suggest, then we are allowing them to exist, but shirk their duties to further strengthen our family."

I gulp. "Well, I don't believe it is a flaw. Certainly, there has been no link between gay evians and any other weaknesses of intellect or physicality. I believe it's a normal variance, like skin, eye color, or hair color."

"Those are things that can be changed," Inara says.

"Fine," I say. "Like height, then, or nose shape."

"So you recommend that we keep them and perpetuate these bloodlines?" Mother glances at Dad.

He doesn't react at all, other than to shrug. I wonder if he's upset that I'm using what he taught me to defend gay evians.

"I do," I say.

"And yet, keeping them won't preserve their bloodline," Mother says. "As they would fail to create children, given their proclivities." She taps her chin with her free hand. "It's a conundrum."

"They could have children," I say. "Especially now, with the advent of a procedure called in vitro fertilization. Most of you likely haven't heard of it, but it's been around since before I was born for humans who couldn't otherwise procreate, mostly. The point is that it could be used here, for those who wouldn't have biological children without scientific intervention."

She spins on her heel and pins Job with a glare. "Is what Melina says true? About this procedure, and also the research? Is there no correlation between gayness and other deficiencies?"

Job gulps. "For obvious reasons, the evians I have interacted with have been reticent to classify themselves as 'gay,' but from the human studies and a very limited sample of evians, I believe that to be correct. Certainly, a change in the law to something less drastic might allow us to obtain better information on the subject."

I'm relieved that it seems true. It was more of a hunch than anything else. I clear my throat. "And beyond that, even if it is a 'genetic anomaly,' we don't eliminate other individuals with genetic imperfections. For example, we might exclude someone who can't perform appearance modification from a security placement, but we don't kill them. Our treatment of gay evians has always been out of line with the scientific support."

Mother's lips purse momentarily, and then she sighs. "Very well. I grant your request and issue a new law, pending confirmation of these assumptions. If an evian is determined to be 'gay' or romantically interested in members of the same gender, it will no longer be grounds for execution. At worst, we will banish them, and only to another family that does not punish their . . . desires. . . with death. Does anyone know which families that might be?"

"Lenora," I say. "And also Analessa. Adora has recently discussed it, but I'm not sure of the status."

"You've given this a lot of thought." Mother grunts. "If Job can confirm it's not a genetic deletion, we will welcome gay evians from other families here. It might be a good way to recruit." She laughs. "We could be a gay sanctuary."

I breathe a sigh of relief and suppress the urge to dance and shout.

"However," Mother says, "they must comply with my law to bear their share of the burden to continue our family lines and bolster the strength of our people."

Huh?

Mother turns again to Job. "What's the average number of children borne by a female evian during their lifetime? Limit it to the term of my reign."

"Seventy-four, over the last nine hundred years," he says. "Although that number has been in decline for the past hundred years or so."

"Fine," Mother says. "Then any gay evians will be required to give birth to one full-blooded evian baby per ten year period, but once they have had . . ." She turns toward me. "What do you think? How many will we require?"

How many what? Babies? I try not to show her how disturbing I find this question. "I don't understand. We're going to *force* the gay citizens to bear children?"

"If it's not a flaw, which is the assumption on which we're changing the law, then they must contribute."

"I thought we were changing it because it's barbaric, senseless, and evil to kill people for something that doesn't harm anyone."

Mother grits her teeth.

If she's already angry. . . "Will you force the women to then raise these children they didn't choose? What kind of life will that be for the child? And how will they select a father?"

Mother waves her hand in the air. "I'll raise them if these ungrateful mothers don't want to do it. They'll become Alamecha foundlings."

"They'll be forced to have children on a schedule, and you'll *take* the children when they're born?" My eyebrows shoot upward. How could she require the very thing that nearly destroyed us last year?

"I've done it," she says. "But, no. I won't take them. They have the option to keep and raise them, and failing that desire, I will take the care of the children on myself. I think it's more than fair."

It's abominable, but sadly, it's still a huge improvement over the prior law. If I continue to argue, Mother will demand to know why. I'm not ready to divulge the reason yet. Especially since we haven't yet confirmed it's not a genetic flaw, and I don't know what Mother will decide if it is. Arguing could yet get me banished at a base line, and depending on where I'm banished to, killed.

"Sure," I say. "Require them to give birth to somewhat less than the average, since it's declining." I can't quite keep myself from pointing out another problem with her solution. "Although, this law forces this only on women. That hardly seems fair."

Mother sits back down on her throne and leans back, her fingers tapping on the armrests. "Fine." Her eyelids flutter. "Then require the men to provide samples for use by the women, if you want them to be obligated to do something as well."

Because that's the same. I try not to groan.

"If you don't have a suggestion for the number, then fifty," Mother says. "Once a woman has provided fifty evian children in her lifetime, the obligation to produce a child once a decade will be fulfilled."

I want to ask what happens if they fail to pop out a baby, but I fear that the answer will be horrible. Maybe leaving this vague is better. I can argue for things that will mitigate the impact later. It's not perfect, but it's a huge leap forward. "I believe if the mothers don't wish to raise their children, then the male who provided a *sample*—" I clear my throat. "Should be given the chance to care for the child. Only if both parents have passed on the opportunity should the child be ceded to Alamecha for his or her care."

"Fine, fine," Mother says. "Then I've reached a decision. Your complaint and demand are denied Lionel. Gareth, you may continue in your position without fear of any harm or punishment as long as you comply with the provision of samples as required. Also, you're obligated to submit whatever Job requires in order to confirm these theories."

Gareth nods his head vigorously, a tear streaking down one cheek. "Thank you, Your Majesty. Thank you."

It sickens me that he's so grateful to be remanded as a voluntary lab rat and sperm donor, and to have his entire life on trial for being who he is, but at least the immediate threat to his life is gone. That's a lot of progress, and I want to run to my room so no one sees if I start to cry. Also, guilt eats at me. It hadn't even occurred to me two years ago that the law was unjust, much less that I should do anything about it. I didn't begin to care until it impacted me personally.

For a brief moment, I wonder whether God might have put me here for a reason. Maybe I'm here, maybe I am who I am, because I understand. But none of that makes me less emotional, so I still escape the very second I'm able.

When I reach my room, there's already a text waiting for me.

YOU'RE AMAZING.

My heart lifts. I WISH I HAD DONE MORE.

Aline texts back immediately. YOU DID MORE THAN ANYONE ELSE EVER HAS. IT'S ENOUGH.

Not by a long shot, but it's progress, and I was part of it. I'm smiling when I drift off to sleep.

15

THE PAST: 2001

In twenty-one years, I've never been shaken awake. Mother's lips are tight, her eyes flinty. I cast around for my phone. Did she find it? Does she know I've been texting Aline? Am I to be the next subject of Job's experiments?

"Get dressed." Mother releases my shoulders and stands. "Meet me in my room immediately."

"What's going on?" I ask. "Is the baby okay?"

She breathes in and out slowly. "The baby is fine."

"Oh." What made her suspect? Was it my passionate defense of Gareth? What will she do now that she knows?

"We're under attack."

My heart races, and I hate myself. Lives are being lost, and I'm relieved that *we're being attacked,* because it means I'm not in trouble.

I'm a terrible person.

"Who's attacking us?" I glance at the clock. Four-twenty-six in the morning. Who would attack us in the middle of the night? I do the math. It's just after nine in the morning in New York City, and just after two p.m. in London.

"We haven't worked that out yet." Mother ducks out of my door, not quite closing it. Her footfalls are accompanied by at least three others as she rushes toward her room.

I bolt out of bed and into my bathroom to change into something appropriate for a war council. Three minutes later, I'm speeding toward Mother's door with Lucas and Jonah pelting along behind me. Inara races from the other direction with Gideon at her heels, and Dad jogs along behind them.

"What's going on?" I ask.

Dad shakes his head. "Inside."

Lucas, Gideon, and Jonah line up next to Mother's guards in the hall as Dad, Inara, and I enter. Frederick stands inside the door, back to the wall, eyes on Mother as she paces back and forth. Balthasar's on the telephone, and Mother's computer keeps binging.

"What do we know?" Inara asks. "Where were we attacked? London? New York? Los Angeles?"

"We don't know nearly enough," Balthasar growls. "A plane crashed into one of the World Trade Center towers at around eight in the morning in New York."

"A plane?" Inara's shoulders relax. "So it's not an attack."

"We didn't initially believe so." Balthasar covers the phone with his hand. "But then another plane hit the second tower a few moments ago. Both planes were bound for Boston."

And unlikely to be on a flight path over downtown New York.

"Two planes hit two different towers?" Dad asks. "Directly next to one another? That's definitely not a coincidence."

"No," Mother says. "It's not. Both flights were headed

from Boston to Los Angeles. Someone used commercial flights to attack us."

"That doesn't sound like one of the Five," Inara says.

"How many people were injured?" I ask. "Obviously the passengers on the flight, but hopefully the towers weren't too crowded that early."

"Ninety passengers on one plane and sixty or so on the other," Frederick volunteers. "But we don't know about the individuals in the towers, not yet."

"They're evacuating, right?" Inara asks.

"Of course." Balthasar ends his call. "And—"

Mother's computer brings up a video of the World Trade Center towers, smoke billowing from the top of both. Firefighters teem around the bottom in their black jackets with florescent yellow stripes.

"Who would do that?" I ask. "Who would attack the towers with commercial flights?"

"We're in the process of figuring that out," Balthasar says. "But clearly I'm not on site."

Ohmygosh. "Alora." I choke. "Is she?" I can't ask anything else.

"She's alright. She's going to coordinate our efforts on the ground for now," Mother says.

"Will Balthasar be going to New York too?" I ask.

He shakes his head fiercely. "I won't leave your Mother here alone, but I'm compiling a list and sending backup for Alora."

"We need to ground all commercial flights," Mother says.

Balthasar's phone rings again and he answers. Then he swears.

"What?" Mother asks.

He hangs up. "Another plane crashed into the Pentagon a few moments ago. He's sending you the feed."

I've never heard Mother swear, not until that moment. She crosses the room to her computer and clicks some links. A video pops up, showing a commercial airliner crashing into the southwest corner of the building. I close my eyes. I can't watch any more. But I can't close my ears.

Balthasar swears again. What now?

Mother gasps and I open my eyes just in time to watch another video. Of the south tower collapsing. "How could that happen?" I ask. "The plane hit at the top."

"An impact like that would create fire and a lot of heat," Inara says quietly. "It probably burned down to the foundation of the building."

"But the other tower hasn't fallen," Dad says.

But it falls too, half an hour later.

It takes the rest of the day and into the next to discover that it wasn't any of the Five Families. They all express true regret at the travesty. Upon investigation into the identities of the hijackers, it's clear that it wasn't a move against us by Mother's enemies. It was a move by desperate humans who credit our rule with the difficulties of the past few decades.

I wish I could blame them, but they're kind of right. Although the way they went about attempting to show their displeasure couldn't have been more awful. We were clearly unprepared to deal with humans attempting to inflict significant damage to our family specifically. A large number of evians worked in the towers, the Pentagon, and the smaller 7 World Trade Center tower next door.

The al-Qaeda eliminated 197 Alamecha evians, and twenty-three from other families. All six of the empresses are livid, including Melamecha who controls the regions where the hostiles are located. She hasn't bothered to do much with Afghanistan in years, but I wonder to what extent that will change.

The next week passes in a blur of investigation, security

measures, operations reports, and plans to remediate and heal New York City. The human leaders are reeling and need more guidance than ever before. Melamecha offers to join in a battle against our attackers, but Mother quickly develops a better plan. She can bring the humans in America together, thanks to this attack, and bind them behind her against a common enemy. Anyone who would senselessly kill, a terrorist, deserves to be despised by everyone, and Mother wants to punish them herself.

Which means that, ironically, the terrorists made the bulk of our job easier in their attempt to inflict maximum damage. We've been having daily war councils, and today, there's finally news to report.

"We have been able to identify that the attacks were coordinated and planned by a man named Osama bin Laden," Balthasar says. "He's currently in Afghanistan, as we suspected. He works closely with the local leadership there, the Taliban."

"We're going to bomb them out of existence," Mother says.

"I think we should offer the local government the opportunity to surrender all the individuals involved," Dad says.

"Why does that not surprise me?" Mother asks.

Dad frowns. "We should demand they hand over all the terrorists—leaders and supporters alike. Demand they dismantle all training camps. Require them to release every imprisoned foreign national, and give us full access to verify that they have complied. But at least allow the humans the chance to avoid this, or we're as bad as they are."

Mother's nostrils flare. "Adriana, Katalina, Richard, Wallace—"

"I lost people I care for, too," Dad says. "But it doesn't justify the wholesale destruction of an entire country."

Mother turns toward Inara. "And do you agree?"

Inara nods tightly.

"And what about you?" Mother glares at me. "Are you worried that I'm turning into a despot, hurling the lives of these people away for no reason?"

I sigh. "We should at least give them the chance to do the right thing," I say. "You and I both know they're unlikely to comply with all of those demands."

"Fine," Mother says. "Do it. Send your little list. But Balthasar?"

He grunts.

"Prepare a plan to pulverize the entire country."

"I would like to fly over myself," Dad says. "I'd like to talk to them as a show of good faith. You can send me as the American ambassador—not letting on who I am, if that makes you feel better, but this happened because they feel disenfranchised and angry. They know someone powerful is pulling the strings and they're lashing out in the only way they can imagine. I believe I can broker a peace agreement that will make this type of attack less likely in the future. Security measures help, especially with the weaponization of commercial travel, but there are too many ways for them to harm the innocent. Sending a sweeping ultimatum isn't the same thing as letting them feel *heard.*"

Mother hasn't yet had the ultrasound that will tell us the gender of her child, what with the world turning upside down, but it's clearly on her mind. Her right hand rests over her not-quite-flat-anymore belly—and even though no one else has likely noticed, I know. Worse, Dad knows, and he's still asking to leave. "You want to fly across the world and negotiate with the people who attacked us?" She lifts one eyebrow. "Right now?"

Oh, Dad, relent. Don't press this issue. Things between

you and Mother aren't good, but leaving will make them worse. I feel it in my bone marrow.

"The entire country didn't attack us," he says. "It was a very small group of dissidents who felt they had no other choice."

"Fine," Mother says. "Go." She spins around and looks out the window at the waves crashing against the beach outside.

"Enora," he says. "Talk to me first. Let's discuss this without everyone else and come to a decision."

"Get out of my room." Mother's tone brooks no argument, and she's not meeting anyone's eye, opting to stare out the window instead.

Dad glares at her back for a moment, but finally shakes his head, his eyes steely.

We all march out after Dad, leaving Mother to confer with Balthasar, Frederick, and Miles. It's not lost on me that Mother's working out the details of the attack she'll launch when Dad's attempt fails.

"You really ticked her off in there," Inara says. "Was that wise?"

"She's not being rational right now," Dad says. "She'll realize that I was trying to spare us and them. I'm just trying to work this out in the best way possible. A surgical extraction is always a better option than fifty pounds of C4."

"I think that's the right call," Gideon says.

"You would think that." I wish I could slap my hand over my mouth. I'm not sure why I'm angry with Gideon. It's not his fault that Dad and Mother fight, and it's not his fault Dad married Mother instead of. . . Well, I don't know what. It's not his fault, any of it. "I'm sorry. I'm stressed out, I think."

Inara places a hand on my shoulder. "We all are."

"I'd like to go along," Gideon says. "It might be nice to have someone else with the same goal. You're only one person. You can't be everywhere at once."

"That's a good idea," Inara says. "It's always good to have someone to watch your back."

Dad meets her eye and smiles. "Yes, although I've nearly forgotten what that feels like. Thank you."

"You two be safe, okay?" Inara wraps one arm around each of their shoulders.

"We will," Dad says.

Mother refuses to come outside, but Inara and I watch their plane take off, waving at them. Dad smiles at me and throws me the cheesiest thumbs up I've ever seen.

I stumble back toward my room, my mind on Dad's task—attempting to avert a war that will kill thousands upon thousands of humans. He really does live by his beliefs, even when they make his life harder. The next few days are sprinkled with reports of Dad's progress.

Or rather, his lack of progress.

He and Gideon make every effort to come to terms, to impress upon the local leaders the importance of relinquishing all ties with the terrorists sheltered under their wings. But their hatred is deep-seated, and their faith is nearly as strong as Dad's, in its misguided way.

He calls me each day with an update. Every time, I hope he has something good to report.

"Any progress?" I ask.

"Oh, sweetheart, every time we take a step forward, we take another back. We're doing our best to convince them that the al-Qaeda aren't on their side, but they have a long history of grievances with the United States."

"With Mother."

"Same thing," he says.

"So. . . no progress at all."

"No," he admits. "Not yet. But I'm hopeful. Tomorrow we have a meeting that they promise will be attended by a representative of Osama bin Laden himself. The leaders of the Taliban have indicated that they want to avoid a war if there's any possible way."

"That sounds promising."

"I hope so," Dad says.

I've just hung up when Douglas comes with a message. "Your mother would like to invite you to the infirmary. She wanted me to assure you that she's okay."

She's doing the ultrasound, and Dad's not even here. I knew Mother was angry, but this is spiteful.

"Fine." I try not to stomp down the hall, but I'm not very successful. As angry as I am, my feet move more and more quickly until I'm practically running.

"What's going on?" Lucas asks. "Why are we sprinting toward the infirmary?"

We reach the door and I stop and place a hand on his chest. "I'm sorry, but you have to wait outside. I'll tell you just as soon as I'm able."

He shrugs. He's used to me by now.

Only Job and Mother are inside the room. The ultrasound machine is on, and Job's holding jelly in his hands. Mother smiles at me. "While we wait on your father's efforts, we finally have time to breathe. I thought we might as well face this."

I still can't hear another heartbeat, but Mother thinks it should be audible any day now. I want to tell her that doing this when Dad's not here is mean. Spiteful. Beneath her. But I can't handle any more arguments or yelling, not right now.

"Go ahead," I say.

Job squirts the jelly on the small bulge on Mother's stomach and begins to move the ultrasound wand. My eyes fly to the screen, transfixed. *Please be a girl, please be a girl, please be a girl.*

"Well, that's unexpected," Job says.

"What?" I peer at the blurry images. I can't tell what I'm seeing exactly. It looks like a heart shape, or maybe a head and a belly. "What is that? Is the baby okay? Can you tell whether it's a boy or a girl, or is it still too early?"

"Well, *it* is a girl." He shifts the probe and I can see a face—nose, eyes mouth. Then he shifts it again and I realize it wasn't a head and a belly. It was two heads. "But it's not just one girl. And one of them appears to be. . ." He cocks his head and leans closer. "Shoving the other one."

Mother closes her eyes, her mouth a tear across her face, her chest heaving. "Twins," she finally whispers.

"You are having two little girls," Job says. "And I'm so very sorry to be the one to tell you."

I was so worried about whether Mother would have a boy—desperate to be freed by a girl and avoid the horror of losing another sibling. I prayed and prayed and prayed that my life would selfishly be improved. But two girls?

Mother doesn't need to explain why this is catastrophic. I know my history. The Peloponnesian War, the Seleucid-Parthia War, the Hundred Years' War. All of them caused by twin daughters at the end of the empresses' line of succession.

I prayed and prayed and prayed for a girl so hard that God gave us two, and now one of them must be murdered.

It's all my fault.

❧ 16 ❧

THE PAST: 2001

The Empress of Alamecha never cries. Tears are weak. Sobbing is undignified. And besides all of that, it makes your face blotchy. The Empress would never have a blotchy face.

But tears stream down Mother's face and I'm powerless to stop them. I know I should hug her, or squeeze her hand, or offer words of encouragement and solace or something. I have no words to offer, no comfort to provide. In fact, if Mother knew what I did, how hard I prayed for this, she'd probably kick me out. At a baseline, she would yell and scream.

Maybe I should confess. It would be better than this quiet, miserable pain.

Job pulls her against him and she sobs on his shoulder. I had no idea they were so close. "It's going to be alright." He strokes her hair softly.

He's a liar.

I sit as still as a corpse and wait. I don't know what else to do. It feels like I'll be waiting until the babies come, like somehow we will never leave this room. The sun will set and rise again, over and over, and we'll still be here. Mother sobbing, Job rubbing her back and whispering softly to her, and me, wallowing in a puddle of guilt.

God sure did show me not to be a greedy little brat. I asked for something entirely so that I could get what I wanted, without regard for anything else, and look what happened. I broke everything.

But the moment doesn't last forever. Eventually, Mother straightens. She leans her head against the wall behind the infirmary bed and inhales. Then she exhales. Job's shoulders relax the tiniest bit.

Mother takes my hand and I jump.

"I'm sorry I startled you," she whispers. "I have a favor to ask, and it's a large one."

"Anything," I say. "Whatever you need."

"I know with absolute certainty that one of these babies —" She chokes.

I squeeze her hand.

"One of these babies," she continues, "must die. But I'm not entirely sure that I can bring myself to do it. My mind recoils at the thought."

My stomach churns.

"I want you to promise me that you will force me to do it. It's for the good of Alamecha, and that's your duty. You're my Heir, and I need you to do this, as your last act in that role. Can you make me that promise?"

"Perhaps me," Job says, "or Balthasar, or Eamon, or Frederick. One of us could make you that promise."

Mother shakes her head. "None of you can countermand me. Only my Heir can issue a challenge."

"But once the children are born," Job says, "she will no longer be your Heir."

Mother waves her hand. "The Charter holds that a

newborn must survive the first twenty-four hours to become my legal Heir."

"I don't recall—"

Mother cuts Job off. "You're not an expert on the Charter, are you?" Mother closes her eyes. "Melina will be able to contest this if I can't do the right thing. She's the only one who can."

"You want me to force you to kill one of your children on the very day she's born?" I ask.

"I do," Mother says.

I wish I didn't feel God's hand in this, but it's fitting that I should have to repair the damage I created when I so flippantly demanded a boon. "I'll do it." I stand up. "I vow it."

"Thank you." Mother's eyes close, her hands resting on her belly.

"You're welcome." I step toward the door. "May I be released?"

Mother doesn't reply, but I take that as consent.

Lucas is wise enough not to ask me any questions when I emerge. The walk to my room is a blur, and I'm not sure how long I sob on my bed before the tap at the door.

Inara.

Somehow, she always knows when I'm upset, and she always says the right thing. She's the daughter Mother deserves, the Heir the family needs. The second I open the door, she throws her arms around me.

"How do you know?" I ask, my words muffled by her hair.

"Mother had Job tell me. She's not receiving anyone right now, which is probably for the best."

"She looked worse than me."

Inara releases me and crosses the room to sit down in one of my armchairs.

I follow her over and take a chair across from her. "After Jered." I choke. "I thought this couldn't possibly be worse. I thought nothing could be as hard as that, as losing him."

"I am sorry, Melina. Job told me what she made you promise and it's not fair. She shouldn't put that on you."

I can't help it. I break down and sob into my hands.

She leaps to her feet and kneels down in front of me. "What did I say? What's wrong?"

It takes me a moment to calm down enough to speak. "It's my fault," I say. "I deserve to fix it."

Inara frowns. "How could it possibly be your fault? Obviously you aren't the father, and you can't magic twins into existence, last I checked."

I drop my face back into my hands. I should never have said anything at all. Trying to tell Dad was a total mistake. But a burning desire to be honest with someone consumes me—no, not with someone. I want to tell my dearest friend, my cherished sister. If I can't tell Inara, I can't tell anyone.

My eyelids flutter and I swallow. Then I swallow again. "I—"

Inara looks into my eyes. "You can tell me anything. You know that."

"Remember the law I asked Mother to change?"

Inara nods.

"I might have wanted her to change it for selfish reasons."

She tilts her head and her mouth opens slightly.

I need to just say it. "I think I'm gay."

"You *think* you're gay?"

I shake my head. "I am gay. I met—well, you met Aline too—at the Games. And it was like lightning struck me or something. I just knew."

"Okay." Inara doesn't move. She doesn't tense or scowl

or glare, but she doesn't wrap me in a hug or say anything that tells me what she's thinking.

"I didn't do anything about it, but when she and her brother attended Mother's party. . . I've been texting her ever since."

Inara sits down cross-legged on the floor. "I don't understand."

"I was confused at first," I say. "I thought maybe I only liked Aline." I choke. "Of course, I do only like her. But what I mean is that I've realized that I do find the female form—"

Inara shakes her head. "No, no, not about all that. I should have seen that before. I'm sorry that I didn't, and I'm sorry that you've been so alone with all of this." She sighs. "I've been wracking my brain and I can't think of an explanation for what that possibly has to do with Mother's pregnancy and twins."

Oh. "Well." I sigh. "You know that Dad believes in God and that he's been teaching me."

Inara shrugs.

"And I have slowly been kind of figuring out what that means to me. After Mother told me she was pregnant, well. I prayed. It's the first time I've pleaded for anything, and I begged God to please let Mother have a girl. It would keep us from repeating Jered's—" I choke again. I can't bring myself to say it. "But also, it would free me. I could leave, and Mother wouldn't even mind. I could be with Aline, maybe. Especially with Mother's new law. It's not illegal— it's not punishable by death anymore."

She rises to her knees again and pulls me toward her for a hug. Her body is shaking, and I worry that she's sobbing now, distressed by my confession. I hurt everything I touch.

Until I realize that she's laughing.

I shove her back. "What's so funny?"

"Oh, sweet Melina. I'm sure your father would be touched by your faith, but you can't *pray* twins into existence. It's a biological phenomenon. This is no more your fault than the terrorist attack. Sometimes things happen and we don't have any control over it at all. In fact, I think that's the strongest argument against Eamon's fanatic faith. What kind of God would punish a child he loved by putting her through something like this?"

I shake my head. "I feel it in my bones. This is because I begged. . ." I drop my voice until it's a bare whisper. "For something wicked."

Inara's shoulders slump. "Oh, Melina. I can't convince you in this moment, but one day you'll see that it isn't so. This isn't a punishment, I promise you that. It's just something that happened."

"You're saying that I begged and begged God for something, something that would enable me to pursue a relationship that most religions on earth agree is wrong, and that it's totally not connected to Mother's situation? Because what she's asking me feels a lot like penance or some kind of divine message."

"Not everything is about you," Inara says. "And not everything is a message. Sometimes all we can do is survive until things improve."

"Accept the world as it is," I say.

"You are doing things to change it, and you're making great strides in the right direction, I believe," Inara says. "What does Aline think?"

I blush. "I haven't mentioned any of the news about Mother to her."

"Of course. I mean about Mother being pregnant at all, or about your recent law changes."

"I didn't tell her about Mother's pregnancy either," I say.

"I didn't want to get her hopes up. And until you and I spoke, I hadn't really admitted to myself that my prayers were about Aline. I kind of told myself it was about avoiding another Jered situation."

"It's about that too," Inara says. "I'm sure of it. People are multifaceted. We aren't all right or all wrong, and your motivations are complex. But that also doesn't mean that anything but altruism is evil."

She's right that people aren't all good or all bad, but she's wrong about the rest. This is God's answer to my demand—her comforting words don't alter the truth. If Inara believed in God, or religion of any kind, maybe she would get it. I don't have the energy to argue with her though, not now. "I'll think about it."

A banging at my door drags me to my feet. "What could possibly be wrong now?"

Inara follows me, her eyes weary. "I'm beginning to dread waking up in the morning. But take cheer. Things can't get much worse, can they?"

I yank the door open. A young boy is waiting on the threshold, trembling slightly. He won't meet my eye, his gaze trained on his shiny black boots. "What is it?"

He glances upward, and I recognize him. His name is Edam, and he was Mother's spur of the moment purchase a few years ago. He's the little boy who was raised by his mother, Senah, until her death. Then his sister decided to sell him. He's always dragging around the palace, eyes downcast, hands wringing, alone. I've frequently wondered what I could do to help him, but I can't ever think of anything. I have my own problems.

He holds a piece of paper up in the air like a prayer.

I take it and scan the writing. *Meeting was a trap. Gideon and Eamon both killed along with fourteen humans. Remains to ship immediately. Condolences. -M*

M must stand for Melamecha. My brain focuses on that. Melamecha is sending us a message. But wait, why would she send this to me? "Why didn't you take this to the Empress?"

Little Edam still won't meet my eye. "She won't answer the door. Balthasar told me to fetch you, and I wasn't supposed to bring this, but I thought you needed to know." His voice drops to a whisper. "He didn't notice I took it. Maybe you could not mention that."

It's not a trick or a miscommunication. Which means. . . Dad is dead. My hands begin trembling, gradually worsening until I drop the paper. Inara bends over to pick it up slowly, as though she's moving in some kind of time-delay. I can't decide whether it's my brain boycotting its job, or whether she's actually moving that slowly.

She reads the note and begins shaking her head, as though she can shake the truth into fantasy. As if she can dislodge the harmful truths of today from her brain entirely.

1. I have to murder my infant sister.

2. My father is dead.

My big, brave sister collapses on the floor in a heap, totally incoherent. Somehow, I'm handling this better than her. How can that be? But of course. Her best friend of a very, very long time died right alongside my dad. Gideon and Eamon both gone, in a single attack. Those terrorists are canny enemies. Or, perhaps they're simply tools.

Inara may not have thought that the first occurrence was a punishment, but there's no doubt in my mind, now. I angered God with my demands, and he has answered me with these tremendous penances. Dad tasked me to follow God's plan, and I was supposed to be learning how to find it. Dad is just like me. Was just like me, and now thanks to me, he's dead.

Instead of being selfish, I should have done what Dad taught me. I should have been selfless. I should never have asked like I did. I need to go and tell Mother what happened. I need to clean up the mess I've made. But before that, I need to show God that I hear him.

I pry the crumpled message out of Inara's hand and hold it out to Edam. He snatches it back gratefully. "Take this back with you so you won't get in trouble, and tell Balthasar I'm coming."

He nods and rushes off. I close the door before Lucas or Douglas, who surely overheard, can push their way through to make sure I'm okay. Of course I'm not okay, and a hug or a few words of comfort won't help. It's time for me to stop trying to fight against what Dad wanted of me. It's time for me to fulfill the destiny he laid out.

And that means making the right choices, no matter how hard they seem. No matter how miserable they make me. It's time to follow in the footsteps of my dad, to do what he asked me to do, and not what I selfishly want instead.

I pick up my phone. I have perfect recall, so this isn't really going to prevent me from contacting her, but the action has significance to me. I text Aline. FATHER IS DEAD. YOU AND ME ARE ALL WRONG. PLEASE DON'T CONTACT ME AGAIN.

I don't wait for a reply, and when she calls me, I don't answer. But I do delete and then block her number. And I delete our text chain, and hardest of all, I purge every photo she has ever sent me.

All evidence of Aline is gone, and I'm ready to make the decisions I should have made from the start, no matter how hard. Because all we have are our choices and mine will never be so epically wrong again.

❧ 17 ❧

THE PAST: 2001 & 2002

Inara curls up into a ball on my floor and cannot be consoled. She doesn't even seem to understand any of the words I'm speaking. I don't have a best friend like Gideon was to her—except maybe for her. If she died. I choke at the thought. It would destroy me.

After a few moments, I give up and walk down the hall toward Mother.

Lucas doesn't ask a thing, just follows me silently. Which, of course, makes me want to tell him. But not until after Mother knows.

Her solid door was created to withstand direct gunfire, even an explosion. It blocks most noise, but not all, thanks to evian hearing. I begin by calling out softly. When that doesn't work, I yell. Finally, I bang on the door. Repeatedly. Eventually, my concern at her reaction evaporates in frustration. And rage. Why does it fall to me to deliver this news? I'm as upset as she is about the twins, and I've been tasked with eliminating one if she can't bring herself to do it.

Isn't that enough?

But apparently it isn't. No matter how loudly I scream or how hard I pound, Mother refuses to answer. Even the fire of indignation burning in my heart isn't quite strong enough to compel me to scream the news through the solid wood of the door. I finally slump to the ground in front of her room with my back to the wall and sob into my knees.

The door opens behind me, and I twist around immediately.

"You couldn't give me a few hours?" Mother's face is puffy and red, and her words sting like a slap.

"I'm sorry," I say. "I really am sorry."

"What?" she asks. "What do you need from me that I could possibly give right now?"

I stand up and look her in the eyes. "It's not something I need." My voice cracks and tears leak silently down my cheeks. "I have more news."

Her eyes widen. "What?"

"Dad is dead," I say. "An explosion at the meeting, prepared for evians, apparently. There were no survivors."

Mother freezes and then her hands clench at her sides. "Balthasar!" She pushes past me and strides down the hall. "Balthasar!"

Guards, hers and mine, scatter behind her like bowling pins, hurrying to re-form and follow. I stumble along after her like I'm on a leash. I want to curl up like Inara and bawl, but something finally broke through the fog of sorrow around Mother and I need to see what she does about it.

Her cheeks are dry when we reach the Security office. Her hands are relaxed at her sides.

"Enora?" Balthasar swallows heavily, and then as he takes in her demeanor, he quiets. His voice is barely a whisper when he says, "You know."

She nods slightly. "I do."

"What are you going to do about it?"

She inhales slowly, her exhalation quick and sharp. Her lower lip trembles. "Bomb that entire country into a crater."

Which is exactly what Dad wouldn't have wanted, but I don't have the heart to stop her.

Mother spins on her heel and walks back to her room one measured step at a time. She pauses once and her shoulders sag, but she squares them again and continues on until she reaches her room. She doesn't rush back inside to hide like I expected.

No, she continues past, and turns into the throne room. "Frederick, please let the citizens know that I have news."

Oh, Mother. I take my seat at her side. "Do you want to take some time to process this first?"

She shakes her head tightly. "I can't. I can't process all of this quickly. An empress's first duty, always, is to her people. Ours deserve to know, all of it." She stares straight ahead as citizens filter in and then stream through the doors at a steady clip.

I hate all of the murmurs. "Another law change?" "No, she's declaring war." "War on Melamecha. It's about time." "Maybe Melina's finally got a boyfriend."

Mother waits longer than I would have. The room is nearly full when she finally stands. All the whispering immediately ceases. "I've asked you here without any notice, and for that I am very sorry. I know it's hard when something unexpected interrupts your day. You're probably also wondering what news I bear today."

Her heart is steady and strong. Her eyes are clear. Her hands are relaxed and still. Mother doesn't look like a woman whose heart has been ripped out today—twice. And yet, I know that's exactly who she is.

"As many of you know, less than a month ago, a group of

humans who learned of our existence decided to attack us. They chose Alamecha as their target because we are the epitome of what is quintessentially evian. We are strong, fearless, and we offer no quarter. My Consort, Eamon ne'Godeena ex'Alamecha, wished to offer the humans who weren't involved in the attack the opportunity to surrender the insurgents. He wanted to spare their lives."

Mother pauses and looks from one end of the room to the other. Not a soul so much as takes a breath.

"Today, he was meant to meet with the leaders of these innocent humans in an attempt to finalize the details of a deal. Instead of gratitude at his offers of mercy, instead of the respect they should have shown to someone of his station, these *innocent* humans prepared an explosion that killed my Consort and the head of my daughter Inara's personal guard, Gideon ne'Leamarta ex'Alamecha. Five other evians attended them to see to their protection. None of them survived."

Gasps and then utter silence.

"These humans don't comprehend what they have done, but they will. I am Enora Alamecha. When my last Consort was killed at Pearl Harbor, I fully committed to a war that I didn't want to fight. It culminated with destruction on a scale that the humans had not previously imagined. I didn't drop those bombs at Hiroshima and Nagasaki lightly or out of rage. I dropped them to show the world what we can do."

Mother sits down on her throne.

"I wouldn't dream of using such weapons on these vermin. They don't deserve a quick and clean ending. No, I will slowly, carefully, and intentionally destroy them incrementally. I will dismantle any faith they have in their ability to stand against us now or at any point in the future. At all times, they shall be allowed to cling to hope, so that I might rip it from their filthy, undeserving hands. They will despise the individuals who crossed Alamecha, and then they will burn too. Slowly, painfully."

Every face in the room mirrors Mother's fury and resolve.

"And there is one other piece of news I need to share." She swallows and inhales slowly. "I recently discovered that I am pregnant. With female twins."

A thousand faces fall. Two thousand eyes widen.

"All of you know that with my Consort dead and my age nearing nine-hundred, these may likely be my last female children. But this will not break us, not Alamecha. We have learned the lessons from history. We are too strong to succumb to the kind of senseless warfare that usually follows this type of thing. Believe me when I promise you: We will emerge from these trials stronger than ever. Accept the world as it is."

The entire gathering repeats the second part of the family motto back to Mother in unison. "Or do something to change it."

Mother marches out of the room galvanized, as if she has drawn strength from her people. Maybe she has. That same sense of purpose pulls her along for months. I stand by her side as she systematically destroys the government of Afghanistan, eliminating or driving all the leadership into neighboring Pakistan. Melamecha swears to deal with the threat they pose immediately. Of course we believe her —what empress wants evian-hating zealots in their backyard?

I assert my influence to temper Mother's less prudent attacks, especially the ones that will unduly harm civilians. It's what Dad would have wanted. Women and children and farmers aren't to blame for the Taliban and al-Qaeda threat. Melamecha isn't pleased when Mother sets up bases all over Afghanistan, but she doesn't dare complain publicly.

Before I realize how much time has passed, it's 2002 and Mother's belly has grown significantly. I attend each ultrasound, forcing myself to watch as the babies grow, both of them infuriatingly healthy and strong. But as the urgency of the war wanes, Mother spends more and more time alone in her room.

She also eats less than she should. Far less.

"You can't subsist on two eggs," Angel says one morning. "It's not even enough for you, much less two more growing bodies."

Mother shoves the plate away. "I don't take orders from you."

Angel leans toward her. "You do about what you eat."

"Is that so?" Mother leaps to her feet, surprisingly agile for a woman with such a large belly. She snatches a sword off the wall. "Prove it."

Angel whips a dagger from her boot. "Fine. You think I won't attack a pregnant lady? At least if I take action, you'll die quickly, not one painstaking day at a time."

Mother swears under her breath and drops the sword. It clatters against the floor and Frederick rushes into her room, his eyes wild. "What's going on?"

"Nothing," Mother says. "I'm being an idiot, that's all."

"I think Frederick needs a day off," I say. "He hasn't left your door since October."

"Agreed." Mother meets his eye. "I don't want to see you anywhere near me for two days. And that doesn't mean you leave here to spend time in the security office working on my rotations. Do something that isn't work."

"I won't." He squares his shoulder and looks at the wall.

"You people are all ridiculous," Mother says.

"You're lucky to have people who love you," I say. "Let

Lyssa fill in for Frederick, or Balthasar. And listen to Angel. She's trying to help her friend, just as I want to help my mother."

"Fine." Mother slumps in her chair and shovels food into her mouth as though she's unaware of what she's even doing.

It worsens day by day. No one even mentions a birthday party, and the day of her birthday comes and goes without any celebration. I walk into her room with a cupcake and she immediately turns away. Inara isn't much better. She's not pregnant and she's not empress so no one cajoles her and badgers her and hovers over her, but she barely leaves her room. I have to force feed her more often than not. She loses weight, a lot of weight. But I don't have time to run the family business and deal with both of them, and Mother's in worse shape.

By late March, near the due date of the babies, Mother stops getting out of bed except to use the restroom. She won't climb out, even to eat, no matter how much I cajole. I finally shove the tray onto the coverlet next to her and call Angel. Mother leans forward enough to eat when Angel yells at her, and then rolls over and pulls the covers up over her stomach. It's like she's an incubator for the babies, nothing more.

Frederick is on another forced day off, so Lyssa's standing outside Mother's door with Jaclyn and Jonathan. Angel rushes back to the kitchen, but I am reaching the end of my patience. I need a solution.

"I don't know what to do," I say.

"We do what we can do," Lyssa says. "Take things one day at a time, with our goal as basic survival. She made it through after Althuselah's death, so I know that she'll emerge on the other side of this too."

"It doesn't feel like it," I say.

Lyssa hugs me. "She will."

"What about Inara?"

"She'll survive too," she says. "Losing a best friend is like losing a limb. Your mother and your sister will slowly recover, but we can't expect things to return to normal in a day. This pregnancy is making everything harder, I think."

I don't mention that I've been doing everything while Inara and Mother take a leave of absence from life. Hearing petitions, meeting with Larena, acting as Empress—I hate every second of it. But I don't need to complain, because Lyssa already knows. She's doing everything that I'm not, and filling in to keep Frederick from falling over to boot.

Less than a week before the babies' due date, I make Frederick unlock the door when Mother won't answer my banging. I don't have a great feeling about her retreating further and further. Things were hard enough with Jered. This is going to be that much harder. Killing her own. . . I can't even make myself think the words.

Mother's in bed, as always, and I start across the room. But an ink pot has tipped over at the top of her desk, a black blot spreading even as I watch. She was up? And writing something? "Mother?" I call.

No response, as usual. I don't know whether she's asleep or just ignoring me. She hasn't taken an active interest in management in so long, I'm dying to know what roused her interest. I look down at the paper, black ink creeping downward. I can only make out the last few lines.

With the might and power of God, the Eldest shall destroy all in her path and unite my children as one. Only through her blood can the stone be restored to the mountain. Together, with the strength of her strongest supporter, she shall open the Garden of Eden, that the miracle of God shall go unto all the Earth to save my children from utter destruction.

My heart practically stops. I lean closer, anxious to read

the words written before that passage, but all that now exists is the ink blot, spreading to cover the rest of the words in darkness. It must be the prophecy Dad mentioned but never saw. I have it now, the actual text. I just have no idea why Mother was writing it down, or who she was sharing it with.

The Eldest. Dad was convinced the prophecy he heard snatches of was about me—and I now have younger sisters on the way. Which makes me the eldest of Dad's children. The eldest of this round of Enora's heirs. What if it *is* talking about me? Utter destruction. Like the kind that follows twin sisters battling over a throne?

"Mother." I reluctantly leave the paper, confident the ink will soon eliminate all evidence that it ever existed. "Who were you writing?" I draw close enough to see that she's asleep, as usual.

She has been sleeping far, far too often. I should tell Job. She's due for an ultrasound today anyway. Hopefully he'll have some advice to offer.

Job grumbles at first, when I tell him Mother won't be coming to the infirmary. "Does she know how annoying it is to haul this thing to her room?" He points at the cumbersome ultrasound cart.

"She's not getting up for anything other than peeing anymore. Frederick had to unlock her room this morning—she wouldn't even come to the door."

"Wait. She's not getting out of bed? For how long?"

I shrug. "A few days. Maybe a week."

"Why hasn't anyone mentioned this before?" Job walks toward the hall, the wheels on the ultrasound machine rattling.

"I don't. . ." I struggle to keep up when he rounds the bend and reaches the straight part of our walk. "I assumed you knew."

"She walked down to see me last week. You're saying she's staying in bed, what, almost all day?"

"We've all been helping, okay? Angel makes sure she eats, and Lyssa and Jaclyn help her to the bathroom two or three times a day."

Job stops without warning and I run into the back of him, shoving the machine clattering down the hall.

"She has no appetite? She must be *helped* to the bathroom?"

"No one told you?" I ask.

He spins around, his eyes flashing. "Who would have told me, exactly?"

I shake my head.

"Can you hear the babies' heartbeats?"

I try to remember. I'm sure I must be able to. . . "I—I think so."

"You think so?" Job takes off down the hall at a sprint, grabbing the ultrasound machine and carrying it, the wheels pivoting uselessly below.

I race to catch up, my heart hammering faster than my exertion would require. Why didn't I tell Job before? Mother's been acting essentially like this for weeks now, but it was so gradual that I didn't really think about it. She lost her Consort, she's facing a hard time, and that's the reason.

Right?

Job doesn't wait to ask permission to enter. He barges through Mother's door and slams the cart against the ground. I hope it's not broken. He jogs across the floor to her bedside. His voice is surprisingly light, unconcerned, when he finally says, "What's this I hear about you not going to the bathroom without help?"

Mother doesn't move.

I listen carefully for heartbeats. Job pauses and I assume

he's doing the same. Two are slow and steady. One is erratic. "Something's wrong."

Job tosses his head. "Tell Frederick to get help. Now."

I run for the door, but Frederick has been listening. He bellows so loud it makes my ears ring. "Balthasar—get down here. And Angel, and Lyssa, and Larena, and Inara. Now. No, I don't care what they're doing or whether they're busy. Now!" He pushes past me and in through the doorway himself. "Is she alright?"

Job is turning Mother from her side to her back and pressing his head to her belly. Mother's eyes are shut, but there are dark bags under them. Her skin is ashen. Job asks me to assist while he checks her cervix, which I've now seen more times than I thought possible. But Dad's not here to sit with her, so it falls to me.

"She's not dilated, not at all."

"Then what's wrong?" I climb up on the far side of the bed and scoot toward her. "Is she going to be alright?"

"I believe she's being poisoned," Job says. "Either her, or the babies, or both."

"How could we not have noticed?" I ask.

"That's what I'd like to know," he says.

I take her hand and squeeze. Her head turns toward me slightly, but she doesn't return the pressure on my hand.

"The first thing we need to do is remove these babies immediately. Her body is diverting resources to care for them that she needs to recover from whatever has been done to her."

"No." Mother tries to sit up and coughs. "They must be kept safe."

"They will be," Job says. "It's only a few days from your due date. They'll be fine."

She falls back against her pillows and closes her eyes.

"This is going to hurt," Job says. "You have always

waited for labor to begin, but this time I'm going to have to cut them out."

Mother nods.

Inara's face appears in the doorway and shortly after, so does Lyssa's.

Job says, "Frederick, send someone for Wessington. Tell him I need the anesthesia."

Mother cries out. "Don't wait. Do it now."

Job bites his lip. "I think—"

"Do it." Mother's eyes flash.

Somehow, Mother's anger reassures me. She can't be dying, not if she's still issuing orders and demanding that Job cut her open like a filet of fish.

Job shakes his head. "At the very least, I need a scalpel."

Mother turns to look at me.

I sigh and slide my forearm dagger from its sheath. "You can use this."

"You two aren't normal," Job mutters. "Daggers and no anesthesia. This isn't battle. It's childbirth."

Mother smiles. "Same difference."

Inara snorts from the doorway. She looks haggard and far too thin, but she's here. That's encouraging. "For someone with no children, I've been around a lot of newborns. She's not far off."

"Just do it," Mother begs. "Please."

Job takes the dagger from my hand reluctantly and examines the edge. "Fine." He shoves Mother's shirt upward, exposing her stomach, and yanks the sheets down. "Give her something to bite on."

Mother rolls her eyes. "I don't need to bite down. Just do it, Job. I'm not a child."

"And I'm not a warrior, in the habit of slicing people open with impunity."

"I'll heal," Mother says.

I hope she's right.

Job brings the dagger down at the top of her belly. His hand shakes as he applies pressure, the shaking worsening as the dagger slices Mother's skin.

I place my hand on his shoulder. "Tell me what to do and I'll take over. You're going to slice the babies with all that nervous twitching."

He throws his shoulder, dislodging my hand. "No, I can do this." He straightens and closes his eyes. When he reopens them, his hand is steady. He presses down, harder this time, and a line of red appears, sliding downward. "I'll need to make it a little deeper, but I wanted to make sure I didn't cut the babies."

"Do it quickly," I say.

Mother's stomach is already healing up.

Job uses a combination of words I've never heard together. Creative, confusing, and disgusting all at once. "Okay, this time it's going to be a little deeper."

Mother grunts. "If I knew you were going to dig them out with a spoon, I might have asked for that numbing medicine."

"I'm sorry," Job says. "I've never done this before."

"Clearly."

"Okay, I'm through the abdomen. The next incision is through the uterus." Job's hands are still steady, thankfully.

I lean closer, ready to see my sisters. As my dagger separates the uterine wall, a tiny hand pokes through. All I've seen are four tiny fingers and a thumb, and I'm already in love. The fingers are splayed, and it flexes. Then it disappears back into Mother's belly. I lean closer.

Job reaches inside the incision and pulls a baby through. "Here's the first one." He cuts the umbilical cord and passes her to me, covered in blood, wriggling, and this time, it's my hands that shake. I press her against my chest and she curls against me as if she's cold. I suppose I might be cold too, if I were naked and tiny.

She doesn't even cry. "Hello, darling." Her head turns toward me and she smiles. I nearly drop her. I can't kill someone who's smiling at me. I can't do it.

Job has to slice the uterus open again—it has already healed shut— and the second he does, two hands reach through and take hold of his fingers.

"What's going on?" I ask.

"I've never seen anything like this. I sliced the sack earlier when I removed the first baby, but this one is clawing its way out." He dislodges the tiny hands grasping his fingers and slides his hand in further to lift the other newborn out of Mother's uterus.

I glance at her face, which is contorted with something that looks a lot like rage.

The second child begins to howl, and I swear that she's as loud as an adult.

"Do something," I shout. "What's wrong with her?"

Inara rushes inside and takes the screeching baby, tucking the child against her side. As soon as her fury has decreased somewhat in volume, Inara inches closer to Mother.

"What can you do for her?" Inara asks. "Job! Mother needs help."

He shakes his head. "Enora will either heal from the delivery and recover from this poison, or she won't. I could test her blood and try and find some kind of antidote, but that will take far too long."

The baby in Inara's arms has returned to howling full force, but all my big sister's attention is on our mother. She raises her voice to be heard over the complaining baby. "Do it then! Do it now!" Inara shrieks for Jonathan, who rushes inside. "Job's going to give you a sample. Rush it down to the infirmary. Tell his minions to test it. Now."

Job sighs and grabs a cup from the bedside counter. He scrapes the blood coating his hands into the cup. "There. That's not totally clean, but there should be plenty. Tell Wessington to test for heavy metals, CBC, CMP, and run a basic tox panel."

I scooch toward Mother on the bed and hold the happy newborn near her face. "Look, Mother. I know you can hear me. Your babies are both out, and they're beautiful and healthy. You kept them safe, but your job isn't done. They still need you."

My voice drops to the barest of whispers. "I need you. I can't lose you and Dad both in the same year. Come back, please."

Mother's eyelids flutter.

I shift Mother's arms around and notice her abdomen is healing, albeit slowly. "She needs broth, or something," I say. "Her body needs healthy calories. It's been at a deficit for too long. Is Angel close?"

Angel steps into the room. "I'm here."

"Make something simple. I don't care what as long as it's fast and easy to digest. A smoothie, or yogurt, or I don't know. Bring it yourself. Now."

She nods and runs out the door.

I shift the sheets and set the cheerful newborn right in front of Mother. I gently angle her face so that Mother can see the baby. "Look," I say softly. "She's perfect. She's beautiful. I know the past few months have been hard. The past few years, really. But things will improve, I promise. Things will only be better from here on out. Take a chance on us, Mother. Come back. We need you more than ever."

Mother inhales deeply. The slice on her stomach heals the rest of the way, but her eyes still don't open.

"Look at your baby," I plead.

She does, and for the first time in months, Mother's mouth turns upward with joy. And that darling, tiny angel beams right back at her.

"Her name is Chancery," Enora says softly. "She will be good and fair and true, and because of her, I'm taking a chance on loving, one last time."

❧ 18 ❧

THE PAST: 2002

Angel shoots through the door with a glass in her hand a moment later. It's a toss-up as to what Mother needs more—motivation to heal, or the nutrition with which to do it. Eventually, she shifts her head the other direction and drinks the entire smoothie through the straw Angel had the foresight to bring.

Not long afterward, Mother sits up and picks up Chancery. I wasn't wrong. That tiny baby snuggles against Mother the same way she did against me. No one speaks. Not Inara, who has finally calmed the other baby. Not Lyssa or Angel, who are standing shoulder to shoulder against the window. Not Job, who looks like he has been bleached, washed, and wrung out. Not even Frederick or Balthasar, who stand stiffly on either side of the open doorway.

When the second newborn begins to cry again, Mother shifts Chancery into her left arm and holds out her right. "Bring her to me."

I hold out my hand. "Is that wise? Maybe you shouldn't bond with both of them." Because I already want to spare

Chancery instead of the crying one—probably because I've held her and she has a name. To do what needs to be done, it might be easier not to think of the other infant as anything other than number two.

"Bring her now," Mother says. "That's an order."

I can't argue with her again, not now, not minutes after we nearly lost her. "Fine." I wave at Inara, who crosses the room stiffly. She places the second baby girl in Mother's right arm, and baby number two immediately quiets, as if she already knows that she's finally where she should have been all along.

How will Mother ever choose which one to keep? I shudder. What if she doesn't? But she must, or the task falls to me.

"You're seventh generation," Mother says to the second child. "Both of you are. But you're my youngest child, by a minute or two, right Job?" She looks up expectantly.

"Right," I say. "About ninety seconds. And she's a fire-cracker. She clawed her way out of the uterus. I think she was upset that Chancery was already out here, schmoozing people."

Mother smiles. "You're the one who was always pushing Chancery around. You're the fighter. I'll name you Judica. In Chaldean numerology, that's the number seven, and it also means judge. Because you will not shy away from doing what's hard, from making the right decision no matter the cost."

I suppose that settles which one will be Heir, but that means that sweet little Chancery. . . I close my eyes. *Why God? Why?*

Why doesn't He ever answer? Why are we left alone here, to do everything ourselves? The cost is unbearably steep. Perhaps this kind of thing is what will prepare Judica to be as strong, as relentless, and as fierce as Mother—

ready to rule her people with the iron fist I could never manage.

Mother eventually allows me to wipe Chancery down with a washcloth, and Inara takes care of Judica. We dress and swaddle and return the babes to her waiting arms. Lyssa has been busy helping Mother while we've worked on the babies. She looks much improved, and she's eating a bowl of stew. Color has returned to her cheeks, and no part of her trembles anymore. "Here's Chancery." I hand her off, but I wonder how to ask about Mother's plans without getting my head snapped off.

"You're wondering which child," Mother whispers.

"I assume it's this one." A profound sadness tugs at my heart. Sweet, happy Chancery. She'd be eaten alive here, surrounded by sharks. But it still pains me to consider ending her life before it has even begun.

Inara circles around behind me and places Judica on Mother's other side. "I think they may need to eat."

"I'll bring bottles right away," Angel says.

"Wait." Mother hands Judica to Lyssa. "Get Judica a bottle, but I want to nurse this one." Chancery. The one who isn't going to be kept.

Why would she do this to herself? It's prolonging the inevitable—it's basically torture. For the first time, I understand why Mother gave Jered up. Every day she kept him, she suffered a little more. He rubbed salt in the wound of her guilt, and here she is, doing it again. "I think that's a mistake."

"Spending time with her?" Mother lifts her shirt and Frederick and Balthasar spin on their heels to face the wall with matching looks of horror on their faces.

If things weren't so awful, it would make me laugh.

"All of it." I force myself to be blunt. "If you know

Chancery has to die, why not do it *before* it becomes impossibly hard?"

Chancery latches onto Mother's breast, and Mother sighs and closes her eyes. "Don't lie to yourself, Melina. It's going to be impossibly hard no matter what way we do this. No one should ever kill their own child. Ever."

She's right of course. It's another in a long line of the ghastly realities of our life. "But in this case." The wars march through my head. Thousands upon thousands dead in each circumstance. Humans, which Mother won't care about, but evians too. So many evians. "This isn't my fault." Even though it actually might be.

"It's no one's fault," Mother says. "But I can't kill her before I even know her." Her arms curl up around Chancery, and she sighs in contentment.

"I can't watch it," I say. "I can't. And I made you a promise that I will fulfill. Now that you're alright, I'm going to leave. I will return tonight, sometime after six. More than nine hours from now. I can't give you more than that."

"You won't need to," Mother says. "I promise."

When I return at seven-thirty, because I lied and I want her to have as much time as possible, I expect her to be prepared to do what needs to be done. I secretly hope it has already been resolved.

Frederick touches my arm when I reach her room. "Try to understand."

Understand what? I open the door and brace myself. There's only one baby in a bassinet near Mother's bed. I don't see anyone else around. What's going on? I cross the room quickly and pick up the baby. They look identical, but this newborn beams up at me with the sweetest smile I've ever seen. At once like Jered and nothing like him.

And I know.

This isn't Judica. Mother hasn't done it. I'm holding sweet Chancery in my arms. I breathe her in, and the lotion is coconut lime. I put that lotion on her myself. "Oh, Chancery. Mother can't do it."

I'm not sure where it comes from, but suddenly I'm singing. A stupid human song about a blackbird in the night. It came to mind because of the concept of broken things, I assume. Chancery curls into me, like before, and I realize it's the only way I can do it, and possibly the only time. "You were only waiting for this moment to be free," I sing. And then I cover poor Chancery's mouth with her own blanket, and I hold it there.

Her small body spasms, bucks, and struggles, but she's too small. And I don't have a choice. I want to release her, to snuggle her, to feed her, and to love her. But I think of the two hundred evians dead in the attack on the towers, and the nearly three thousand humans. In my mind, I multiply that number by a hundred, by a thousand, by ten thousand.

"This is the only way," I murmur. "Mother can't do what needs to be done. I don't want to do it, but if she won't, I don't have a choice."

Mother opens the bathroom door and stands in the doorway, cradling a mewling Judica in her arms. "Melina! No." She looks around frantically, which makes no sense. She knew I was coming. I warned everyone.

I want to drop the blanket from sweet Chancery's face. I don't want to be a villain, but Mother made me promise. I swore to her—because it's my fault, and I have to fix it, no matter how awful. No matter how it blackens my soul. And maybe this has been my destiny all along. Maybe this is the first step in staving off the utter destruction that the prophecy mentions.

It would be worse if hundreds of thousands—humans

and evians—died because no one was brave enough to take the life of this darling, precious little baby.

Blood drips down Mother's leg to pool on the floor below, and I finally understand. She and Inara were in the bathroom tending to Mother's delayed recovery—only holding Judica because she was crying. Thanks to the poison, Mother's still healing, still passing the extra uterine blood, which is why she lost track of time. Or maybe she didn't believe me, not really. I'm not known for being savage or a stickler. That has always been Mother's job.

But she was struggling with her health, for perhaps the first time in her life. And then I stole her baby out from under her nose. And I'm killing her. At least Chancery's no longer struggling as much. She almost looks like she's falling asleep in my arms.

"You can't keep her, Mother." Poor Chancery's arms and legs are barely moving. The life is slowly draining from her strong young body. "You can't. You know that as well as I do, but you're not thinking straight." I look at the blood dripping onto the floor below Mother.

Inara pushes past her and heads for me. "This isn't your decision to make," she says. "It's Mother's."

"She made the wrong one." As she worried she might, but when she was in her right mind, she made me promise to do what needed to be done.

"Only history will tell," Inara says.

"I'm telling you now—if we don't learn from history, then what's the point?" Chancery's perfect little arms go limp. "I know it's hard, so blame me. I can take it." Or at least, I hope I can, and if I can't, it doesn't matter. Because after today, I don't matter anymore.

"You're the reason I needed a new heir in the first place," Mother says. "You're flawed."

I stiffen, my grip on the blanket slipping. Inara sees her

moment and grabs Chancery. I'm too broken to resist, and flawed, like Mother said. But does she mean my failure at the games? My kindness and compassion? Or does she know about Aline?

Sweet, kind baby Chancery breathes in huge, rasping breaths, pinking up before my eyes. I shouldn't have let Inara take her. I could have snapped her neck, or just evaded Inara's attempts to recover her. Like me, she knows what should happen. She knows the risk Mother is taking, and who will pay for her gamble if it goes wrong.

Inara's acting like she's the angel of mercy, Mother's obedient child—and I'm the failure, again. Just like I lost in the games. Just like I have always lost, because I am my father's child. My father, who is dead, who was like me. No matter what I do, it's wrong. I won Sovereignty, but it wasn't enough. I gave up Aline, never even letting on that I loved the wrong person, never besmirching our family name, and it still wasn't enough.

Mother believes I'm flawed; she still finds me lacking.

Chancery and Judica may look perfect, they may have the same pedigree as me, but I know the truth. They aren't perfect either. None of us are, least of all Mother. And I shouldn't have been forced to be someone I'm not for this long. "I am exactly who I was always meant to be. You can't ignore the hard truths and you can't pick and choose who and what to love based on what fits your worldview. Love is many things, but convenient isn't one of them."

"I don't need or want your help," Enora says.

"You do need it though," I say. "More than you realize."

Inara backs away from me, as though my flaws might be contagious.

"You never meant for me to have your throne, no matter what, did you? Not from the second you found out." She hasn't looked at me the same since Brazil. But was it losing at Weaponry, or looking at Aline the way Dad looked at Gideon? Regardless, if I'm not exactly like her, I'm useless.

And now look at her, unable to kill her sweet, smiley daughter. Even the great Enora Alamecha is not hard enough, apparently. Oh, the irony.

"I won't lie and say I wasn't relieved to discover I was pregnant again," Mother says.

I've spent months agonizing over this moment, wondering how I could possibly do what Mother made me promise I would. And now it has come to this, the words bubble out of my mouth easily. I still don't want to rule. I have zero desire to spend another second here in Ni'ihau, and yet, I can't let Mother make this epic mistake. I can't let her divide our people against themselves.

"I challenge you, Enora Alamecha, for the good of our family. I challenge your leadership, your competence, and your abilities."

Mother's entire face crumples. "Your sisters aren't even one day old. You're challenging me now?"

She's the one who told me it had to be today. Mother demanded this—I can't tell if she's groggy from the lingering effects of the poison, or whether she really and truly forgot. "You've left me no alternative. I take no joy in this."

"So be it," Mother says.

"If I wait until tomorrow, I don't have the power to do what you can't. You'll be answerable to no one."

"And you believe this is a fair fight?" Mother tightens her grip on Judica and gestures with her other hand to the blood that has pooled around her feet. "You think that history will remember you as. . . what? Some kind of freedom fighter? You are Eamon's child, through and through. A zealot, misguided, and too weak to follow through on anything you want." Mother passes Judica to Inara. "Keep them both safe, no matter what."

Inara meets my eyes, hers more tortured than mine.

Mother crosses the room to stand next to me. "I almost hope you do kill me. For once in your life, you'd be following through on something, no matter how difficult. But you'd better be prepared, because I won't hesitate to kill you, not now, not after this."

❧ 19 ☙

THE PAST: 2002

I don't expect Inara to knock at my door, not minutes before my challenge with Mother.

"Oh Melina." She wraps me in her arms the second I let her inside.

"I don't know what to do."

"This entire situation is horrible. But I had to come by and tell you that it's not your fault, and it's not your job to clean this up. Mother had no right to demand that promise of you."

I think about my assumption for the past few months, that it was my prayer that caused this, my greed and my selfishness. And then I repeat the words of the prophecy in my head. If God really means me to save the world from utter destruction as Dad believed, and I think few people spent more time trying to align with God's will than my father, then it seems unlikely God would punish me in this way.

"These babies," Inara says. "I love them dearly, and I hate them too. Before they came, everything was fine."

I sit on my bed. "Fine?"

"Yes," Inara says. "Before we knew about them, Gideon was alive. Eamon was alive. Then we find out they're twins, and the world just goes to pieces."

I'm not the only one who's confused about where to lay blame. "I seriously doubt their birth had anything to do with Dad's death."

Inara's nostrils flare. "Either way, the whole world fell apart when they entered it."

I can't argue with that.

"And now you're going to fight Mother and one of you will die." Her shoulders slump, her head bows, and her hands fall to her sides, limp. "I just, I can't handle losing either of you—" Her voice cracks, her breath heaves in great sobs.

"I'm sorry."

"Back out of it," Inara begs. "There's no good solution here."

My eyes widen. "Those babies, one of them must die. Don't you see that?"

Inara stands up and takes my hand. "Absolutely I do, but there are ways to do that where you don't wind up dead, or the one who murdered Mother. She's not in her right mind. She will come around, like she did with Jered. Remember?"

I yank my hand away. "You think *that* was the right decision? Giving him away?"

"Selling him, you mean?" She sighs. "It was a hard decision, but he was making Mother miserable, and the practice exists for a reason. We need options for Consorts who are raised by us, people we can trust, like Gideon. He was purchased, and he was never miserable. He was probably happier here than he would have been with Lenora."

"I can't get into this," I say. "Not right now. I wish I could delay, but Inara, this is my only chance. Mother made me promise, because I'm the only one who can set things right. I'm Heir until midnight tonight, and not after that. I'll have been displaced, replaced by, well, if I fail, replaced by two little girls. That gives us a very small window. I'll have to do what needs to be done, and hope God will forgive me if I choose wrong."

Inara leans across my nightstand and plucks my sword from its mount on the wall. "If you have to do this, then you need to go into it with the right frame of mind. You can't believe in your heart of hearts that the existence of these girls is your fault. You're not cleaning up a mistake. Things happen, Melina, and they aren't always anyone's fault." She hands me the sword. "You're strong, beautiful, wise, generous, and intelligent. And you care for people. All of those things are gifts of God. All of them are wonderful. Mother was wrong. Eamon wasn't flawed, and neither are you. If she can't see that, then the flaw lies with her."

"But at the Games, when I met Aline—"

Inara shakes her head. "That changes nothing. God loves you, and I love you, and anyone else is wrong. Accept that, and accept yourself. Until you do that, I'm not letting you leave this room."

If I accept that, I won't be able to fight Mother. I close my eyes and consider what she's telling me. The Eldest shall destroy everything in her path. . . to save the world from utter destruction. How am I supposed to destroy everything in my path and also save the world? It feels as impossible as eliminating one of my darling, perfect, precious baby sisters to prevent a future war.

And yet, both must be done.

"I accept it," I say. "And I still think I'm doing what must be done. I think this is the only path to peace. It's hard, but that doesn't mean it's wrong."

Inara steps aside to let me pass, but when I walk next to

her, she hugs me again. "I love you. I love Mother too, but I think I love you more. Please, please don't die."

My heart thaws a little, hearing her words. Mother may have immediately cast me aside, but Inara knows my darkest secret, and she loves me still. I hold that truth close to my heart the entire walk into the ballroom, repurposed now with a raised combat dais. The entire room is jammed with our people.

Every single one is glaring at me, the monster who would challenge their Empress on the very day she gave birth. Their Empress who was being poisoned. They probably assume that I was poisoning her, my own mother.

But it doesn't matter what they believe. It's not true. I would never harm Mother if there was any other way.

I step into the ring, my sword in my right hand, my dagger in place over my left forearm. Oh how I wish this was only to first major.

Balthasar steps into the ring and offers Mother a hand. She shakes her head stiffly and swings up alone. She grasps her sword with both hands. Her white pants are immaculate, no sign of blood. I hope she has recovered, that at least it's a fair fight.

My hands shake slightly as I stand across from her. Not for a sparring match, not this time. We're facing one another in a fight to the death, because I want her to kill my little sister.

How did I get here?

I want to run away screaming. I try to imagine what Dad would say to me right now. Mother made me promise to do this, exactly what I'm doing. She taught me the history lessons herself so that I would know what happens when an empress's youngest girls are twins. Dad never knew about them, but he would have hated the idea that one life could cause thousands and thousands of deaths. He would hate that they could be pitted against one another. But he might hate the idea of one of them dying more. I miss him more than ever. He fought with Mother bitterly, but the idea of one of us killing the other? That would be a terrible blow for him, for anyone really, but especially for him. His wife and his daughter.

"On my cue." Balthasar scowls at me, and then claps. The other gathered citizens clap with him.

After the third clap, Mother leaps forward and strikes immediately, so fast I'm totally unprepared. I throw my hand out to block her and the edge of her blade nearly severs it.

She's going to kill me before I even hear her song.

My heart hammers in my chest, shoving more blood through my veins. It pours from the gaping wound at my wrist and spreads across the floor. But Mother isn't pushing pause. She doesn't seem to notice how badly she injured me, or maybe she just doesn't care. Her sword comes at me again, this time from the right side. I block one-handed with my blade this time, but the shock of the hit reverberates through me.

I back up and twist toward her on the right, holding my left hand so that the wound is closed and can heal, forcing her to slide across the pool of my blood if she wants to press her attack. Pain tears through me as my nerves heal and tissues reconnect. But Mother isn't giving me time to recover. She leaps over the pool and spins into a kick.

She never kicks in sparring, and when her heel connects with my solar plexus, I hear something I've never heard. The first notes of her harmony.

Mother is blunt, forceful, and strong. She's a hurricane, knocking down all obstacles, giving no quarter. And yet here she is, killing her eldest daughter to spare the weak, smiling one. It doesn't add up, but the answer is there, somewhere in her harmony.

I desperately hope it's something that allows me to back off. I don't want to do this any more than she wants me to do this. I fall backward, my head striking the mat, but my left hand is healed, which I bet Mother hasn't noticed. She lifts her blade to spear me through the heart and I hold position, as though I can't move, until the last second.

When I use my left hand to shove to the right, Mother's not expecting it. Her sword sinks deep into the mat, because she meant to cleave my heart in two. It firms up my resolve. Mother's not in her right mind. She begged me to do this. She shouldn't be so angry at me for keeping the promise she forced from me. I leap to my feet and shake my dagger into my left hand, ready for her this time.

Her melody beats like a drum line, dark, hard, staccato, but the harmony I heard begins to form into a real counterpoint. She's all the things I knew, but there's more. It must be something to do with my father, something I'm missing. "You believe Dad was flawed."

Mother lifts her chin and then launches a series of hits that I block easily, moving backward and then spinning around so she's forced to course correct.

"You think I'm flawed like him."

Mother, predictably, accelerates her attack. But I'm not as lost as I was before, not as unsure. She prepared me for this, the expected, the boring.

"I'm not flawed," I say. "Mercy isn't a flaw. It's just not one of your strengths."

She tosses her head. "Your father wasn't only merciful. He deceived me."

She's talking about Gideon, about my father's secret. Something hits me then, striking more painfully than a blade. I'm about to kill my mother, or she's going to kill me, and she'll never know the truth about me. She'll never understand my struggle, my pain, or my fears.

My own mother won't know me at all.

"I stood up for Gareth," I say, "because I'm like him. I'm gay, Mother. That's how I know it's not a flaw. It doesn't weaken me. It strengthens me. Hiding who I am is the only thing that weakens me."

Mother's mouth opens, but she doesn't speak. She splutters, like, well, like a human.

"But if it was a flaw, that would be alright too." I risk a glance around me. Everyone is leaning forward, eyes wide, breathing heavy. "You're all so caught up with the idea of being perfect that you're missing the point of life. Perfection is boring. It's the flaws that give life meaning."

Mother strikes me again, but this time, I hear her melody, her harmony wrapping around it like a soft caress. I could close my eyes and predict her strikes, and not because I've learned something about Mother. No, I can hear her because I finally understand myself.

We move faster and faster, but I'm blocking, not striking. I need some time to think about what I really want. I didn't block Aline's number only to punish myself. I did it because I'm a coward. I was afraid that even if I risked everything, disappointed everyone, that I'd still end up like my parents.

I've been afraid that I really am flawed, but not by being gay. I'm afraid I don't know how to love.

But Dad never accepted who he was, who he loved, or what he needed. I've done what he never did—confessed the truth to Mother. I have exposed my true self. It's as though shackles have fallen from my soul, allowing me to rise. I stop blocking and begin striking. Mother isn't sure what has happened. She thought she knew me, but I'm not who I was yesterday, last month, or even last year.

I may be flawed, but if I am, I'm stronger for it.

I show her, one slice, one slash, and one strike at a time. Until she stumbles. Maybe she's exhausted. Maybe it's the poison, or the babies. Maybe this wasn't a fair fight.

But nothing in my life has ever been fair.

I stab Mother in the stomach with my sword. The blade slides up, up, up and through until the tip of it emerges from her back. All I need to do is slam it upward and I can end this. I will be honoring Mother's own demands—fulfilling the promise I made at her request.

I would be opening up the world for the change it so desperately needs. Dad might even want me to kill her, the woman who never accepted him, who never really loved him.

But my life yawns before me and one thing is perfectly clear. I'm not the killer Mother has always hoped I would be. I'm not the fierce, unyielding warrior. No, I'm merciful. I'm kind. I'm caring.

I am Eamon's daughter, not Enora's.

I withdraw the blade, slowly. "You forced me into this ring," I say. "You knew you'd need me to clean up your mess. But I'm not going to do that. I'm not going to remove you from this world that is so confusing, a world that is changing faster than you can process. It's a world you don't understand, but it's the only one we have."

I'm the Eldest. I have work to do, but before I try to fulfill any prophecy, I'm going to live life on my terms.

I'm going to call Aline.

Mother collapses to the ground in front of me. "You're not going to kill me?"

I shake my head. "You said it yourself. You wanted that, but that's not me. It never has been. You're going to have to deal with what God has given you on your own. I'm not going to do it for you."

She shoves herself up to her feet. "Well, if you're not killing me, then I'm still Empress."

I nod.

"I can order your death."

I shrug. "You can."

Mother meets my gaze with her own, conflicted eyes. "Melina Alamecha, you are hereby banished from family Alamecha, but not in the usual way. You're forbidden to make contact with any royals of our family, but you will not leave Alamecha soil, either. Instead, I assign you to reside in Austin, Texas. I'll assign Marselle to watch over you, and you will comply with all of her commands. Should you fail to honor these restrictions, I'll order your immediate death. Is that clear?"

I bow. "It is, Your Majesty."

I don't bother trying to explain to her how or why or what I am. Instead, I climb out of the ring, walk to my room to gather my things, and flip open my phone. I dial the number I've been thinking about every day.

"Hello," Aline says, slightly breathless.

"It's me," I say.

"I know."

"Are you so mad you don't want to talk to me?"

"Never," she says.

"Good. Then how do you feel about Austin, Texas?"

"I've heard it's a little weird."

"I think they like to keep it that way," I say. "That might be one of the reasons I was thinking of taking a trip there."

"I look amazing in cowboy hats," she jokes.

"So that's a yes to Austin?"

"I like kicking people while wearing heeled boots. I

think we can figure the rest out," Aline says. "When should I book a flight?"

"I'll be there tonight."

"That's the best news I've heard all year."

Actually, it is for me too.

THE PRESENT

I haven't left Austin in almost twenty years, so it feels beyond strange to be sitting on a plane. My knee bounces and I don't bother stilling it, because for almost two decades, as long as I ever spent in Ni'ihau, I've been free. It hasn't mattered whether I frowned or smiled or cried. No one important was watching and evaluating my reactions to anything.

Dad would be proud, I hope, that I never gave up on his goal of finding God's purpose. Even stuck in Austin, I've made significant progress into studying the prophecy I saw on the very day I was banished. I almost sent Aline on several occasions—but I've always felt like I needed to do this myself.

And now my sweet, smiling little sister, the true Eldest, has set me free. Thanks to Chancery, no one is watching me, ready to put a bolt through my heart the second I step out of bounds.

"Beginning our descent."

"It was brilliant for you to insist we take our own plane," Aline says. "Quick thinking."

I shrug. "With Judica's hatred of me, which is legitimate, it was an obvious request. I probably could have explained in more detail what I wanted, but. . ."

"You don't know her very well, and talking about sleeper cells set up by your Mother's enemies sounds—"

"Wacky?" I ask.

Aline laughs. "Sure, let's go with that."

"Alright," I say. "Let's review what we know. We don't have much time before Chancery will start asking questions about what took us so long. We need to get in and get out."

"You should have sent me years ago," Aline says.

I reach for her hand and she takes mine immediately, our fingers interlacing. "It's too dangerous."

"You sent me to kill your sister," Aline says.

"That was different," I say.

"She shot me in the face."

"That was before I even sent you, and it was a huge miscalculation on my part." I squeeze her hand. "You know I'd never have put you at risk like that."

"You worried I'd fail," Aline says.

"I believe that whoever Mother has stationed to watch over the site will be reticent to shoot the third in line to the throne. I doubt they'd even pause for a millisecond before shooting you."

"I hope you're right."

"My hope is all focused on these caverns having what Dad's journal indicated."

"A replica of the inscription over the gate to the Garden."

Precisely. I review the details we know. Dad had coordinates and a brief description from one of his men that was gathered before Mother's intelligence network disappeared it all. "Fifteen hundred feet down a sheer canyon wall."

Aline's heart rate picks up.

"Where would you position a watch, if you were Mother? He's got to be right on the edge, right?"

"It's the Grand Canyon," Aline says. "I imagine the location of the guards will be pretty obvious."

"What I want to know is, if Shenoah had this information, why didn't she share it? Or do something with it."

Angel shakes her head. "First of all, evian royals aren't exactly known for their willingness to share. But beyond that, I doubt Shenoah even knew what it was. Eamon's journal said the group Malimba sent were led by her rival—and that she believed they should be following the creed of Shenoah, whatever that means."

"You think that Malimba sent them for two reasons, right?" I ask. "To eliminate a threat—her sister, and to set up a civilization to challenge Mother's power here?"

"Actually," Angel says, "I think you'll find a whole lot of nothing. I think Eamon was unable to verify a thing, and he was pinning his hopes on rumor and speculation."

Great. I might be stopping over, and possibly alienating the little trust Chancery has in me, for no reason at all. "Well, it's the last lead I haven't been able to investigate. I need to check it out, at least. AND it's on the way."

"You have plenty of other things that will help Chancery," Angel says. "We've discovered four possible locations for the Garden—all likely for different reasons. That's doable for Chancery to investigate—totally reasonable. You've also formulated several powerful theories for the utter destruction that may be coming. It will allow her to prepare for them, both mentally and physically."

"But there's a whole puzzle piece we've been missing," I say. "We still don't know the *when*."

"We have too many guesses and not enough hard facts," Aline says.

"No prophecy contains hard facts." Lucas crosses his arms. "Which is what makes this so hard. Eve predicted our struggle six thousand years ago and explained it as best she could. Then we were morons and lost and scattered her directions. It's no wonder we're casting about in the dark."

Lucas has been a voice of reason for twenty years. I'm so lucky that many of my guards came along when I was banished, but I've relied on Lucas most of all. The plane lands. "I hope we can shed a little light on it today."

"I hope so too," Angel says. "But I wouldn't count on it."

Angel's people are waiting for us when we arrive on the tiny, private runway. "The transport is ready," a tall man in fatigues says.

Seconds later, the engine on the helicopter turns over and the wind beats against us in erratic gusts. The blades speed up steadily and the sound and wind normalize. "Who exactly is going?" the man in fatigues asks.

"Me," I say.

Unfortunately, Lucas, Angel, and Aline say it too.

"We've been over this," I say. "I think I should go alone."

"You're outvoted," Angel says. "And this isn't a monarchy."

As I am reminded daily. "Fine."

We all pile into the helicopter. Thankfully, the Sikorsky could hold more than ten people easily, so six is no problem.

"You trust these people, right?" I ask.

Angel smiles. "Absolutely."

Because falling out of the air into the Grand Canyon would really suck.

"You're lucky you didn't come a week ago," the tall

human pilot says into our headphones. "Everything was still blanketed in snow."

Snow? Ugh. Trying to scale the drop would have been much worse if it was icy.

"Where exactly are we going?" I ask.

"The point you gave us is on the southeast side. It's not in view of the tourist overlooks, so that makes it easier."

Two coincidences? Although, the location being masked is likely by Mother's design. She would have approved any decisions about tourist overlooks.

"I can't go down into the canyon," he says. "It's not safe to descend at that point. But I can drop you off less than a mile from the checkpoint without them seeing or hearing us."

"Wait, without who seeing us? What's the checkpoint?" I ask.

The pilot turns around and looks at me. "Where the guards are stationed."

I glare at Angel. "Did you already know?"

She shakes her head and mouths, "They're human. I didn't tell them too much."

Well, at least we know where the danger lies.

True to his word, he drops us off a few miles south of the Little Colorado River Gorge, then he gives pretty specific directions.

"How can you know exactly where we should go?" I ask. "If there are guards?"

"They shot at me," he says. "I won't forget where they're at, not any time soon."

I suppose I wouldn't either.

"What are they guarding?" he asks.

I shrug. "We didn't know they were there at all."

"What do you *think* they're guarding?" he presses.

I shake my head.

He steps closer and Lucas and Aline both tense next to me.

"Is it aliens?" His eyes light up and it takes every ounce of my restraint to keep from laughing.

"Uh, yes. We suspect that there may have been a UFO that crashed in the gorge there. We're scientists evaluating the risk of radiation to tourists who come to see the canyon."

His eyes widen. "Wait, there's radiation?"

"Unknown quantities, but yes. We're here to evaluate the risk."

He gulps. "I'm safe here?"

I nod. "But I wouldn't go any closer."

"No," he says. "Right, we'll wait here." He climbs back into the helicopter where his co-pilot is still sitting.

"Perfect," I say.

We race away, wasting no more time than we absolutely must. When the guard tower comes into view—Mother must be air dropping them supplies as there are no roads out here—everyone halts.

"I'll take it alone from here," I say. "You'll be more valuable as backup than charging ahead. And there's a chance, as I previously mentioned, that he might let me past when he would block you."

Aline sets her jaw and I prepare for an argument, but she surprises me. Even after twenty years, she still surprises me sometimes. "Fine. We'll provide cover." She pulls out her Thompson Center single shot, which is how I know she's serious.

Lucas and Angel carefully work their way out from here, preparing to cover different angles. Once they all nod, I walk toward the black tower near the edge of the cliff. Covert doesn't work when there's nothing but dirt and rock on a plateau.

But when I reach the tower and look inside, the one guard present. . . is asleep. I roll my eyes. They've either slacked off since Mother's death—confusion isn't usually a great motivator—or this was never a high priority outpost. I wave the others over, slide through the door and begin removing the woman's weapons slowly. I'm tugging a dagger out of her boot when Aline reaches us.

Her snort of disgust wakes up the errant guard. "What? Who are you?" She sits up and looks around, her eyes widening as she takes in my face and Angel's. "You're. . . you're wanted."

Angel smiles. "A true statement on many levels, but I believe you're right that your boss would greatly like to apprehend me and force me back to Ni'ihau."

The brunette guard gulps.

"However, as you may have noticed, you're outnumbered and outmaneuvered." Angel smiles. "I won't be making a return trip today."

"Will you stay with her while I scale the wall?" I ask.

The guard frowns. "Why would you scale the wall when there's a—" She claps a hand over her mouth.

Ridiculous. "I really should have sent you years ago," I admit.

Aline doesn't say I told you so, which is one of the many reasons I love her. She does, however, insist on scrambling down the ladder with me, all the way to the bottom. The sun is setting soon, which means the shadows are lengthening, but even in the sketchy light, the entrance to the caves is clear, and right there, over the very outmost door is a magnificent carving. How could Mother not have seen this for what it was?

A replica of the archway over the gate to the Garden of Eden—unless Dad was very, very wrong.

"So Eve gave Mahalesh the prophecy," Aline says.

"But she gave Shenoah the task of keeping the Garden a secret. Or at least, Dad believes that was Shenoah's task. The records he found indicated that Eve tasked someone with keeping it safe when she decided to abandon it."

"And by now, the descendants of Shenoah don't even remember that job themselves, they've become so caught up in politics?" Aline shakes her head. "We suck at the greater good, don't we?"

I shrug. "Or perhaps Shenoah felt the best way to keep the Garden safe was to eliminate the temptation of sharing the secret, even from her own daughter."

"You think she removed references to it because she didn't even trust her own children?" Aline says. "No trust at all—that's sad."

My mother wouldn't have shared it with me. Perhaps Shenoah didn't have confidence in her heir either. We'll probably never know. I reach into my bag and pull out the etching paper. I make an etching as carefully as I can, and then Aline takes photos and videos from every angle. Finally, I turn on my phone camera and we take a few more, just in case the lighting matters.

"Do you think we have what we need?" Aline asks.

"It's a long way to come back if we don't." I duck through the doorway, a tiny bit uneasy that it will collapse on me. It would be just like fate to kill me in a collapse after allowing me easy access to this point. But the stone that has held for centuries doesn't give out, and I enter a large room.

I hold up my phone light for a moment, wishing it was more powerful, before Aline pulls a lantern from her bag. Another reason I love her—she's always prepared. It illuminates the cavern much better than my phone would have, well enough to display doorways branching out in all directions.

I wonder how many people lived in these caves and what happened to them. By the time Dad's man, Kincaid, found them, there were only remnants left behind. He used them to piece together who lived here, but the image of the doorway was overexposed, only showing enough to realize it perfectly matched the description of the Gate to the Garden Dad heard his Mother talk to his aunt about long ago.

He would be overflowing with joy to be here, to have the images and an etching in his hands. I'm filled with an overwhelming sense of gratitude that, finally, after all these years, I'm bringing some of his work to fruition. He would be so very, very proud of Chancery and the steps she's taking. I'm sure he's looking down on her, on us, from up in heaven, beaming.

"Time to go," I say. "As much as I'd love to investigate those doorways, we can't risk the additional time, not with the sun setting, and not with Chancery waiting."

We race up the ladder, a harder climb than descent, thanks to the failing light. Angel and Lucas are still waiting up top, apparently having had no issues with the guard. "Let's go," I say. "And we better bring her. Can't have her letting anyone know we were here."

"Agreed," Angel says. "I'll integrate her into my network." She shuffles around near the edge of the plateau, a few yards from the rope.

"What are you doing?" I ask.

"Giving them an explanation." She points at the edge, and then drops a small ball with a blinking light into a crevice a few feet away.

"Wait, that's not—"

Lucas grabs my arm and wrenches me away and toward the helicopter. I finally realize her plan, as I'm pelting away. "How long do we have?"

"Two minutes," Angel says. "More than enough time."

We've nearly reached the copter when we hear the explosion. "Better rush now," she says. "Wouldn't want them to catch sight of us in the air or it'll ruin all my hard work creating a rock-sheer avalanche."

"They could excavate," I say. "And they'd realize there was no body."

Angel smiles. "They sure could. But I really doubt they will."

We rush back to the helicopter and board quickly, the guard not even attempting to escape. It's too easy, and the skin on the back of my neck crawls, waiting for something terrible to happen. But it never does. We reach the plane, where Lucas and Aline and I board, and Angel stays.

"Be careful," I say.

"I will."

"Be safe." I hug her. "And keep looking."

"I actually recently had a small break through," she says.

I stop, two steps up the stairs onto the plane. "What?"

"You know that whoever Nereus is, he wiped the cameras anywhere near the location where he or she bought the poison."

I nod. "And?"

"But I finally managed to obtain the shop owner's old files. He had them stored in a safehouse, which is why it took me so long."

"Why does that help?" I ask.

"He noted the purchase of the poison used for your mother in his books as 'N.' "

"I knew that," I say.

"There's another notation of a purchase by N," Angel says. "Dating to 2002."

My jaw drops. "You think it's the same person—and that they poisoned Mother twice."

"But the second time, they got the dosage right and it worked."

I gulp. "But we still don't know anything. It just says, 'N,' right?"

Angel smiles. "Nereus wiped the cameras that would have betrayed his or her identity from this year, but I doubt he went back and found every single bit of camera footage from 2002. It would be too onerous, and looking for that footage would draw too much attention. No, I'm guessing that if there were any security cameras live in 2002, they caught Nereus on film—and they're still around."

"But they probably weren't digital, not back then."

Angel shrugs. "A lot of them would have been digital, but I'm hoping that some weren't and that the old tapes are in a box somewhere, frozen in time."

"Because if they are. . ."

"We can bring Chancery quite a gift." Angel beams at me. "Enora's murderer on a silver platter."

⚜ 21 ⚜

THE PRESENT

N i'ihau is way more humid than I recall it being, and that's saying something. Because Austin can be downright muggy.

I close my eyes and pinch the bridge of my nose. As an evian, I never get headaches. I mean, I've been shot in the head twice, and that hurt pretty badly. I've also been kicked, hit, slammed and whacked in the cranium more times than I can count. But I've never actually had a pounding in my brain due to exhaustion, fatigue, or illness.

Until right now.

"You need to take a break." Aline sits on the table in front of me, forcing me to back away from the enlarged image. "Your brain is going to explode if you don't."

"The world is going to implode if I do," I say.

Aline laughs. "It has been thousands and thousands of years since this message was chiseled into the gate over the Garden, and it has been more than a thousand since it was replicated in the Grand Canyon. I think it can wait a few more days."

I shake my head. "You don't get it. There's always a reason for this kind of timing. God's hand—"

Aline smiles and brushes my hair back from my face. "You are a good and faithful person. Your father would be very proud. But the world will not explode any sooner if you uncross your eyes for a moment and eat something. Besides, your brain cells will work better with nourishment."

As if her words prompt my neurons to fire, I recognize the smell. "Is that picanha? And coxinha?" My mouth waters and my stomach growls. "Maybe a five minute break wouldn't hurt."

"And we can talk it over while you eat," she says. "That always clarifies things for you. What have you figured out?"

Since I've completely covered the kitchen table with various blown up images, I wonder where she's thinking we'll eat. "Five minutes. No more." I stand up.

Aline laughs. "With anyone else, I'd say no way. But I've seen the way you inhale food. Five minutes should be fine." She shakes her head. "American through and through, and always in a rush." She launches off the table's edge—Aline never walks or meanders; she's always moving at top speed. For someone who criticizes Americans for eating fast, she's quick at everything else. She jogs toward the back patio that overlooks the water. I should have known. The doorway muffled the smell—she must have barbecued it outside too.

"We could have the kitchens send us food, you know," I say. "It's a perk for guests."

She picks up a plate and hands it to me. "You can't always trust something made by someone else, and also, I like my food."

"So do I." I load up my plate. She clearly went all out. I must have been pretty out of it to miss that. The second I begin filling my plate, it's like a cattle call. Everyone who came with me appears as if out of thin air.

"Lunch time?" Lucas asks.

"Aline!" Horatio says. "This smells amazing. Throw that harpy over and marry me instead."

My gorgeous wife puts a hand on her hip and raises one eyebrow. "You think saying you want to marry me because of my *cooking skills* is wise?"

Horatio drops one hand to the hilt of his sword. "I figured it might liven up the training later."

I can't help think of the men and women I've lost in the past few weeks in my attempts to eliminate Judica. I still believe she's a threat, and I worry that Chancery will see her as the 'strongest supporter' when I believe that's me. But for now, I'm holding to peace. I hope that's not a mistake.

Which is another reason I need to translate the inscription on the doorway now, not over the course of several weeks. I shovel food into my mouth, a little guilty at my failure to savor it properly. The spice in the acarajé—or technically, the vatapá filling—never fails to make my eyes water, but that's part of the reason I love it.

"Okay, what have you already figured out?" Lucas asks.

"It's not Egyptian," I say. "I knew that from the outset. The team that found it told Dad it was, but that would have been too easy."

"Is it Adamic?" Aline asks.

I shake my head. "Not Adamic. And not Sanskrit."

"Any guesses?" Lucas asks.

"I'm afraid it's a *sprachbund*—a mixture of Sumerian and Amorite—heavy on the Sumerian, unfortunately. That one's harder to decipher. I'm worried I'll need to appeal to Chancery for access to Mother's library. I'm sure she has several texts that would help me decode it more quickly and accurately."

"You are making progress, then?" Aline asks.

I nod. "I've got the first line. It reads: My children, so pure and precious, a task I set before you—the price of your power."

"That sounds promising," Lucas says. "Why do you sound so. . . hesitant?"

"Think about the importance of a single word," I say. "Think of how much its placement and purpose can change the tone of a sentence. For example, if I were to say, 'Let's eat,' and then pause, and say, 'Lucas,' you would know I was asking you to eat *with me*. If, however, I said 'Let's eat Lucas,' you might be concerned I planned to *eat you*."

Aline and Lucas and the others laugh, but I don't find this very funny. A single word used wrong and I could totally misunderstand the point of the prophecy.

"At least that admonition works in the framework of what we believe," Aline says. "Because it is a prescription for Eve's children, right? Think about what the gate to the Garden of Eden might say. It makes sense that it would give them a task—your Dad was always saying we've lost our purpose—and then the next few lines will hopefully guide us on exactly what to do so we can narrow down the problem Chancery faces, and the timeline for when she'll face it."

"And hopefully how to solve it," Lucas says. "That might be nice. Like, 'be sure to kill the wicked twin,' or maybe 'practice your ancient Sumerian so you'll know how to play a wicked game of chess. You'll need that to defeat the devil and close the gates of hell.'"

I frown. "This isn't a joke, and the biggest risk is that my own preconceived notions will impact my translation."

Lucas sighs. "I know it's not. The fact that you found a

carved entrance stone to vast caverns below the Grand Canyon is weird enough. But don't fault me if I hope all of this utter destruction stuff is a little overblown." He looks pointedly at the tattoo on my arm.

I didn't get the tattoo for my benefit. Those words have been carved in my mind since I first saw them on Mother's desk, disappearing even as I read them. It all felt awfully symbolic, and I've thought about it often. How many times has a few days mattered? Or a few hours? A few moments? If Dad had forgone that meeting and come home early, he'd have been around to guide Enora and his youngest daughters. He'd have been around to teach me and to smooth things over. If I had walked into Mother's room a few moments earlier on the twins' birthday, I would have seen the entire prophecy before the ink erased it. Or if we had ever forgiven one another—I could have asked Mother to share the prophecy in its fulness. I thought we had loads of time, yet. If I knew the actual timeline, would it have changed my actions?

I don't know.

The people who came with me when I left, more people than I deserved, and the people who have joined me over the years since, none of them really understand. They didn't see the importance of the prophecy, or how its knowledge gave me purpose when I had none. Dad expected great things of me, and I ran away to hide. Similarly, that prophecy has been hidden from our people for far too long—millennia. It's time for the world to know what's coming so we can prepare. The only way I could think to impress upon my followers the importance of it was to do something drastic.

A tattoo made of platinum is painful, and the discomfort never quite disappears. After all, my body healed around it, but it's still a foreign substance. I've had it touched up three times, and even now a few words are beginning to fade.

I stand up and walk back inside, my belly full, my brain whirring, ready to crack the riddle of what's going to happen. What is our task, Eve? What is the path we must take to avoid the utter destruction? How can I make Dad proud? How can I serve my sister in her difficult calling?

Slowly, one excruciating word at a time, I work my way through the carving. In a few spots, the stone had chipped and broken and it's impossible to know exactly what was meant. But most of it, I think the majority of it, is solid.

As I translate the last line, the hair on my arms stands straight up. My mouth goes dry. My hands begin to tremble. *The rift must be healed before the bisection in convergence of the ringed with the largest and the smaller in the seventh generation. . . or the time is past and the end begins, never to renew.*

The end begins, never to renew. That sounds uncomfortably similar to utter destruction. The ringed and the largest converge. What does that mean? The ringed? Does it have to do with the rings Chancery is assembling? I think about the timeframe of the prophecy. The prophecy on my arm came from Eve, but we aren't sure when. But the words from this were carved over the gate to the Garden. That means the prophecy was given before Eve grew old—before she would have split the staridium. Before there were rings.

Also, the word I translated doesn't mean jewelry. The base word is more like, encircled. I translated it as ringed, but it could also be the surrounded, or encircled and the most big, or most grand, or perhaps most weighty. Why can't these things be clearer?

Perhaps it's the nature of language—ever changing—that makes it so difficult to prophesy anything that will truly help. The odds of it even making sense are slim enough. Okay, I review it again. This feels like the timeline we've been hunting to find. *The rift must be healed.* I'll leave that for now. Then it continues with 'before the bisection in convergence.' Bisection in convergence? Bisecting something means to split it in half, or to divide something into equal parts.

I have no idea what a bisection in convergence could mean. Split something in half so that you can join it again? I growl in frustration.

"What's up?" Aline has become extremely American, and she doesn't even realize it.

I point at the last section of the gate. "I hate this. It makes no sense."

"Want another perspective?" She tilts her head, as if that will make ancient Sumerian a snap. It's ridiculous enough that it defuses some of my frustration.

"I think I have the translation, but it's not helpful or clear. Like, not at all."

"Maybe you could try reading it to me."

I inhale slowly and then exhale. "Yes, that's a good idea. I think what it says is, 'The rift must be healed before the bisection in convergence of the ringed with the largest and the smaller in the seventh generation. . . or the time is past and the end begins, never to renew.' I think that's our time-line, if I can make heads or tails of it."

"What part doesn't make sense to you?" She collapses into a chair. "I feel like it's all a big jumble."

"I think that the first part is clear. The rift must be healed."

"What's the rift?" she asks.

"Oh, I have no idea about that. Or, I suppose I have a lot of ideas, but no solid knowledge. But at least I get what it's saying. Fix the problem, and then it gives the timeline, and then it says, 'or the time is past and the end begins, never to renew.' That sounds horrible, right?"

"Like we've entered the last winter and spring will never return."

I nod. "But the timeline is nonsense. I mean, it starts with the bisection in convergence. What could that be? The bisection, so splitting, in convergence, so joining."

"What if it's the bisection, and then pause, in the first item—a convergence between the ringed and the largest. . . and the second item is the seventh generation?"

My brain cycles, trying to understand her point. Their syntax is odd. I look at the symbols again.

"Okay so you're saying maybe it means when the ringed and the largest converge, that's one event, and then when the seventh generation. . . what? I mean, for it to be the bisection of two events, there has to be, like, an event."

She points at the symbols. "Is that completely accurate? It says, 'the smaller in the seventh generation.' The smaller what?"

I shake my head. "It's not a modifier like in English. This literally means small. I mean, the rock is chipped here." I point. "But you can assume that the line at the bottom would have continued."

"What if it didn't continue?" she asks. "What if there was a space?"

I think about it for a moment. "It might mean the smallest child?"

"So could it be the convergence of the ringed and the larger with. . . the smaller child in the seventh generation?" Aline asks.

"Smaller." I tap my lip. "What if it meant. . . weaker? Those ideas were fairly fluid." Again though, my own guesses might be coloring my interpretation.

"So the weaker child of the seventh generation—

Chancery?" Aline asks. "Could it mean, when she's born? The 'Eldest'?"

I nod my head. "It's describing an event that would be universal and then pinpointing it to Chancery's life, maybe."

"Ringed and largest," Aline says. "Something cosmic, like planets or stars."

"When you say it like that, I feel really dumb."

"Okay," Lucas says from across the room. "Because I'm thinking, geez, it must be Jupiter and Saturn, right? The convergence of Jupiter and Saturn?"

I smack my head. "Of course. That happens pretty often, I think. Like—"

Lucas holds up his phone. "Once every twenty years. The last one was in 2000."

"Every twenty years?" My heart accelerates. "The last time was 2000?"

Lucas nods. "It happens again at the end of this year, December 21, 2020."

"Still think we've got loads of time?" I close my eyes. "We barely have seven months until the end of the world, and we don't even know what's going to cause it, much less how to stop it." I stand up. "I really need to talk to my sister."

✦ 22 ✦

THE PRESENT

Except Chancery's on her way to war, so I can't really stop her to explain my news. If she comes home with another stone, that's probably more important than knowing her deadline anyway. Unfortunately, it doesn't make waiting on her return easier.

Time is funny—I was stuck in Austin for years, but I wasn't sitting on specific information regarding the end of the world. Now that I am, my hands cast about for something to do. My knees bounce when I sit. My eyes can't focus on much of anything.

"I'm going for a jog," I say. "I need to get out and into the air."

Aline frowns. "They put guards on us. You know that, right?"

"Of course I do. I'm not an idiot." I get snappy when I'm forced to wait.

"You are the least patient person I know," Aline says. "They went to war. It's going to take a while."

"This failing has served me quite well over the years." I

sit on the couch and cross my arms. But two minutes later, my mind is reviewing the characters I've already translated, and my knees are jerking up and down again. My fingers rub the strange tassels on the throw pillows over and over until whoops. I've yanked one off.

I stare at it dumbly.

"I will just have to tell the guards they're going for a run too." I leap to my feet and walk outside. In addition to the two guards out front, there are two more on the south, east, and north sides of the building. Eight guards? I suppose there are twenty-six of us. "Hello," I say.

The taller man in the front salutes. "Yes, your highness?"

"Umm, you don't look familiar. Who are you?" I ask. "And please don't call me your highness."

"You're third in line for the throne, after Her Majesty's twin sister."

I have not missed this. "Okay, but you're guarding me right now for a reason. No one trusts me, which I understand. The point is, I would like to go for a run—well, I'd rather go for a ride, but I doubt that's likely to happen. I can't sit around any longer. Is that something you can accommodate?"

The man taps his ear. Why would he tap his ear?

"Melina is requesting to go for a ride. Is that allowed?"

Coms. Duh.

"They're checking. I'll let you know in a moment. Many of the top personnel are out right now, as I think you know."

For Chancery's war. I offer up a silent prayer that it's going well. They should be on the ground by now, probably prepping to attack. "I do."

A tiny squeaking sound comes from his ear, but I can't

make out the words. Quite an impressive bit of technology if our ears can't pick up on the response. He looks up and meets my eyes again. "You've been granted permission to ride—but you'll be accompanied."

Of course. "To ride?" My eyes light up. "That's wonderful news."

"I'm to escort you to the stable," he says.

"Perfect. Let me just. . ." I turn around and shout. "I'm going for a ride! I'll be back in less than two hours."

Lucas shoots out the front door, sword waving, shoelaces untied.

I don't roll my eyes, but it's difficult. What is he doing?

"I'm nearly ready." Lucas slides his sword into the sheath on his back and slams his foot down hard until his heel finally reaches the bottom. "Just let me tie these."

The guard by me tilts his head and lifts one eyebrow. "You require a guard of your own? Let me call to clear that."

I put my hand on his arm. "No, don't bother." I step toward Lucas. "I'll be fine. This may not be home anymore, but it used to be. And other than Judica, no one hates me here. Not now, not anymore."

Lucas straightens, his dark eyes flashing. "You don't know that. You haven't been here in twenty years. You won't go out alone." He lowers his voice, which is pointless since we can all still hear him. "Aline agrees with me."

But she hates horses, so she's sending him instead. Ridiculous. "Fine, fine. Do you mind calling again?"

The tall guard shakes his head. "Not at all. We're on tight rotations right now, down to eight guards from twelve because Her Majesty took quite a few Motherless with her. I'll need to ask for a rotation to replace us from the royal guard." He transfers the message and waits. Luckily, they approve his request.

"Do we have to hang out until the new guards arrive?" I ask.

He begins walking by way of answer, his partner falling right into step on the other side of Lucas and me. "I'm Philip, and this is Fernando."

A tight nod is all that dark, sour faced Fernando offers. I doubt he's super excited to be stuck here guarding me instead of off fighting for Chancery.

"Thank you for your help, Philip. It has been such a long time since I took a ride, and I'm really looking forward to it."

"It's my pleasure. I hear quite a few of your purchased sons went with you when you were banished. Is he one of them?" Philip tosses his head at Lucas.

"I'm capable of speaking for myself," Lucas says. "And yes." His lip curls. "I was *purchased* for Melina, but it wasn't her fault. When she left, I preferred the idea of working for someone I chose, instead of someone I'd been assigned to serve."

Philip smiles. "I'm glad that's the reason."

"You said the Motherless," I say. "Is that—are you—"

"We were all purchased during the last half a dozen centuries, yes. I was purchased by Lainina, but Denah was my mother."

"So you aren't really Motherless," Lucas says.

"No one is biologically motherless," Philip says. "But in all the ways that mattered, I had no mother."

Fair enough. "I'm sorry you went through that."

"Chancery is the first Empress to promise to end the practice," he says. "Among many, many other positive changes. So if you're wondering how dedicated we are to serving her." He shakes his head. "We'll cut you down without hesitation if you move against her."

I laugh. "I hope that's true. It gives me hope for her yet.

But as it happens, we're on the same side. I want to see her succeed—in all her sweeping reforms."

"Then we won't have any issues," Philip says.

"That's wonderful news." We're nearly to the stable. As we approach, I notice a familiar face waiting for me.

"Melina!"

I freeze for a split second, and then I sprint toward Inara. The only other time I've seen her in the past twenty years was when she was in the middle of seeing Chancery and company off for war. She opens her arms and I leap into a hug.

"I've missed you," I say.

When we finally pull apart, tears stream down her face freely. "I should have come to Austin more often, but the twins and Mother needed me."

I shake my head. "It's fine. I understand. You called me regularly. I'm not upset."

"I am so happy that you and Chancery are speaking. It's about time that rift was mended."

"She's not like Mother, is she?"

Inara laughs. "Not the Mother you knew, no."

"She changed?"

"Chancery changed her." Inara touches my hair. "She was softer. Kinder. Closer to the woman she might have been if life hadn't been so hard. Mother put the family first for century upon century. Chancery taught her that sometimes, maybe something else might matter more."

It hurts that I didn't change her—that Dad didn't change her. But I suppose I should be glad that something did. "It's a powerful person who can alter the gravitational pull of Enora Alamecha."

"People thought Chancery was weak, spineless even," Inara says. "They were all quite wrong. It has been one of the most amazing joys of my life, watching her learn and grow and serving at her side."

"I look forward to it as well." Motion behind Inara catches my eye for the first time and my jaw drops. "Is that?"

Inara beams. "He's still alive." She frowns. "And kicking the grooms far too often."

I run past her and toward the crossties where Splash is already saddled and throw my arms around his neck. He tosses his head and I release him. Of course he doesn't remember me. It has been far too long. "Thank you," I say. "Thank you, thank you."

After I bridle Splash, and Inara has provided horses for the rest of us, we head out, turning immediately for my favorite trail. Inara and I used to race Gideon straight down toward the sand as quickly as the horses could run. It doesn't feel right to make Splash sprint, not now that he's closing in on thirty.

But he hasn't changed much. The second Inara pulls up even with us on her chestnut, Splash pulls on the bit. "Okay, old boy. Let's not get carried away, but I won't hold you back either."

Inara and I pull pretty far ahead of the others, but by the time Splash's neck is coated with sweat, I force him to slow.

"I think he remembers you," Inara says.

I shrug. "Unlikely, but he rides just the same." I lean forward and hug his neck. "I've missed this."

"Me too." Inara sighs. "Speaking of people I miss, is Angel coming back?"

"So you can clap her in chains?"

"We wouldn't do that," Inara says. "You've talked to Chancery some. She's extremely fair. She would hear her out."

"After she kidnapped Judica, do you think they'd listen to anything she said?"

"Well," Inara says. "You're here."

She's right about that. "Angel's helping me with one last detail, and then maybe she will come home. I think she'd like to do that, if it was safe."

"It's safe for anyone who's innocent," Inara says.

"Then it should be perfectly fine for her," Melina says. "I promise you, she had nothing to do with Mother's death. She has been mourning the loss deeply—and Lyssa's loss struck her hard as well. These past few weeks have been harrowing for us all."

Difficult discussions notwithstanding, the ride with Inara, even with Lucas and Philip and bitter Fernando along, is therapeutic. Healing, even. It prepares me for more boring waiting. I review my list of front runners for the eminent danger, narrowing it down to three possible events. But by the third day, I pace the living room of the guest house for far too long.

"They're going to have to replace the carpet," Aline says, "if you don't stop that."

"Who cares about the carpet?" I fume. "I should have gone with her."

"Judica would have cut you down." Aline puts one hand on her hip. "I like you in one piece."

"You think she'd defeat me?" I narrow my eyes at her. "I could have killed her twenty years ago, and I could kill her now."

Aline laughs. "I think you forgot a few nots in that sentence. You couldn't bring yourself to kill her then, and as many times as you sent me to try, I doubt you could do it now, either. Even when you had the certainty of your version of the prophecy behind you."

That worries me, sometimes. How many times what we

believe is true about these predictions turns out to be wrong. I sit down at the table and review the translation again, checking and re-checking every word. I start to make notations about the word 'rift.' The symbol is for breakage —a crack between something. Could 'rift' be wrong? Maybe I should say 'the fracture must be healed' instead. And then there's the word 'lost.' It's not like something that people can't find—it's more like something people don't know about.

I hate translations. And trying to figure out the nuances behind symbols that haven't been used in thousands of years is the worst of all.

"So are we never eating on this table again?" Horatio asks. "Because the weather is nice outside, but it's kind of annoying to traipse out to the back patio every single time I want to eat something. Not to mention, we have two random guys staring at us. What's with the guards here, anyway? Why don't they have any women?"

"Chancery asked her personal guard to watch over us," I say absently, still thinking about the symbol for 'lost.'

"So Chancery's the one who's kind of sexist," Aline says.

Lucas snorts. "Those guards call themselves the Motherless. They're here because she issued a proclamation."

"I did hear about that," Horatio says. "And technically, it includes me. Maybe I could go join, and then I'd be the one guarding us."

Aline laughs. "Yes, do it!"

"If I keep having to eat outside, I might look into it. Yesterday it started raining and ruined my sandwich. Like, literally, the bread fell apart and I was holding a piece of turkey and a slice of cheese. For the record, mayonnaise on turkey and cheese with mushy wet bread sliding off it looks disgusting and tastes even worse. Like, really gross."

I take in the mess I've made on the table. Fretting over

the same symbols over and over without any additional information isn't helping.

"Fine. I hear you." I gather the images carefully into a stack. "I probably ought to put these somewhere safe, anyway." I look around the cottage. It's well made, obviously, and spacious for a beach cottage, with five large bedrooms, but the living areas aren't overly large, and with twenty-something people crammed in here, there's not a lot of extra space.

"What about that?" Aline points at the fireplace in the center of the living room. "I mean, who needs a fire in Hawaii?"

She has a point. I lift the damper and shove the images and my notes up into the flue. The damper's a little bent and won't close all the way, but that's not a big deal. It's not like we'll forget it's there and start a fire, not when it's seventy degrees outside. Which feels like just the sort of thing I would think, and then it would happen, randomly.

"Everyone, report to the den," I shout.

My people, my family really, filter in quickly. "This is probably a silly thing to announce to you, but I hid the images we recovered in the fireplace, okay? No one get any oddball ideas and burn it all up."

"She's talking to you, Paolo," Kira says. "Because none of us would do anything that stupid."

I roll my eyes. "Seems like hubris to hide it and not tell anyone."

"But if it does burn," Aline says, "you've still got the translation locked up here." She taps the side of her head. "And we have the images on our phones."

I shrug. "I took a lot of notes, and as you noticed, I need to check and recheck sometimes."

"Alright," I say. "You can go."

My phone rings and I pull it from my pocket.

"It's Angel?" Aline asks.

I nod, and I notice that everyone freezes. We've all been hoping that she'll find the footage we discussed. "Hello?"

"Melina," she says. "I hope you're well."

"I am," I say. "And you?"

"I've left Arizona, and I'm still safe."

"Glad to hear it. Is that why you called?"

Angel barks a laugh. "It's not."

"You're being mean," I say. "Just tell me."

"I located the video," she says. "And it's bad, Melina." Her voice drops to a whisper. "Like, I can't tell you anything over the phone, bad."

I don't drop my cell. I regulate my heart rate, but it's hard. "Okay."

"I'm sending you the video, because you will need it as evidence. And I'm also sending the record books as verification. You're going to need all of it to pull this off."

"Okay." Names cycle through my head of members of Chancery's inner circle. Judica. Edam. Balthasar. Inara. Alora. Marselle. Larena. Maxmillian. Franco. Frederick. Job. It must be one of them or she would tell me now. Anyone else, Chancery would hold on my word. Or maybe it's one of the rival empresses. Melisania, Analessa, Lainina, Melamecha. Or could it be Chancery's stray, Noah? The one who can disguise himself as anyone? The abomination?

No, he couldn't possibly have poisoned Mother—he wasn't even here yet. "How will you send it?"

"I can't tell you over the phone," Angel says. "But it's the same way I sent you the update that Enora died, but in reverse."

"Absolutely," I say. "I remember."

"Stay safe," Angel says. "Predators are at their most dangerous when you're closing in on them. They can sense it."

I wish she could just tell me who it is, but if she could, she already would have. "Accept the world as it is," I say.

"Or do something to change it." Angel hangs up the phone.

"How long have we been hanging around," Aline says, "just waiting to hear news on Chancery's attack?"

I shrug. "Too long. Two full days."

"Isn't someone supposed to update us?" Lucas asks. "Will we even find out if things go poorly?"

I shake my head. "We aren't in the inner circle yet, but we will get there. As soon as she's back, I'll let her know that we have a lot to discuss."

"I can't just sit around here." Aline says. "And now we're waiting on those files from Angel too. I'm going crazy, just watching you slowly going crazy."

Aline doesn't like to ride, but she does love to run. "Why don't you go out?" I suggest. "Let's ask the guards. I bet they'd let you."

"It's raining," she says. "I'd get soaked."

"So take this." I toss her a hooded windbreaker. "In fifteen minutes the rain will stop and you can tie it around your waist. I think it would do you a lot of good. I felt much better after my ride."

She glances around the room at the twenty some-odd guards. "Oh fine. I suppose you're safe enough."

Apparently, Aline poses more of a threat than I do, because they send *three* guards with her. But they don't even radio in to ask for permission this time. Either they've set up some kind of protocol, or the royal guards who are currently stationed to relieve the Motherless aren't quite as nervous about making decisions.

Not half an hour after she leaves, there's a knock at the door. I suppose her run wasn't quite as energizing as I hoped it would be. I open it, but it's not Aline's hooded face standing on the other side.

It's Inara's.

THE PRESENT

"Hey." I smile and wave her inside. "I was wondering if you'd come."

She steps inside the doorframe and stops.

"Come in before you're completely soaked." I move aside so she can pass more easily.

I hope Aline comes back soon. I didn't realize it was raining quite so hard. At this rate, she'll soak the floor of the entire cottage when she returns.

Inara walks through the door and glances around the room, noting that every seat is taken.

"Oh," I say. "We're a little cramped in here, not that I'm complaining. But you can have a seat at the kitchen table."

"I can't stay," Inara says.

"Oh." Fear worms its way into my heart. "Did things not go well with Chancery?" I clear my throat. "Tell me she's alright."

"You're still in contact with Angel?" Inara asks.

I blink. "Yes. She's fine, as far as I know."

"She called you earlier?" She glances around the room.

"And you took the call here, where everyone could hear you."

The worm of fear grows, but in a totally new direction. "What are you asking me about, Inara?" Years and years of memories crash over me, and Inara is in all of them. Bathing me as a child, riding horses together, eating meal after meal, attending so many events I lost track, playing checkers and then trying to help me with my chess game. Cheering for me during the Games. Hundreds and hundreds of others from the mundane to the exciting. Sure, she stayed with Mother when I was banished and only came to visit a handful of times. We haven't been as close, but I never once doubted whether she loves me. And more than me, I've always known she loved Mother.

She was on the list of possibilities, but I can't even fathom it might have been her who poisoned Mother. My throat is tight when I ask, "Inara, why are you here?"

"So they all heard?"

"Heard what?"

Inara reaches into her pocket and withdraws a grey ball, roughly the size of a tennis ball.

"What is that?" I step closer.

"I hate that things have happened this way, but I don't have a choice, not if they all know about Angel's video." Inara hurls the ball at the fireplace and it explodes with a flash of light. Smoke pours out of the center of the room, rolling toward us quickly. My mind churns to try and make sense of what's happening. Inara isn't threatening me, she's merely standing in front of me, but she's here because she somehow heard the phone call Angel made.

The call where she told me she had the murderer on video, with enough evidence to convict.

It's Inara. She killed Mother. She's the threat to Chancery's throne.

She's the traitor.

I try to turn around and reach for my sword. Any weapon. A kitchen knife would be fine. But I can't move, not a finger. I can't even make my mouth move to talk.

"The ocean is full of all kinds of interesting things," Inara says softly. "Mother really should have spent a little more time exploring its depths."

Few things in my life have been more constant than pain. From birth, I was taught to withstand it, from first steps, I was taught to embrace and move beyond it, so that I could do what had to be done. But nothing prepared me to watch, frozen, as my sister, my most beloved family member, beheads every member of my team. Tears leak down my face, but I can't even close my eyes. She moves out of view, but I hear the sounds—utter silence but for the thwack of her blade. No sound, other than the whump of a head hitting the floor, and the slither of the body following suit. Blood sprays on my arm as she kills Lucas behind me, and I want to die, too. I want her to mow me down along with everyone I love.

But she doesn't. She circles back, spattered with blood, her face impassive. I don't know Inara at all. Everything I thought was a lie.

At least Aline is on a run. At least Aline is on a run. At least Aline is on a run.

"Where's your wife?" Her eyes are almost kind, like she regrets having done this. As if any regret, real or imaginary, could ever atone for her actions. For her deep and abiding evil.

"Oh." Her eyebrow lifts in frustration. "I forgot. You can't talk. You need the antidote." She opens a vial underneath my nose and waits. Then she closes it up again and tucks it into her pocket. "I've only given you half a dose.

Can't have you freaking out on me. It takes ten seconds or so to work."

My arms begin to tremble with rage like I've never before felt. My hands move, finally, but it feels like I'm dragging them through wet cement. I stumble forward and catch myself, barely, on the back of a chair.

"Time to go," Inara says. "I'll have to question you later. Chancery's just arriving. This couldn't have happened at a worse time."

"Sorry to inconvenience you," I slur. Blinking my eyes is like lifting a ton of bricks. I'll never reach my own sword. But Lucas's was half drawn when he froze. I could grab it. I look away from his head and the blood and focus on reaching that hilt.

Inara laughs. "Really, Melina. Come on." She knocks the sword away easily and shoves me toward the door. She pulls her hood down even further over her face and spins the knob. When I resist, she drags me through behind her.

I fumble for the doorframe and then the railing, but my hands aren't working right. I can't seem to get a firm hold on anything. That antidote sucks.

"Stop, stop!" I can't leave them all, but Inara won't let me stay. She tugs me harder. Aline will return and find all the bodies. "Why would you do that?"

"I had no choice," Inara says. "My hand was forced from the first day. It had to happen, and this does too. Stop struggling."

Angel's sending me the video. Inara heard, since she's running security section currently, and they're obviously monitoring my calls. She had to eliminate everyone who knew. Except she hasn't killed me. "You're Nereus," I say. "You must be. Which means you killed her."

Mother. She must have, but that's the part I can't wrap

my head around. Inara loved Mother, always, I'm sure of it. Why would she ever do something like that?

Inara's hand tightens on my arm and shoves me backward until my groggy head slams into the open doorframe and everything goes blessedly black.

❧ 24 ❧

THE PRESENT

I open my eyes and close them again. No difference. When my eyes are open, it's black. When they're closed, it's still black. Where am I? My hands are bound behind me and I'm lying on my side. The ground is cool, damp dirt and rock. The air is cool as well.

Underground cool.

Mother has a bunker just off the courtyard to her room. Am I in it? A horrible thought springs into my mind. Am I below it?

I crawl forward until I face-plant into a wall of rock and dirt. I spit repeatedly until my mouth is nearly clean. It's time for me to gain some mobility. Using the weight of my body and the leverage of the cuffs, I break my left wrist and slide it out of the metal restraints. Once it has healed, I crawl on my hands and knees to map the area around me. It's at least nine feet tall, as I can't reach the ceiling, and it's about seven feet long and four feet wide.

I'm in a pit in the ground. It feels like a grave.

There's a weighty feel to the air, like it's old and the circulation is poor. Like I'm way, way down and there's no way I could ever dig my way out, not without collapsing under the rubble of any attempt. I wonder how much air I have. Without any idea how long I've been down here, it's hard to know. The air quality seems fine, if a bit earthy. I'm wearing the same clothing I had on before, my blue shirt and black pants, covered now with the blood spatter of my friends.

An image of the room as we were leaving slams its way into my brain and I can't shake it. I can't open my eyes and look around—and I can't stop thinking about them—almost everyone who mattered the most to me in the world, dead. Evians live brutal lives—especially in times of war. We're a bloodthirsty people, and execution is our most likely punishment. But Paolo, Lucas, Horatio, Kira, Douglas. I choke. It's too much. All of them, gone forever.

By the hand of my most beloved sister. Oh, Inara. Why?

She was displaced when I was born, but she never seemed to mind. She was further displaced when the twins were born, but—

Something hits me like a fist to the jaw. Angel knows it's Inara because . . . Inara bought the poison that almost killed Mother when the twins were born.

Which means that Inara tried to kill Mother twice. Or maybe she tried to kill the twins and failed, and then killed Mother. Either way, I don't understand how it could be her. Why support me and Mother and then completely burn it all down? She said she had no choice, but why? Could she be in trouble? It would make more sense than some bizarre, newly found thirst for power.

On the other hand, Inara is patient. She always advocates a long game. If she did feel threatened by me, she might not move on it right away. But when she found out Mother was pregnant, she might feel compelled to take some kind of action. I think of the thousands of moments we spent together. The rides, the talks, her support and advice. She couldn't have been plotting that entire time. Right?

Was she trying to kill Mother with that poison or the babies? Did she regret it when it didn't work?

I blamed Judica for intercepting my letters to Chancery, but it must have been Inara all along. She read my impassioned pleas, and she kept my little sister from seeing them. Why? What could she gain? If she wanted to rule, but she loved me as I believe she does. . . Could she have intended to kill Mother and the twins and then ascend the throne? She had to know I never want to rule. I've told her as much.

But why now? If that was her plan, why not kill the twins when they were small? She could have challenged Mother and killed her when I couldn't. I wouldn't even have faulted her. Why wait? What precipitated this?

I'm not sure how long I lay on my back in the dirt before I hear a noise, like a grinding, far up and to the left. It's faint, but I can make it out distinctly because it's a noise I've heard before. It's the sound the door in the ground makes when it's opening into the tunnel down to Mother's bunker.

Shortly after, I hear the rolling of the locks in the keypad entry to the main bunker area. It's closer, but still far to the left and above my location.

When a sequence of clicks sounds a few dozen feet away, I scramble to my feet. When a bright yellow light appears over my head, my body shakes, and when Inara's face appears at the top of the pit, garish in the glow of a handheld incandescent lantern, I can't help my sob.

I was hoping somehow I hallucinated, that it wasn't really her. That someone else was pretending. Maybe the Noah person who can make himself look like others. But only Inara and perhaps Chancery or Judica would have access to Mother's bunker, and my older sister is glaring down at me right now.

Which means it really was her.

"Why?" I ask. "Why would you do that? What do you want?"

"You cast off the restraints and then quit? Why didn't you scale the walls?" She's leaning over a ledge about eleven feet in the air. I could have carved out handholds and climbed to the top. "You aren't even trying."

To escape. I should be, I suppose. "Judica would have."

Inara frowns. "All of us would have."

Except me. "I've never had the burning rage that you and Judica appear to share." I think of Aline. She wasn't there, she wasn't murdered with Lucas, with Paolo, with Horatio, with Kira, with everyone. "You killed them all." I can barely bring myself to ask the next question. "Did you —" I swallow. Aline's delicately strong hands, her nails always buffed evenly, her graceful neck, her dark, cascading hair, her hugely expressive eyes. I can't ask. And I'll die if I don't find out.

"I didn't kill your girlfriend."

"My wife," I growl, the words a low hum in my throat.

"Whatever. She's still alive."

"She's with Chancery?" I ask.

Inara laughs. "Wouldn't you love that? No, I'm not that idiotic. I'm sure she heard the same intel that they all heard."

"She didn't." I frown, because of course she did. But Inara can't possibly know that.

"Nice try," Inara says. "She already figured out that's the reason I captured her."

"Why didn't you kill her, then?"

Inara drops a woven rope over the edge. Her voice is

resigned when she says, "Climb up." Aline is alive because Inara still needs something from me. She knows I'll never help her without leverage.

Aline is a bargaining chip.

I take the ladder rungs slowly, evaluating. I'm in a pit below Mother's bunker. It was probably a storage hole, judging by the size. "Why didn't this fill with water?" I ask. "Isn't it below sea level?"

Inara rolls her eyes. "You're wasting your questions on logistics? Mother employed the best engineers to create this place, you know. You don't have to worry about your pit flooding, at least, not unless there's a tsunami. There are several of those areas, locations for pumping out any water that might threaten the main bunker."

I reach the top and climb out, wiping my hands on my pants. I'm sure I look like a ten-year-old child, caught making mud pies. "Why am I in a pit? Why did you kill everyone I loved?"

"I was one of those people you loved once." Inara pulls the ladder up and winds it around a pole before dropping it to the ground.

"I love you still," I say.

"After I killed all your people?" She shakes her head. "I wish I had thought of any other way. I wish I hadn't had to do that, but animals always fight back when their back is to the wall."

"If anyone will understand making hard decisions, it's me," I say. "My whole life has been one miserable decision after another." I think about the people I lost trying to slay Judica. I wonder how much of that was because I felt it was right, and how much was because I wanted to be important, the salvation Dad told me I'd be. Then I remember their faces, my people, as Inara mowed them down. I shudder.

"We need to talk," Inara says. "But first you need a shower."

Why would she allow me that? Why is she letting me out of the pit at all? Why not just demand that I give her what she needs and threaten Aline's life if I don't comply? I try not to think about the fact that Inara will never release Aline, not with what she knows. Inara won't be safe as long as my wife is alive.

I follow my sister through the doorway and into the main part of the bunker—coming through the back of a large storage room and into the third bedroom. "You will shower. There are clothes for you to change into once you have."

Inara's sword is in place on her back, but otherwise, she looks completely calm, unthreatening. The same as she always has. My heart lurches. How can we be here? How can the woman who rocked me, who sang to me, who taught me to dance, who helped me learn to cook with Angel, who gave me the best, most thoughtful birthday gifts, how can she have murdered our mother? How could she have mowed down all my friends without even pausing?

She's the same woman who stood by Mother's side as she executed criminals. Did she see us as criminals?

I walk into the shower, numb, and I half expect acid to rain down on me from the shower head. Only warm water emerges. I throw my soiled clothing, thankfully too dirty to differentiate between blood and dirt, in a pile in the corner. Once I'm clean, I dry off and put on the clothing she chose. Her own clothing, I assume. By the time I emerge, I'm calmer, and I've come to a conclusion.

"You didn't kill Aline because you need a bargaining chip." I sit on the edge of the bed. "What do you want from me? You know me well enough to know that you're better off if you're up front about it."

"Mother and Eamon fought constantly. Your entire childhood was one desperate attempt to please them after another. It never worked. You made one happy or the other, but nothing satisfied both your parents." Inara folds her arms. "Would you do the same thing again?"

I don't understand.

Inara leans against the doorframe. "I don't need anything from you, Melina. I should have killed you, and I should have killed Aline. My failure to do so was a major mistake no matter how I look at it. But I want the opportunity to tell you what I've done and why, and I guess I'm hoping you'll be able to forgive me."

For murdering twenty-four of my friends. For killing our mother.

"You forgave Mother often. You saw her attack, you saw her execute, you saw her destroy. I did too. You didn't see her with Chancery—she became a *mom* for the first time in her life. Instead of putting her people first, instead of foisting Alamecha above all things, she put her *child* first." Inara shakes her head. "It almost makes me wish. . ."

"And that's all?" I ask. "You have no end game, other than trying to explain your actions to me?"

Inara's nostrils flare. "I want you to hear everything I have done, all my mistakes, all my missteps, and love me anyway."

When I realized I was gay, Dad told me to make better choices. Mother couldn't kick me out fast enough. But Inara, she never batted an eye. I should at least listen to what sent us to this place. "But Chancery—"

She waves her hand through the air. "She's safe. She's fine."

"You don't want her to know you killed Mother."

"She can never know," Inara says. "She won't understand, not ever. Mother was different with her. She was. . .

softer. . . she was what a mother should be. She sacrificed for her. Sometimes I think that Mother would have sacrificed anything in the world for Chancery."

Inara's jealous.

But hearing this account, I can understand why. Chancery was minutes old when Mother cast me aside for her. But jealous or not, I would never put Chancery's prophetic calling at risk. I would never harm her. I'm not sure I can say the same of Inara. And a warning niggles at the back of my mind. Inara says she needs nothing from me, but Angel has a video on her. She may have killed or captured all the people on the island who knew about it, but the video is out there. And Angel is canny, resourceful, and connected. And free.

Inara might never catch her. Angel might yet reach Chancery with the evidence needed to convict my big sister. Inara needs me to reel Angel in or destroy the video. And she probably needs to blame Angel for Mother's death in order to satisfy Chancery. It's what I'd do if I were in her shoes.

Which means she's lying to me, right to my face. That hurts almost as much as watching her kill my people. But I can't let her know. Not if I want any hope of outsmarting her and escaping to warn Chancery. "If you want me to listen to you, if you want me to try and forgive you, I need to see Aline. I want her—"

"Sure, yes."

"I can see her?"

"She can stay here with you, even. It's riskier to have you together, but keeping two separate prisoners has its complications as well."

I snap my mouth closed. I didn't expect her to agree, and I certainly didn't expect to be kept with her.

"But." Inara holds up one finger. "You have to promise

me that you'll be patient and let me tell my entire story. You must vow not to try to escape or move against me until I'm entirely done with explaining my side. Is that a promise you're prepared to keep?"

We have months before the end is nigh. It's sooner than I expected, but we have months to gather the stones, find the Garden, and stop the destruction. And I'll have Aline, here with me.

Inara's right that Mother and Dad fought all the time. I never had a moment of happiness or peace, and for years I struggled with the knowledge that choosing to be with a woman would disappoint both of them. My decision would devastate both of the people I had tried—and failed—my entire life to please.

But once I accepted Aline, once I accepted who I really was, I let go of that perceived failure. "I promise neither myself, nor Aline, will attempt to escape or move against you until we hear the entirety of your story. We will not make any attempts until you've completed your explanation."

Inara stares at me for a moment, but seeing my sincerity, she nods her head. She leaves then, barricading the door on her way out. But when she returns a while later, carrying my unconscious wife in her arms, my heart floods with relief. I wanted to believe Inara, but seeing Aline eases the anxiety I didn't realize plagued me.

I want to fulfill Dad's destiny and avoid the utter destruction. I want to help Chancery, but if I can't, if my life ends early, at least I found my purpose, my safety, my home. I take her from Inara and set her on the bed. As I do, I recall one of the last things Aline had me do: hide the translations in the chimney. If that explosive Inara threw didn't burn it all up, Aline's hiding spot might convey one last piece of information to Chancery before it's too late. Ah, Aline. Still saving us, even now.

I brush her hair back from her face. "How long will she be unconscious?"

Inara shrugs. "Another hour at least."

"And if we listen to your explanation and I can't forgive your actions?" I straighten my shoulders. "Is that when you kill me?"

Her eyes widen. "I don't know whether I could ever do that."

She probably shouldn't admit that to her captive, but the combination of shock and horror on her face is more convincing than I expected it to be.

"I love you, Melina, like I would if you were my own daughter. I've always loved you, from the moment you were born."

"You tried to kill Mother when she was pregnant with the twins and you almost succeeded. How could you do that? Why didn't you love them like you love me?"

"It's complicated," she says. "Really, really complicated."

"Well, I have at least an hour to kill," I say. "So you may as well get started."

"I don't have time right now," she says. "I've already been away for too long. But I will return, and when I do, I'll explain all of it."

"Fair warning, though. I doubt there's much you can say that will erase what you've done. I love you, but—" I cough and shake my head. I will never forget what she did today. Mother wasn't perfect, but my people did nothing to Inara that she didn't cause by her own actions.

"I know that," she says. "But I want to the chance to try."

"Understood."

"While I'm gone, I want you to think about something," Inara says. "You're not the first heir to believe there was something wrong with you. I thought I was broken beyond repair. I thought I would never love anyone, not ever, or at least, not romantically."

"What?"

"You met Aline when you were only twenty, and I'm guessing you were already wondering what was wrong with you. I bet you wished a million times that you could just fall in love with Lucas."

I flinch when she speaks his name. Lucas was one of my most devoted friends, and she killed him.

"I was one hundred and forty-five years old before I felt the smallest bit of interest in anyone at all," Inara says.

A hundred and forty-five?

"When I did fall in love, the warp and weft of my being shifted, rewoven anew. I would have done anything at all, killed anyone, destroyed everything, to make him love me back."

"I'm still confused."

"I'll be back soon to explain," she says.

"Okay."

"But just like yours, mine is a love story." Inara glances back at Aline. "Only mine has a tragic ending." She reaches for my hand but pulls back at the last second. Her voice is the barest of whispers. "I didn't have a choice, Melina. Not in the end. I hope you'll see that."

Except, we always have choices. Even when things are hard, even when they seem unfair, even when a decision splits us right down the middle, we must choose. I made a lot of decisions before I left Ni'ihau the last time, and not all of them were easy. I sacrificed so much of who I wanted to be in order to be true to who I already was.

My wife knows exactly who I am today. If Inara fails to convince me, Aline won't be surprised when I risk our lives to do the right thing. Because like me, Aline knows that good and bad exist. She knows that we must choose good, no matter the sacrifice.

But the more I hear from my sister, the more I worry that Inara doesn't know that basic principle. I'm terribly afraid that Inara chose badly, and I may be the only one who can repair the damage.

As Mother would say, failure is a choice. And no matter the cost, I will not fail Chancery. Not this time.

❧

The next volume in Chancery's epic journey, Disavowed, releases May 15, 2020 and it's already up for preorder. Read on for a sneak peek of the first chapter!

And Inara's story, unRepentant is up for preorder now, too.

Finally, if you'd like a FREE full length novel, you can grab my standalone ya romantic suspense, Already Gone, if you join my newsletter at www.BridgetEBakerWrites.com.

❧ 25 ❧

APPENDIX: THE SIX FAMILIES

I. ALAMECHA: United States of America, England, Ireland, Scotland, Canada, Cuba, Puerto Rico
Eve
Mahalesh 3226 BC
Alamecha 2312 BC
Meridalina 1446 BC
Corlamecha 553 BC
Cainina 273 AD
Enora 1120 AD
Chancery 2002 AD
H. Judica 2002 AD

2. MALESSA: Germany, France, Netherlands, Switzerland, Norway, Sweden, Finland, Australia, New Zealand, Papau New Guinea, Iceland
Eve
Mahalesh 3226 BC
Malessa 2353 BC
Adorna 1451 BC

Selah 618 BC
Lenamecha 211 AD
Senah 1022 AD (Denah dead twin)
Analessa 1820 AD
H. DeLannia 1942

3. LENORA: All of South America (including Chile, Argentina, Brazil), Mexico, Spain, Portugal
Eve
Mahalesh 3226 BC
Lenora 2365 BC
Ablinina 1453 BC
Leddite 652 BC
Selamecha 379 BC
Priena 460 AD
Leamarta 1198 AD
Melisania 1897 AD
H. Marde 1987

4. ADORA: India, Japan, Korea, Indonesia, Thailand
Eve
Mahalesh 3226 BC
Adora 2368 BC
Manocha 1461 BC
Alela 590 BC
Radosha 192 BC
Esheth 638 AD
Lainina 1444 AD
H. Ranana 1967

.   .   .

5. SHAMECHA: Russia, Mongolia, Kazakhstan, Pakistan, Uzbekistan, Philippines

Eve

Mahalesh 3226 BC

Shamecha 2472 BC

Madalena 1639 BC

Shenoa 968 BC

Abalorna 299 BC

Venoah 333 AD

Reshaka 936 AD

Melamecha 1509 AD

H. Venagra 2000

6. SHENOAH: Continent of Africa, Saudi Arabia, Iran, Iraq, Turkey, Greece, Italy, Jordan, Afghanistan

Eve

Shenoah 3227 BC

Adelornamecha 2385 BC

Kankera 1544 BC

Avina 670 BC

Sela 467 BC

Jericha 135 AD

Sethora 399 AD

Malimba 708 AD

Adika 1507 AD

H. Vela 1990

SAMPLE CHAPTER OF
DISAVOWED

For the first six thousand and five hundred days of my life, my mom took care of everything.

If another family threatened ours, she eradicated their armies and leveled their military bases. If I couldn't comb out a knot in my hair, she made short work of it. If an assassin tried to kill me, she removed their head from their neck slowly, so they suffered. If I was hungry, she handed me a bag of goldfish—the rainbow kind I preferred. I went to sleep every single night with the knowledge that I was safe, treasured, and valuable.

Then, not long ago, she died. She left me her crown, but it's up to me to keep it.

For the vast majority of my life, I slept easily because I knew my mom would take care of me. With the faith of a child, I never doubted. And when she was suddenly gone, that belief that others could be relied upon shifted, but it didn't disappear. I believed that my family and friends would be there for me.

I was a total chump.

One of my trusted confidantes poisoned Mom right here in our palace. That same person abducted my older sister Melina right out from under my nose after killing almost her entire retinue.

"You're saying we have no idea who did this?" I ask.

My Warlord and former Chief Security Officer, Balthasar, shrugs. "I can give you a list of who it isn't. A huge contingent of us weren't even on the island when this happened, and many more had only just returned."

"Gather every guard who has watched that villa in the last few days, and compile a list of people who *were* present. I also want to know who could have modified the guard placement around Melina's cottage." I close my eyes. I'm no closer to rooting out the traitor who killed my mom today than I was on the day she died. And if Melina's accusation in the security feed is correct, the same person just killed twenty-four more people on my watch.

"Technically, the Chief Security Officer should be doing this," Balthasar says.

I slam my hand down on the table. "He's in the infirmary, because I blew up my friends. I think you can step in for a second."

Balthasar's eyes widen.

I drop my voice to a whisper. "Just do it, okay?"

As badly as the sheltered, scared little girl inside me wants to trust someone, when I look around now, I don't see allies. I see threats. I see risks. I see liabilities. Even Balthasar, my mother's brother in law, is suspect. After all, he arrived just before I did. He might have been here in time to butcher those people. And if anyone has the skill. . . But why would he want Melina's people dead? How could he possibly stand to gain anything from her disappearance or death?

I wish I knew what motivated the people who have surrounded me my entire life.

But I feel like I don't know any of them at all. Not the twin sister I've wasted years hating, not the fiancé I love to kiss but struggle to trust, and not either of the older sisters I've admired my entire life. In fact, the one person who has told me the least about himself may be the person I trust most. At least he's honest about the fact that I don't know a thing about his motives.

And we have no idea where he is, or if he's even alive.

"Whoa," Balthasar says. "What happened to you?" His hand touches my side and I wince and leap away from him.

The pain in my side has become like a second heart-beat, heavier when I breathe, but constant, unending. I glance down to see what he noticed.

There's a hole in my shirt and my pants beneath. Clothing that was completely fine when I flopped out of the ocean and onto the sand. Both the pants and shirt clung to the gash above my hip that won't heal. It takes effort, but I don't grit my teeth when I cover the hole with my hand. The hole in my side is sticky with a mixture of blood and something else. "It's no big deal."

"Wait." His eyes widen as he takes me in. "You're injured right now? From the blast? Why hasn't it healed?"

I shake my head. "It's not a big deal," I repeat. "And it's not from the blast. When I was fighting Adika she sliced me, and there was something on her blade. Or that's what Edam thinks."

"Edam!" Balthasar bellows. "That idiot is sitting calmly on a bed in the infirmary while I do his job for him. Mean-while Job's hovering at his bedside for a little blunt force trauma to the head, and his queen is actively *bleeding* from a wound she received *yesterday?*"

"It barely even hurts." As long as I don't breathe. Or move. Or think about it. "And I meant to see Job about it immediately, before. . ." I gesture at the screen where we just watched my sister hauled away by someone who is likely Mom's killer.

"Well, now you've seen the video, and you're headed straight to the infirmary." Balthasar takes my forearm in his hand. "March, missy." He tugs me out the Security headquarters and into the main hallway. The Motherless who found me on the beach straighten up and fall into step behind us.

I practically stumble along behind him, my feet pumping to keep up with his much longer stride. So much for being 'his queen.'

"You should have told me right away," Balthasar says. "Your health always comes first."

"Compared to the twenty four people who just lost their heads, this really isn't that big of a deal," I say. "Adika simply doused her blade in some kind of poison that prevents blood clotting, probably. Or something like that."

Balthasar's head ducks lower, his voice low in my ear. "It has been quite some time. No matter what she used, it should have healed."

He's right. But admitting that scares me, and I can't handle any more terrifying admissions right now.

"Are you okay to walk?" he whispers.

I yank my arm away. "I'm perfectly fine, and I won't have you creating some kind of panic."

"Your majesty." Frederick jogs down the hall, the Motherless parting like curtains.

"Frederick," I say. "Good to see you." Except, I can't help wondering whether it might have been him. He and Mom were quite close, and he has watched over me tirelessly since her death. But what if he killed her and this whole devoted act is just a cover up? He certainly could have poisoned Mom, and he remained behind while I flew to Europe. Or it could have been Balthasar, or at the very least, one of his minions.

Frederick frowns and I realize I've stopped and I'm staring from Frederick to Balthasar and back again. "We're going to the infirmary to check on Edam," I say, silently pleading with Balthasar to concur.

"Right. Security Chief needs to be up and running," Balthasar says.

"Of course." Frederick motions me forward and falls into step on the opposite side of me from Balthasar.

Oh good. The number of people following me is growing. "I will be fine in my own palace." But even I don't believe that lie. Mom, Melina. . . who's next?

"We're simply happy you've returned triumphant," Frederick says with a smile. "Larena wanted me to let you know that Gregor will be visiting your room shortly to find out what kind of setting you'd like for the stones. I hear the two of them have merged into one?"

I nod tightly. "That's correct. Tell him to wait for me at my room. I'll return there as soon as possible."

Frederick bows. "I'll leave you in Balthasar's care, then." He turns to face the six Motherless trailing me. "Hayden, Porter, you two will report to Robert immediately. He'll dispatch the proper attendants per the schedule. The rest of you will stay with her until the assigned guards arrive. I appreciate your help until we can properly integrate her return."

For once, I actually appreciate that he's paying attention to details. I'm hoping some of those details might keep me alive. But first, I need to figure out what's wrong with me. A few dozen yards more and Balthasar and I reach the infirmary.

I hear Edam's voice before I walk through the door. Strong, confident, acutely irritated.

"You can't keep me here," Edam says. "I need to see Chancery."

"She's with Balthasar," Job says with almost no inflection in his voice, as if he's said the same thing a hundred times. "She's fine—and I'm almost done with my final check. You sustained a pretty severe—"

"Actually, she's not fine," Balthasar says. "And that idiot should have been telling you that."

Edam's eyes meet mine and my heart flips. "You're not fine?" His brow furrows. "The poisoned blade?"

Job chokes. "What's this about poison?" I'm guessing he's a little gun-shy about it, what with Mom's recent death due to poison.

"We don't know what is wrong, exactly," I say.

Edam stands up, brushing Job away. "It's still not better?"

I shake my head.

Edam crosses the room in a few steps, sliding effortlessly past Balthasar, and sweeps me upward. His arms slide under my back and knees and he carries me to the bed he just vacated. "Adika fought dirty. Something on her blade is keeping Chancery from healing." His steady hands carefully shift the edge of my shirt out of the way, pausing when he notices the hole in my shirt and pants. "What happened here?" He leans closer, his eyes intent.

Job clears his throat. "Unless you've been studying evian anatomy in your free time instead of lifting weights, I think I might be better qualified to determine the answer."

Edam startles. "Right." He steps to the left, allowing

Job to examine me, but staying close enough to touch me too. His hand comes down against my face. "I'm sorry."

I'm not sure what he's apologizing for, but he's done nothing wrong.

"Yeah, yeah," Balthasar says. "You're both so terribly in love, blah blah. If you have this in hand, Job, I'm going to return to the Security office and start doing this lovesick puppy's job." He points at the Motherless. "You four, wait outside." They jump and file out in front of him.

Edam doesn't even huff when his former boss leaves. I'm proud of him for ignoring Balthasar's jab.

"What does he mean, doing your job?" Job asks.

I shake my head. "Let's just say there's been a lot going on and I have some things to catch Edam up on."

Job prods at something and my insides contract.

"Ouch," I say. "Careful."

He shakes his head. "I've never seen anything like this. It happened yesterday, right?"

I nod.

"It should have healed. I'm going to need to test a few samples."

I sigh. "That's fine."

"Do a better job than you did with her mother." Edam's voice practically bristles.

Job frowns. "This is a topical injury. Enora was ingesting something that did her harm."

"Potato, po-tah-to. Figure out what it is and fix it," Edam says. "Because that's *your* only job."

"We can't all have someone else fill in," Job says.

Edam laughs then. "I'm sorry. I get snarly when she's hurt, apparently." He squeezes my hand. "I'll try to be less hostile."

"It's your default setting," I say.

Edam smiles. "I suppose it is."

"That's okay," I say. "You're hot when you're prickly." Actually, he's kind of hot all the time, but he doesn't need to hear that. Certainly not in front of Job.

"Simmer down, you two. From what I hear, you haven't even set a date yet. It's easy to do when you're young and in love, but let's not get ahead of ourselves."

Since he's the only physician for Alamecha, he'd be the first to know if I got pregnant. Which I definitely do *not* have planned for a while. I open my mouth to tell him not to worry when it hits me. I've been focused on who might have known about Mom transferring the throne to me. I've contemplated who might have been upset about my reaction to the stone.

But I've been virtually ignoring one huge clue.

Job crosses the room with a small set of tweezers and several specimen containers. "I'm going to have to take a few samples. It won't be comfortable."

"It's fine," I say. "Go ahead."

He's right, it's not fun, but it's nothing to a stab, slice, or whack with a sword. After he closes the last container and sets it on the counter, I pounce. "Job, I know Mom was pregnant when she died."

He turns toward me slowly.

"And I know you did the autopsy."

"Okay."

"But I don't recall ever seeing a report on the identity of the father."

Job's mouth drops open.

And for the first time, I wonder whether it's him. "Can you tell me who it is?"

He shakes his head. "I don't know."

"How can you not know? Wouldn't you have identified paternity of the child, if only to notify the father?"

"If he knew she was pregnant," he says, "he'd have

known the baby perished with the mother. And if he didn't know, it's because she hadn't told him. I prefer not to violate her trust by disclosing anything she wouldn't want shared."

"But I need to know. What if that had to do with her murder?"

His eyes widen further.

"Why didn't we look into this sooner?" Edam asks.

I shake my head. "There has been a lot going on. But I still feel bad."

What if Job didn't test Mom's baby. . . because he already knew it was his? I shake my head. "I hate to do this, but we're going to need to—"

"I'm not entirely sure that a test will reveal the paternity at this point," he says. "But even if there's enough tissue to test, we'll need to have the father's DNA on file to identify a match."

"I'll make every single person on the entire island submit to a DNA test, if that's the issue," I say. "Because I will have my answers. Patience has lost me another family member. I'm done waiting and hoping."

Job nods. "Let me send these samples off to be analyzed. I have a few ideas, but I need to get the answers on them ASAP." He steps out of the room and I hear him talking to his assistant. When he steps back inside, he motions for me to get up. "No time like the present. Let's go down to the family crypt."

The walk down to the crypt below the main palace is two hundred and thirty six steps. I count every single one, because each of them jars my injury and makes me want to whimper. By the time we reach the bottom, I feel a little guilty. I haven't been down here to pay my respects to Mom since the funeral.

But when Job unlocks her vault and opens the solid

door, I take a step closer. I duck my head to make sure, but it doesn't alter what is right in front of me. Or rather, what isn't.

Mother's vault is empty.

**If you enjoyed this sample, preorder Disavowed today!

ACKNOWLEDGMENTS

My husband, always and forever, is my number one supporter. I couldn't do any of these books justice without his help and solid guidance.

My mother and my son Eli and my daughter Dora are my three biggest fans. Oh, how I love and appreciate them and their enthusiasm.

My editors are phenomenal. My team of sensitivity readers are AMAZING, and my developmental editor Peter is world class. My copy editor Carla and my proofer Mattie are also phenomenal. THANK YOU!

And my Advance Team: thank you so much! You are my first round of feedback, my early cheerleaders, and my best bolsterers when I waiver. I love all of you!

My fans: I don't think I can adequately express what your reviews, your comments, your shares and your kind words mean to me. Your support has MADE this career a success. Without you, my books would serve no purpose at all. Thank you for coming on this journey with me! <3

ABOUT THE AUTHOR

Bridget loves her husband (every day) and all five of her kids (most days). She's a lawyer, but does as little legal work as possible. She has two goofy horses, two scrappy cats, one bouncy dog and backyard chickens. She hates Oxford commas, but she uses them to keep fans from complaining. She makes cookies waaaaay too often and believes they should be their own food group. To keep from blowing up like a puffer fish, she kick boxes every day. So if you don't like her books, her kids, her pets, or her cookies, maybe don't tell her in person.

ALSO BY BRIDGET E. BAKER

❧

The Almost a Billionaire clean romance series:

Finding Faith (1)

Finding Cupid (2)

Finding Spring (3)

Finding Liberty (4)

Finding Holly (5)

Finding Home (6) Coming July 15, 2020!

The Birthright Series:

Displaced (1)

unForgiven (2)

Disillusioned (3)

misUnderstood (4)

Disavowed (5)- coming May 15, 2020

unRepentant (6)- coming September 15, 2020

Destroyed (7) - coming fall 2020

The Sins of Our Ancestors Series:

Marked (1)

Suppressed (2)

Redeemed (3)

A stand alone YA romantic suspense:

Already Gone

Made in the USA
Middletown, DE
30 December 2020

30474736R00166